THE MEDICI MANUSCRIPT

THE GLASS LIBRARY, BOOK #2

C.J. ARCHER

WWW.CJARCHER.COM

CHAPTER 1

LONDON, SPRING 1920

"*M*oving pictures are the future," Daisy declared, "and I want to be in one."

I slotted the book I'd been trying to read back into its place on the library shelf. It was no use continuing; Daisy was impossible to block out when excitement gripped her. She was like a child who'd been sitting at a desk all day and was finally allowed outside to play with the other children.

I knew she wouldn't leave until satisfied, and she wouldn't be satisfied until I paid her more attention than the pile of books I cradled in my arm. Even so, I was supposed to be working.

"Daisy, can we talk about your acting career later? I need to reshelve these."

"You can reshelve while I talk. All you have to do is listen."

"I want to read a few pages of each to get the gist of them. It's the best way to learn about magic."

She plucked the topmost book off the pile and read the title out loud. "Superstition in the Tribal Cultures of Western

Africa: A Brief History." She hefted the thick book in her hand, weighing it. "Brief? The author isn't fooling anyone."

I gave up attempting to read each book and decided to simply reshelve them. The sooner I listened to her, the sooner she would leave. "Since you spend as much time here as I do, you might as well help. West African superstitions occupy the second and third shelves. They're arranged alphabetically by author."

She studied the spines of the shelved books, some with the title and author printed on them, others blank. With a sigh, she pulled out the blank ones to find the author names. "How do you know it goes on this shelf?"

"Professor Nash's cataloging sequence is based on subject, just like the Dewey Decimal System."

"The what?"

"Never mind. All you need to know is, he created a system that shelves the books on a particular subject together. This entire area is where the books on superstition are kept. They're sub-sorted by Africa which is then organized by region. All of those books are then arranged by author."

"So many books just on superstition in Western Africa! Fascinating."

"If you want to be an actress, you'll have to sound more convincing than that."

"Actually, I won't need to *sound* at all convincing since the audience can't hear the actors. Moving picture acting is all in the facial expressions. Like this." She mimed being fascinated by widening her eyes and ripping one of the books from the shelf and cradling it to her chest.

She needed more practice, but I didn't tell her that. Yesterday she wanted to be an artist, and today she was keen on acting. There was no point offending her; she would probably change her mind again next week.

Daisy slid the book back into its place on the shelf. "You

don't have a list of cataloging numbers to refer to. How did you know the book goes here?"

"I've memorized Professor Nash's system."

"Already? But it's only been just over a week since you started. It would have taken me months."

"When you enjoy what you do, it's not a hardship."

She sighed. "That's why I gave up painting. My art teacher told me to mine my soul for my innermost thoughts, fears and desires, but it was just so *hard*, Sylvia. Honestly, you have no idea how difficult it is to stare at a blank canvas and just *think*." I was about to say something sarcastic about her idea of hardship, but she added, "The only things I could think of were the poor men who died in the war and those who came back damaged beyond repair. And then I felt guilty because I didn't *want* to think about those things anymore." She took another book from the pile I carried and studied the title, but her bowed head didn't quite hide her tear-filled eyes.

It was easy to think of Daisy as somewhat selfish and spoiled, but I knew her well enough now to know she was a kind-hearted and generous soul who chose not to dwell on the past or let troubles overwhelm her. I envied her. After mourning the loss of my brother in the war and my mother to influenza, I'd found it difficult to crawl my way out of the pit of despair these last eighteen months. But I'd recently managed to do it. I still thought about my family every day, but the ache that accompanied those thoughts no longer pressed on my chest until I couldn't breathe. I was ready to move on, and Daisy's cheerful kindness had played a part in me being ready. She'd come into my life when I needed her the most, and I would be forever grateful.

I put my free arm around her. "Thank you for helping me."

She gave me a brief hug then waved the slim volume in

front of my face. "Where do you shelve books on pre-Christian Scottish superstitions?"

I pointed along the aisle. "Down there, top shelf."

She stood on her toes to read the spines of the other books. "Did you find anything more about silver magic in these books?"

"I did, and there is even a mention of a family name here and there, but none that I recognize. The author of the most recent text that mentions silver magic was convinced the lineage ended decades ago. He's wrong. Of course the book was written before Lord and Lady Rycroft met Marianne Folgate in 1891."

The name had been brought to my attention by Mr. Gabriel Glass, the only child of the famous Lady Rycroft, a powerful watchmaker magician. He was artless, like his father, but their family had met many magicians over the years, one of whom was Marianne Folgate. She'd disappeared in 1891 and not been seen or heard of since.

Her whereabouts remained a mystery, as did the history of my own lineage. I never knew my father. My mother refused to discuss him or her family, and we moved from city to city, never settling down, for reasons she refused to divulge. My brother and I gave up asking why, and we stopped asking about our father, too. But neither of us stopped wondering.

After reading my brother's suspicion that we were descended from silver magicians in his diary, I'd tried to learn more from Gabe's mother, thinking she must know a great many magicians. Although she'd gone overseas, Gabe was able to help, and it was he who told me his parents had once met the silver magician named Marianne Folgate. The name meant nothing to me. Without more information, I was unable to continue my search.

Besides, I was no longer sure my brother's suspicions

were correct. I felt nothing when I touched silver. I wasn't drawn to objects made with silver, and according to Gabe, a magician ought to feel a compulsion when near their craft.

With my new job in the Glass Library keeping me busy, I'd shelved my curiosity about my family and thrown myself into work and learning as much as I could about the library's collection of magical texts. It was fulfilling, and my new employer was a delight. Professor Nash was knowledgeable and interesting. His tales of traveling around the world collecting texts with his friend were full of adventure and daring, as if straight out of a book themselves.

Professor Nash peered around the end of the bookshelves. He carried a tray with a tea set and a plate of biscuits. His glasses had slipped down his nose, but with his hands full, he couldn't push them back up. He squinted over the top of them at us. "There you are! Tea?"

We followed him to the larger of the two reading nooks on the first floor. Soft light streamed through the arched window, bathing the leather sofa and armchairs in a warm glow. A book sat on the desk by the window, a leather strip marking the place where a library patron had reached in his reading. He'd asked if he could leave it there until tomorrow, when he planned to return in the morning. With so few patrons visiting the library, the professor gave his permission. We did not loan the books out. Most were too rare to be allowed to leave the premises.

Professor Nash set the tray on the table between sofa and chairs and sat down with a heavy sigh. He pushed his spectacles up his nose with one hand and rubbed his lower back with the other. "Tea, Ladies?"

"Lord, yes." Daisy reached for the plate of biscuits. "I'm starving." She offered the plate to me, as if she were the hostess at an afternoon tea. It was a testament to how comfortable she felt here, and how often she'd dropped in since I'd begun working at the Glass Library. She came so frequently that the professor might feel obliged to pay her a wage soon.

He handed me a cup and saucer. "And what were you two chatting about when I interrupted you?" If my former employer had asked me that question, it would have been said with a sneer and been followed with an accusation that I should be working, not talking to a friend. But Professor Nash was genuinely interested in the answer. He didn't care that Daisy came every day, or that she talked almost non-stop. Indeed, I think he liked the company. As long as my work got done, he didn't mind who visited.

In fact, I wondered if he cared about me working at all. There wasn't a lot to do in the library. Very few patrons came, and although he said he wanted me to catalog some old books that were still stored in the attic, he hadn't shown them to me yet. I was beginning to think he'd agreed to take me on for the company rather than to ease his workload.

Not that Gabe had given him a choice in the matter. After inadvertently getting me dismissed from my last position, he'd found me a place in the Glass Library out of a sense of guilt. Since his parents contributed a great deal of funding, the professor was hardly in a position to refuse. It had bothered me at first. I didn't like feeling that I owed Gabe. But now I was glad his guilt had assaulted him. I liked working in the Glass Library, very much.

"Marianne Folgate," I said in answer to the professor's question.

"Gabriel Glass," Daisy said at the same time.

The professor was more interested in my response than hers. "Folgate?"

I nodded. "Do you remember you told me about a silver magician by the name of Marianne, but you couldn't recall her last name? Gabe...looked into it for me." He'd told me

6

he'd consulted his family store of knowledge to gather the information, after deciding he could trust me. It wasn't my place to mention that store to anyone else. It was likely the professor already knew, but I wouldn't risk disappointing Gabe by speaking out of turn. "He discovered a silver magician known as Marianne Folgate, last seen here in London by his parents in 1891."

His glasses slipped down his nose again, but he did not push them back up. "Folgate. The name rings a bell." He sat heavily in an armchair, his brow furrowed.

Daisy picked up her teacup and held it by the handle, pinky finger extended. When she was sipping cocktails in her flat, she often sat with her shoes off and her feet tucked up underneath her. But when she had tea, she behaved like a genteel lady. She must have been brought up to respect the upper class ritual of a proper afternoon tea. "You would have met the woman named Marianne, too, but had simply forgotten her last name."

"No. I never knew Marianne's last name." The professor's brow grew more and more creased, until he finally deposited the cup back on the saucer with a clatter. He sprang to his feet. "I remember now! Come with me, Sylvia. You too, Miss Carmichael."

"Do call me Daisy. When you call me Miss Carmichael I feel as though I'm in trouble with the teacher."

Ordinarily he would smile at that, but he'd already walked off, distracted. He led the way through the stacks to the far wall and the final row of bookshelves. He tugged on the spine of a book covered in red leather until we heard a *click*. With a firm push on the shelves, the hidden door opened, revealing a small, empty vestibule and another door on the other side.

Daisy gasped. "How thrilling! Sylvia, did you know this existed?"

"I did."

The professor pushed open the second door and Daisy gasped again. "Nice digs, Prof."

Light from the high windows brightened the flat, reaching the far corners of the mezzanine bedroom and the sitting room below. Daisy ran her fingertips across the back of the leather sofa as we passed it, and took in every inch of the place. It reminded me of a gentleman's study, all dark wood, books and interesting curios, most likely picked up during his travels to far-flung places in search of texts about magic.

Daisy bent to inspect a white marble statue of a naked classical goddess. When I shooed her forward after the professor, she gave me an exaggerated wink, jabbed her thumb in Professor Nash's direction and mouthed "Lovely." I wasn't sure if she was referring to his taste in art or women, but her appreciation certainly came through loud and clear. Perhaps she'd make a good moving picture actress after all.

We climbed the spiral staircase to the mezzanine bedroom. The professor grabbed a long pole with a brass hook on the end that I hadn't noticed leaning up against the wall. He used the device to tug on a small loop of rope dangling from the ceiling. A trap door opened and a ladder unfolded.

He returned the pole to its place and grabbed a gas lantern from a shelf. He lit it and indicated we should follow him up the ladder.

Daisy and I exchanged glances then both broke into childish grins and climbed after him. The possibilities of what lay in the attic quickened my pulse. It was a silly dream of mine to find an important document in a dusty old attic, long forgotten in a trunk or hidden among ordinary papers. An undiscovered play by Shakespeare was probably too much to hope for, but I had a feeling I wasn't going to be disappointed with whatever we found.

We could easily stand up in the attic, although the three of us weren't tall. Gabe would have to stoop, and his giant friend, Alex Bailey, would be uncomfortable. Beyond the sphere of our light lurked darkness of indeterminate depth. In my teenage years, I'd devoured novels in which gruesome creatures dwelled in such bleak spaces, emerging when the innocent heroine dared to set foot in its lair. Those old stories and my active imagination had me determined to remain within the lantern's comforting glow.

"Now, where can it be?" The professor held the lantern high. Its light picked out traveling trunks covered in dust, stacks of books and unbound papers, also covered in dust, and artefacts of varying kinds, some so odd that I couldn't work out what they were. They were also dusty.

Daisy sneezed. "I can see your charwoman doesn't come up here."

"I clean my rooms myself," the professor said absently as he bent to inspect a stack of books on the floor.

A beautiful casket with a lid inlaid with different woods looked interesting, but I was hesitant to open it in case something leapt out at me. I was working up my courage when Daisy screamed.

She jumped backward and slammed the top drawer of a desk shut with her foot. I rushed to her side to comfort her.

The professor rushed forward too, his lantern extended as if he'd use it as a weapon against whatever vile creature skulked in the drawer. He drew in a deep breath and slowly, carefully, opened it.

He lowered the lantern and plucked out a dead rat by its tail. "No need to worry about this one, Daisy. It's the live ones that are a problem."

Daisy and I eyed the floor around us.

The professor returned the corpse to the drawer and closed it. "Sometimes I hear them scratching above my head as I try to sleep." He pushed his glasses up his nose and smiled at us. "If you ladies wouldn't mind looking through those books there, while I check these." He set the lantern down on a trunk between the two piles. "I know it's up here somewhere."

"What is?" I prompted, as he seemed to have forgotten he hadn't given us any details.

"An old book with Oscar's handwritten note inside the front cover." He studied the spines in his pile without picking one up. "It's not a book, actually. Not really. It's more of a collection of papers bound between wooden boards, fastened with silver clasps to keep it closed. It's not one of these," he added, moving on to another pile.

Silver. The connection to Marianne Folgate was beginning to become clear.

I checked the books on our pile but immediately discarded all of them. They were old, but were bound in leather, not boards, and they didn't have silver clasps. "What's written on the title page?"

"I don't know. The entire thing is written in a code that neither Oscar nor I could decipher."

I sat back on my haunches and looked around. The book could be anywhere, either in one of the piles or stored in a drawer or trunk, or on a shelf. Being bound with wooden boards and mounted with silver clasps made it unusual, however. Most of the covers were made of leather or thick paper, some were cloth-bound and a few had covers made of soft vellum. There was an entire trunk full of loose papers, and another with what I assumed was parchment sheets, tied together with leather strips. It would take an age to catalog them all.

I couldn't wait to begin.

I opened another trunk and breathed in the distinctive smell of old paper. Some people called the smell musty, but I liked it. To me, it was comforting, reminding me of days tucked up in bed, reading quickly to take in as much as I could before daylight completely disappeared. Or of a diversion made after school to the private library of an elderly couple who liked that I delighted in their collection. I'd always retreated to books when I'd felt sad or lonely. Unfortunately, those times had been too numerous.

They might now be at an end, but I still felt more at ease surrounded by books than I did in a room full of people.

The books in this trunk seemed older, their condition worse. Some were missing covers altogether, or the stitching at their spines frayed or was broken. Where covers still existed, they were either stained or had been nibbled by something with sharp teeth. Some books had torn pages, or the ink was faded, rendering the text illegible in parts.

I pulled them out, one by one, only to pause when a glint caught my eye. Surely it couldn't be the silver clasps. If the books had been up here for a while, neglected, the clasps must have tarnished.

Although if the clasps contained a silver magic spell, glinting was entirely possible.

I rummaged through the rest of the books and pulled out the one with wooden boards used as front and back covers, held closed with two silver clasps. They shone as brightly as if they'd just been polished. Each clasp was decorated with a circle surrounding a *fleur de lis*. The silver felt smooth, yet the engraved pattern was clear and well defined. Either it wasn't as old as I thought, or magic had kept it in excellent condition through the centuries.

I undid the clasps and opened the book. Inside was a torn piece of yellowed paper with a few words written in a neat, modern hand. "I found it."

Daisy crouched beside me, and Professor Nash knelt on my other side. He held the lantern close. "Yes, that's it. That's Oscar's writing."

He hadn't written in complete sentences, but rather just a few words. The single word "Folgate?" complete with question mark, occupied a line of its own. But it wasn't that which caught my eye and had Daisy drawing in a sharp breath. It was the tantalizing words Oscar had written above it.

The Medici Manuscript.

CHAPTER 2

$\mathcal{T}$hose two words, Medici and manuscript, conjured up an old world of art and culture, wealth and power, mystery and ruthlessness. My history was good enough that I knew the Medici family had ruled Renaissance Florence during a time of splendor. Over many years, the family had been bankers, merchants, popes, and dukes. Two Medici women had become queens of France. The men were influential in politics and religion, but had also been patrons of the arts, using their vast riches to fund architects and artists such as Da Vinci, Michaelangelo, and Raphael, among others.

All this I explained to Daisy, with Professor Nash nodding on.

Daisy picked up the piece of paper with Oscar Barratt's handwriting. The professor's friend and traveling companion had helped him bring back the library's collection of books over several decades. He'd not returned to England with the professor when war broke out. He'd stayed in Arabia and subsequently died. Professor Nash often spoke of him as we worked, telling me where a particular book had been discovered and the story behind its purchase or rescue. He always smiled when he talked about his friend, his gaze turning distant. But then he would become sad and change the subject. I suspected he felt as though he'd abandoned Oscar by not being with him at the end.

"There is a question mark after Folgate, but not The Medici Manuscript," Daisy pointed out. "Why is he so sure this book belonged to the Medicis?"

Professor Nash pointed to the first page. On it were five red circles arranged below a blue circle with three golden *fleurs de lis* inside. The colors were vibrant, as though the scribe had painted them only recently. "We couldn't decipher anything else in the manuscript except for this. It's the symbol of the Medicis. These spheres are on their coat of arms. You see them all over Florence, rendered on the buildings they funded. Churches, monuments, palaces...it's everywhere. Sometimes with the blue ball containing the *fleurs de lis*, sometimes without. Sometimes there are more balls, but five is the usual number."

"Isn't the *fleur de lis* a symbol of France?" I asked. "The Medicis were a Florentine family."

"They were bankers to the king of France. He let them use the *fleur de lis* in exchange for wiping some of his debt."

"Nice arrangement," Daisy muttered as she turned the page. Aside from faint marks, it was blank. She turned the page again.

There were no words or letters from the English alphabet on that page, but other pages contained them. They didn't make words in any languages that I recognized, however. They seemed to have been placed in a random order without spaces between. Mixed in among the letters were symbols. Some of the symbols were formed with simple strokes of the pen, while others were more complex, comprising of swirls and even recognizable images. One repeated symbol looked like a snake, for example, and there was also an eye and a knot that appeared regularly. We all agreed it was a code. Considering how old the manuscript was, the key to unlocking the code was probably lost.

I closed the book and stroked my thumb across one of the silver clasps. "Where did you get it?"

"We bought it from an Italian collector and antique dealer, along with several other books," Professor Nash said. "He purchased them from a wealthy American who claimed it originally came from a library established by Cosimo de' Medici. It's not clear whether the American knew it for certain or was simply guessing because of the Medici family symbol on the first page. The antique dealer knew nothing more about the book, but Oscar felt magic in the silver clasps so thought we should purchase it. I suppose he wrote Folgate later after remembering the silver magician, although the question mark indicates he wasn't entirely sure of her name."

"Your friend was a magician?" Daisy asked.

The professor nodded. "Ink was Oscar's specialty. He could make words rise off the page and float in the air." He smiled wistfully and blinked rapidly. "He felt the residual magic in the silver."

I opened the book to the front page again and indicated the Medici family symbol. "He didn't say whether the ink is also magical? The quality is excellent to have survived in such lovely condition for this long."

"Oscar would have mentioned if the ink was magician-made. We believed that page was added later. Look at the paper."

"Don't you mean parchment?" Daisy asked.

"Paper and parchment are different. Paper is made from rotting rags. Parchment is made from animal skin. This is definitely paper."

She screwed up her nose.

I carefully turned a few pages. The professor was right. The front page was different to the rest. It was thinner, but the quality was excellent. It hadn't yellowed like the rest.

Professor Nash took the scrap with Oscar's handwritten note from Daisy. "I suppose he planned to follow up with the silver magician when he had time, hoping that researching her ancestry would lead him to the manuscript's author." He sighed heavily. "But he never got around to it."

I touched his arm but said nothing. There were no words that could soothe someone who'd lost a dear friend. "It's unlikely he would have found Marianne Folgate anyway. After Gabe told me about her, I visited the General Registry Office. If my brother thought we were descended from silver magicians, I wondered if she could be a relative. But I found no reference to her."

"So she was born and died outside of London," he said. "And if she married, she wed elsewhere."

I'd also looked for references to my mother while I was at the GRO, but the clerk found no Alice Ashe in the records.

I skimmed my palm over the front page before closing the book and inspecting the silver clasps. Perhaps Oscar was right. Silver magic was a rare form of magic, so perhaps the magic in the silver had been put there by Marianne Folgate's ancestors. *My* ancestors. It was a wild theory, but I wanted to follow it and see where it led. Oscar had died before he could resume his hunt for the silversmith who'd made the clasps, but the search didn't need to die with him. I could pick up where he left off.

The problem was, where to begin?

I peered into the trunk where the Medici Manuscript had been stored. "Are these the other books you purchased from the Italian collector? Could one of them contain the key to cracking the code?"

The professor shook his head. "We looked. We also wrote

to the American who sold the books to the collector, but he couldn't help us."

Daisy stood and dusted off her skirt at the knees. "You want to decode it, don't you, Sylv?"

"I'd like to try, although I doubt I'll succeed if Professor Nash and Oscar Barratt couldn't." I looked to the professor. "May I take it home with me? I'll take very good care of it."

"I know you will, and of course you can." He picked up the lantern and pushed himself to his feet with a slight wince of pain. He wasn't an elderly man—probably in his sixties— but his back often bothered him.

It was difficult to imagine this frail, studious man adventuring through foreign lands, but I could well believe he'd enjoy it with a more assertive companion. He made Oscar Barratt sound like an interesting fellow. Like me, Oscar was a former journalist who'd changed career. His had been by choice. Mine had been because the men came back from the war and resumed their prior employment. There'd no longer been a position for me at the newspaper.

Not that I was complaining. It had worked out well in the end, and journalism had never really suited me. I enjoyed the research and the writing, but I hated interviewing people and the way I had to twist a story to make it more sensational. Librarianship was a better match for me.

* * *

I SPENT my evening trying to decode the manuscript but had no luck. I'd moved into a new lodging house during the week after staying at Daisy's flat for as long as I could stand it. As much as I liked her company, we were always in one another's way. Her flat simply wasn't big enough for two.

The new lodging house was more private than the last. It was an old house that had been renovated and turned into five separate rooms, each large enough to contain a bed, table, two chairs, a wardrobe and some shelves. It was nice sharing the bathroom with only four other residents instead of dozens, and the landlady cooked all our meals. Nor was she a dragon like the matron at my former residence, although she did insist on a curfew and no male visitors in our rooms. It was more expensive, but I could afford it after having sold a painting given to me by a well-known artist whom I'd mistakenly considered a friend. Thanks to the sale, I had savings in the bank for the first time.

My life was certainly improving, and I had the Glass Library to thank for that—and Gabriel Glass. It wasn't simply that he'd found the job for me. I couldn't quite put my finger on what he'd said or done to make me feel happier, however. It was simply...him. By asking me to help solve the case of the art theft, he'd made me feel as though I had something to offer, that I was valued and important. I hadn't felt that way in a long time, not since my brother and mother died.

I hadn't seen Gabe for over a week. As much as I wanted to visit him, I had no reason to do so. I couldn't simply show up on his doorstep at afternoon tea time. Perhaps if he weren't engaged to be married, I would have called on him.

Or perhaps not. Calling on gentlemen at their homes was not in my nature. Besides, he was a wealthy man from the upper rung of society. He was more dashing and charming than a man had a right to be. I was a rather small and plain librarian with no connections, no money, and an unknown family lineage. The only son of Lord and Lady Rycroft would not associate with me in the way that I wanted, even if he wasn't engaged to a beautiful, elegant and charming woman from a wealthy magician family.

I pushed thoughts of Gabe from my mind and returned to the book. There was a faint mark on the second page that could have been made by water, but I didn't think so. It was too fine and quite intricate. I suspected it had been made by pen and ink, only it had faded over time or been deliberately erased. I went in search of my landlady and borrowed a magnifying glass from her then stood directly under the light-bulb in my room. It definitely wasn't a water mark or smudge of dirt. Indeed, I was quite sure it was writing. I could just make out what appeared to be the letters D and E written in an old-fashioned hand.

I inspected the rest of the pages, but none of the others had similar marks. I needed a stronger magnifying glass to get a proper look.

At some point, I fell asleep with the manuscript beside me on the bed. Fortunately I didn't roll onto it in the night, but having stayed up reading, I'd slept in and was going to be late if I didn't hurry. I quickly changed and carefully tucked the book into my bag. There was no time for a proper break-fast, but my landlady insisted I take a piece of toast to eat on the way.

I arrived at Crooked Lane on time, only to be stopped before I reached the library by a fellow I'd met once and taken an immediate disliking to. This time he was not alone.

Albert Scarrow the journalist removed his homburg and smiled. I wasn't sure if it was the smile or the needle-sharp mustache above his top lip that gave him a sinister edge, but I recoiled at the sight of him.

"Good morning," he said. "You may not remember me, but we've met before."

"I remember."

"You work in the Glass Library." He nodded at the library door.

"What do you want, Mr. Scarrow?"

"I want to know if Mr. Glass will be in today."

"He doesn't work here."

The small flare of a cigarette in the shadows by the solicitor's office drew my attention. Mr. Scarrow's companion blew out a coil of smoke.

"Do you know where I can find him?" Mr. Scarrow asked.

"No."

The companion stepped forward into the light. He was aged around thirty with dark curly hair and the shadow of a beard. He did not attempt a smile but gave me a simple nod in greeting. He addressed Mr. Scarrow. "Let's go."

"Not yet."

"She doesn't know where he is." He spoke with an educated accent but wore the coarse, loose clothes of a laborer. He carried a camera, the professional kind, not the sort that could fit into a pocket, and a battered leather satchel was slung over his shoulder.

"We'll wait. Last time he just turned up here."

The photographer's jaw firmed. "We're wasting our time."

"You are," I said before Mr. Scarrow could speak. "I don't know where Mr. Glass is. I haven't seen him since the last time you saw him here." It wasn't strictly true, but was close enough to the truth that I could lie without qualms.

The photographer drew on his cigarette. At Mr. Scarrow's clicked tongue of frustration, he dug out a tin cigarette case from his pocket. He flipped the lid with his thumb and held it out.

Mr. Scarrow took one. The photographer offered the tin to me, but I declined.

Mr. Scarrow lit his own cigarette then withdrew a business card from his jacket pocket. "If you see him, will you let me know?"

"No!"

"I'll pay you."

"Definitely not. If you'll excuse me, I'm now late for work, thanks to you."

"Do you know how he managed to escape a kidnapping attempt in rather miraculous fashion?"

I'd turned to go, but stopped and faced him again. Mr. Scarrow's face contorted into his unfortunately familiar weaselly smile. Even if I knew the answer to his question, I wouldn't have given it to him. "I don't know what you're talking about. Good day to you."

Mr. Scarrow returned the homburg to his head. "Good day, Miss..."

"Ashe. Sylvia Ashe."

I hurried to the library, pausing before I opened the door. Mr. Scarrow passed through the narrow entrance to the adjoining street, but his photographer had stopped before exiting the lane. He watched me.

I pushed open the door and found Professor Nash seated at the front desk, his head in his hands. He looked up upon my entry.

"Whatever's the matter?" I asked.

He handed me the newspaper he'd been reading. "It says he's all right, but it would have been a traumatic experience. Poor Gabriel."

Poor Gabe indeed. According to the article, there'd been a kidnapping attempt last night. It was the second since I'd met him. The first had taken place outside Burlington House on Piccadilly. In that instance, he'd managed to extricate himself and get the attacker in a headlock. He'd been forced to release him when the kidnapper's accomplice pulled out a gun.

The latest attempt must be the reason behind Mr. Scarrow's renewed interest in Gabe, not the Burlington House attempt. That incident hadn't been reported in the papers, but an earlier event had, and that was his initial reason for wanting to interview Gabe. The Glass Library was the one place Mr. Scarrow knew for certain was associated with Gabe, and had hoped to find him here. He'd succeeded. But Gabe no longer had a reason to come to the library. The case I'd helped him solve was over.

"Apparently this time someone tried to kidnap him outside a restaurant as he was about to enter," I said as I read. "How dreadful." The article went on to say that a witness saw him stopped at gunpoint by a burly figure. Gabe had somehow managed to escape by grabbing the gun and turning it on the kidnapper. He was then forced to release the fellow when a motorcar drove up and someone in the front passenger seat pointed their gun at him.

Except for the location, it was very similar to the previous abduction attempt.

"It's so strange," the professor said with a shake of his head. "Are they after money?"

There must be better ways to obtain money, surely. With his parents overseas, there'd be a delay in paying the ransom. If I were them, I'd kidnap one of Gabe's friends, or his cousin, and make him pay before releasing them. He was a man of principle and honor, and his friends were dear to him.

On the other hand, his greatest friend was the son of a police detective and built like an athletic giant, and his cousin was fearless and carried a gun. It would be easier to bundle a dozen cats into a motorcar. It seemed Gabe was just as difficult to abduct. He'd managed to escape both attempts, rather miraculously, as Mr. Scarrow put it.

Mr. Scarrow's interest had first been piqued when Gabe rescued a child from drowning and tried to save the father. According to the child, Gabe had been under water a long time. The journalist's curiosity had been further piqued when he learned Gabe survived four years of war without serious injury.

I wondered what Mr. Scarrow would think about the time Gabe rescued me from a killer by racing up the stairs extraordinarily quickly. An imaginative person might suggest he'd been *inhumanly* quick.

I dismissed that notion as silly. Gabe was just a very lucky man who was fast on his feet and capable in a crisis.

"I think I'll telephone him," Professor Nash said, reaching for the device. "Just to make sure he's all right. His parents would want me to."

I smiled to myself. It wasn't the first time someone had told me they were looking out for Gabe while his parents were away. He had a lot of people who cared for him. That made him lucky indeed.

I removed the Medici Manuscript from my bag and put my bag into the desk drawer for safe keeping. "May I speak to him when you're finished? There were some people outside looking for him and I want to warn him." I clutched the book to my chest and waited while Professor Nash spoke to Gabe then mentioned I'd like to speak to him.

Instead of handing the telephone over to me, he hung up the receiver. "He's on his way here. He thought it best to hear what you had to say in person rather than over the telephone."

"Oh? Why?"

"He didn't say, but I got the impression he was a little bored and was looking for something to do."

"His friends won't like him leaving the house after last night's incident."

My statement proved to be true. Gabe was accompanied by both Alex and Willie. The former greeted me amiably. The latter scowled, crossed her arms, and stood guard by the door. I wasn't sure if the scowl was for me or for Gabe, for insisting on leaving the house.

Gabe's greeting was cheerful and easy. Too cheerful and easy considering what he'd been through. He seemed unharmed. He bore no marks of a fight and moved with his usual athletic grace. I watched him closely as he leaned against the spiral staircase, just to make sure he hadn't been injured.

Behind me, Willie cleared her throat, and I realized I'd been staring at him longer than appropriate.

I lifted my gaze to see Gabe smiling back at me with that mischievous crooked smile of his. My cheeks burned. "I'm relieved to see you're unharmed, Gabe."

He shrugged a shoulder, as if the kidnapping attempt had been no more of a bother than an uninvited guest dropping in. "They were inept."

"It's the second time. Aren't you worried?"

"The police are looking into it."

"Yes, but...how did the kidnappers know where to find you?"

"I was attending an officers' dinner for the Grenadier Guards. The function was reported in the papers. I suppose the kidnapper realized I would be there, just like they did when I attended the opening day of the Royal Exhibition at Burlington House."

"You need to stop attending society events."

Gabe's gaze shifted to Alex, standing near Willie. They both stood with arms crossed now, glares directed at Gabe. Clearly this was a continuation of an earlier argument.

"I'll go where I please." I got the feeling Gabe's statement was more for their benefit than mine. "But I'll be less predictable in future."

"Then you shouldn't have come here!"

"Aye," Willie said darkly. "If you hadn't telephoned, he wouldn't."

Professor Nash put up a finger. "Actually, it was me that telephoned."

"And I make my own decisions," Gabe told her. "I needed to get out of the house. You two are stifling me." He pushed off from the staircase. "Shall we retreat to the reading nook, Sylvia? You can tell me what you need to say there."

Seeing him again was playing havoc on my nerves. I was very aware of him, and of my reaction to him. I wished I wasn't enamored, but it was impossible not to be. What woman wouldn't want to be the focus of his attention? But it was wrong of me to want it—and to like it. My annoyance with myself made my response a little too curt. "What I have to say can be said here. In fact, it relates to recent events."

He frowned and opened his mouth to speak, but at that moment, the door was thrust open, knocking Willie in the shoulder. She tumbled forward and was only stopped from falling by Alex.

Daisy pushed her bicycle inside. "Have you read the—?" Fortunately she cut herself off. Surprise flitted across her face before she schooled her features into a polite smile. "Good morning, everyone. It's nice to see you again, Gabe, Willie." Her gaze slid sideways. "Alex," she added as afterthought.

"Working hard at your painting again, I see," he said.

She leaned the bicycle against the wall. "Actually I'm changing careers. I'm going to be an actress."

"Is that so? You've got auditions lined up?"

"Not yet."

"Shouldn't you organize that *before* you abandon painting? It's what a sensible person would do."

She gave him a smile laced with condescension. "I never claimed to be sensible."

He grunted a humorless laugh.

"I also don't take career advice from someone who doesn't have a job."

Every muscle in Alex's face twitched with indignation. "I'm a consultant for Scotland Yard."

"Of course you are."

"I am!"

Alex puffed out his chest and Daisy tossed her head in response. It was like watching two peacocks strutting about before engaging in a fight. I couldn't look away. Part of me wondered if there'd be a different outcome to their exchange if they were alone. The air between them was certainly charged, and not altogether in a negative way.

Willie glanced between them and rolled her eyes. "I can see you on stage, Daisy, dancing and singing. I know a few actresses and dancers. Want me to ask how you can get an audition?"

"I can't sing or dance."

Alex barked a laugh.

"I don't want to be on stage," Daisy said tightly. "I want to be in moving pictures."

"I know a producer," Willie said.

"Of course you do," Alex muttered.

Willie put her arm around Daisy's shoulders and steered her through the marble columns to the library proper. Alex watched them go from beneath hooded lids.

Gabe moved up alongside me. "Welcome back to my circus."

I grinned. "It seems I've provided my own clown again."

He laughed softly. "So what is it you needed to tell me?"

"That journalist Scarrow was here looking for you. I spoke to him outside."

His stance had been relaxed but he now straightened, drawing himself up to his full height. "Are you all right? Did he upset you?"

"I'm fine. He left, along with his photographer."

"Photographer?" He shook his head. "Damn it. I'm sorry, Sylvia. I'll call on Scarrow's editor and warn him to stay away."

"He won't back down. They want their story and they won't stop until they get it."

"Then they can try to get it from me, not by bothering my friends." He clasped my arms and dipped his head to study me. "You seem a little rattled. Are you sure you're all right?"

My pulse quickened and my heart thudded in my chest. I shouldn't like having him look at me like that, but I couldn't help it.

As if he suddenly realized how inappropriate it was, he let me go. "Sorry."

"Don't be."

He looked away, either avoiding my gaze or wondering who'd seen us. We were alone, however. Alex and Professor Nash had followed Daisy and Willie into the library. I hadn't noticed them leave.

"Gabe...you seem more worried about Scarrow than the kidnapping attempt."

"Do I?"

"Is that because you know who's trying to abduct you?"

He sighed. "I have no idea who it is, but at least they haven't tried to take anyone else, just me. Whereas Scarrow is bothering you and the professor." His lack of concern for his own safety was astounding. It could be that he'd come back from the war feeling somewhat invincible after having miraculously survived it.

Or it could be that he *was* invincible.

There was that absurd notion again. I shook it off. It was the stuff of childish stories.

"Scarrow is only bothering us because he doesn't know where else to look for you," I pointed out. "He doesn't know where you live. I assume the kidnappers don't know either. They have to guess which events you'll attend. So Alex and Willie are right. You should stay home."

"Thank you for your concern, Sylvia, but I'll be fine if I don't go anywhere too public."

Willie snorted as she approached. "When we tell you to

stay home, you complain about being lectured, but when she says it, you thank her."

"Try using a different tone and I might thank you, too."

She snorted again. "It ain't got nothing to do with tone." She turned to me. "Ivy is real concerned about him too. She called before we left and she's coming to dinner to check on him herself. She told him to stay home today, too, and he was real nice to her on the telephone."

I suspected she was pointing that out to me to ensure I didn't think I was special, and to remind me that he had a fiancée. I wanted to tell her that she had nothing to worry about, but I couldn't. Not in front of Gabe.

He stepped back a few paces and once again glanced around. He looked out of sorts, rather like how I felt. His gaze settled on the Medici Manuscript on the desk. "That looks old. What's it about?"

I picked it up and opened it to the front page. I caught Oscar's note before it slipped out. "We don't know. We discovered it yesterday in the attic." I told him about its magical clasps, its connection to the Medici family, and that no one could decipher it. "The professor and Oscar Barratt wondered if the magic was put in the silver by an ancestor of Marianne Folgate's."

"And therefore an ancestor of yours. No wonder you want to learn more about it." He flipped slowly through the pages as Willie peered on. "I know a very clever mathematician who's good with codes. I can ask him to take a look at it."

"That's a good idea, thank you. I think there's something here that may be useful." I pointed to the faint marks on the second page. "When looking through a magnifying glass, I could just make out a D and an E. The rest was too faint, but I believe it's two words."

"Could be the code's key," Willie said.

Gabe shook his head. "Not in the book itself. It defeats the purpose of using a code in the first place." He held the book to the window for the better light, but it was no use. "We need a stronger magnifier."

The door to the library opened and Mr. Scarrow's photographer stood there, his camera in hand. His gaze fell on Gabe.

CHAPTER 3

The photographer's steady gaze settled on each of us in turn, but didn't linger on Gabe. He didn't recognize him.

I wouldn't enlighten him. "I told Mr. Scarrow that Mr. Glass hasn't been here recently, and I won't answer your questions."

He removed his hat. "That's not why I'm here. I wanted to apologize." He spoke quietly, his voice a low purr. "I didn't realize Scarrow was going to try and get answers from anyone other than Glass himself. If I'd known, I wouldn't have come."

I dared not glance Gabe's way. "Thank you, Mr...."

"Trevelyan. Carl Trevelyan." He glanced around the office and towards the library beyond. "So this is the Glass Library. Where do I sign up to become a member?"

"You don't need to be a member. Anyone can come in and look at the books. Do you have an interest in magic?"

"I do now." His features lifted. It wasn't quite a smile. I suspected Mr. Trevelyan was someone who smiled rarely. That alone made me think he must have fought in the war.

He wasn't the first returned soldier I'd met who'd lost his sense of humor on the battlefields.

"Carl Trevelyan!" Gabe stepped forward, only to have his sleeve grabbed by Willie. Like me, she didn't want him to talk to this man. Mr. Trevelyan may be the photographer, not the journalist, but he was capable of asking questions too. "Carl Trevelyan the war photographer?"

Mr. Trevelyan nodded. "That's right."

Gabe extended his hand. "William Johnson."

Willie and I both blinked at him. He'd taken the masculine version of her name.

Mr. Trevelyan shook Gabe's hand. "Where did you serve?"

"Here and there. Your images were very good. The newspapers wouldn't have sold half as many copies without them."

Mr. Trevelyan gave another nod. He seemed somewhat embarrassed to be praised. "I'll come back later, if that's all right with you, Miss Ashe."

"If you're returning to look at the books, then we close at five," I said.

Mr. Trevelyan made to leave, but Gabe blocked the exit. "Do you have a lens that will make an object appear larger?" he asked.

"No such lens exists," Mr. Trevelyan said. "But a macro bellows will do the trick. I have one back at my studio."

Gabe picked up the book and carefully flipped the pages until he reached the second one with the faded writing. "Will it increase the size of this so we can read it?"

"I'm not sure. It's very faint. But I'll try." Mr. Trevelyan checked the time on his wristwatch. "My studio isn't far if you want to go now."

Gabe looked to me. "Do you think Nash can spare you?"

"It's not necessary for me to come."

"Of course it is. It's your discovery."

I was about to acquiesce when Willie piped up. "Sylvia's right. She should stay here." She poked Gabe in his arm. "And you should go home...*William.*"

He waved off her concern and headed into the library. "I'll speak to the professor."

Willie sighed and muttered something under her breath, throwing in a glare at me for good measure. I followed Gabe. Professor Nash was my employer and this was my job; I ought to be the one who requested time off.

He was very enthusiastic about the idea. "Researching the origins of our books is work, after all," he said.

Gabe handed me the Medici Manuscript and we returned to Mr. Trevelyan, waiting in the front room with Willie. Ordinarily I'd feel sympathy for someone stuck alone with her while she glared at him, but he glared right back, unperturbed. It was like watching a child's game of who would blink first.

Gabe must have suspected the challenge would go on forever because he broke the impasse by stepping between them. "Is your studio close enough to walk there or should I drive?"

"There ain't enough room in the Prince Henry if we all go," Willie said.

Daisy grabbed the handlebars of her bicycle and opened the door. "I'm not coming. I'm going to talk to your producer friend." She kissed Willie's cheek. "You are a dear."

Willie nodded sagely. "Well now, seems like we can all fit in the motor, but only if Alex sits up front with you, *William.* He takes up too much space on account of him liking Mrs. Ling's cakes too much."

"I'm all muscle!" Alex cried.

Daisy pointedly arched her brows at his stomach, which looked flat to me.

Alex tilted his head to the side. "Weren't you leaving?"

She waggled her fingers at us in a wave and walked off, pushing the bicycle, her heels *click clacking* on the cobblestones down the lane.

I tucked the book under my arm and left ahead of the men. Willie caught up to me and pulled me further along, out of earshot.

"You should encourage him," she said. "He likes you."

"But he's engaged to Ivy!"

"I was talking about Trevelyan."

I almost glanced over my shoulder to look at him but managed to stop myself. "What makes you think he likes me? He hasn't been flirtatious."

"Course he has. He was flirting with you like you was a rich debutante at a ball and he an impoverished lord."

"That's a rather specific metaphor."

"Well go on, then."

"What?"

"Go back there and flutter your lashes at him. Make him see that you like him and want to meet up with him later."

"But I don't."

She looked at me like I was a fool. "Why not? He's handsome and has a good job. He's a war hero too, in a way. Them war photographers saw just as much action as the rest of the soldiers. I like his physique, not too large and tall, but nice. And that stubble on his jaw gives him a ruggedness. He ain't soft like most English gen'lemen. He looks like a real man to me."

I smiled. "Perhaps you should be the one flirting with him."

We reached Gabe's cream-colored Vauxhall Prince Henry, parked at the side of the road, and watched as the men approached. Willie had gone quiet, pensive.

"Although he's a little young for you," I added.

She turned sharply to me. "If I wanted him, you wouldn't stand a chance." She climbed into the backseat first and pulled me after her, which left Mr. Trevelyan to sit on my other side. It was very cozy, particularly when he didn't keep his leg to himself. It didn't seem to bother him that his knee bumped up against mine.

He directed Gabe to his studio in St Giles then alighted from the motor after we parked. He extended his hand to me and assisted me onto the pavement. He did the same for Willie, but she ignored his hand and clapping him on the shoulder as she passed instead.

"I know you work with that pigswill, Scarrow, but I like you," she declared. "You ain't a fool."

"High praise," Alex muttered.

Mr. Trevelyan merely nodded. He didn't sport so much as a hint of a smile.

The row of shops were busy with people coming and going, doing their morning shopping and running errands. The rooms above the shops appeared to be residential flats or offices rented by professionals. It was in one of these, above a pharmacy, that Mr. Trevelyan's photographic studio was housed. It was unlike any photographic studio I'd been in. There were no props for subjects to use, no painted backdrops to sit in front of and pretend they were on a tropical beach. The room was small. There was barely enough space for the large desk, covered with photographs, and the padlocked cupboard. A folded tripod leaned against the cupboard. A door behind the desk must lead to the developing room. This was the studio of a photojournalist, not someone who made his living from taking portraits.

Mr. Trevelyan unlocked the cupboard, revealing three shelves of cameras and other photographic equipment. Below the shelves were narrow drawers. I wasn't sure why one person needed so many cameras, even if photography was his profession. The contents of the cupboard must have cost a small fortune.

He removed a larger camera than the one he carried and an accordion-like device which he attached to it. He mounted the lens onto that. "Miss Ashe, please open the book to the required page."

I set the book on the desk while Mr. Trevelyan moved the lamp closer and switched it on. He extended the macro bellows to its full length and placed the lens very close to the page. He took some shots, adjusting the camera's position minutely each time.

After taking nearly a dozen photographs, he stepped back. "These will be developed by tomorrow. If you'd like to come past at ten, Miss Ashe, I'll have them ready."

"We will," Gabe said, emphasizing the 'we.'

"You're busy tomorrow, *William*," Willie said.

Gabe shook his head. "No, I'm not."

"It's Sylvia's work. Let her do it."

"I don't mind." Gabe went to pick up the book, but Mr. Trevelyan grabbed it first.

"May I keep this a little longer? If the first lot don't come out, I'll take more."

I was reluctant to let it out of my sight. The book was rare and valuable. But it ought to be safe here overnight. No one knew about it except us. "Yes, of course."

He stroked the clasps with his thumb. "You seem to have an interesting project, Miss Ashe. I'd like to hear more about it, if you have the time."

"Thank you for doing this," Gabe said quickly. He indicated the door. "After you, Sylvia."

I followed Gabe's lead and did not respond to Mr. Trevelyan's request to discuss the book with him. Whether he liked it or not, he was associated with Mr. Scarrow, and I needed to be careful around him. I didn't want to accidentally let slip that William Johnson was in fact Gabriel Glass. I needed to remember that I couldn't trust this man, even though he'd done us a service.

Downstairs, Gabe opened the motorcar door for me. I slipped onto the backseat and Willie followed. After Gabe closed the door on us, she said, "Trevelyan definitely likes you. You should suggest meeting for dinner."

"I don't want to."

"Then you're mad. He's got a quality about him."

"He works with Scarrow!"

"So? Just keep your trap shut about Gabe and everything'll be fine. Meet up with him, flirt with him a little, and enjoy yourself. You need some fun."

Considering she hardly knew me, it felt like an insult. Was I that dull?

Or was she trying to push me in Mr. Trevelyan's direction because she suspected I liked Gabe more than was appropriate given the circumstances? Perhaps she wasn't as much of a fool as I thought.

Gabe slid into the driver's seat while Alex cranked the motor. "Why does Sylvia need some fun?" he asked.

"Ain't none of your business," Willie said.

Gabe stretched his arm across the back of the seat and turned to her. He gave her a dark, broody look that took me by surprise. He didn't seem to take his cousin seriously most of the time, but now he looked like he wanted to challenge her to a duel.

She sank into the seat and fell into a morose silence.

Alex climbed in and Gabe revved the engine. He drove very fast back to Crooked Lane. Instead of merely dropping me off, he parked and walked with me to the library. Alex and Willie followed, alert to an approach by a potential kidnapper. Gabe didn't seem worried, and nor was I. The kidnappers wouldn't attempt anything while he was in their company.

The reason he escorted me back to the library became clear when he invited Professor Nash and me to dinner. "Ivy will be there, with her family. She mentioned she'd like to see you again, Sylvia. She enjoyed meeting you."

I wanted to see Willie's reaction to that comment, but she was out of my line of sight.

Professor Nash accepted and I followed his lead. It wasn't until Gabe left that I had second thoughts. It wasn't that Ivy would dislike having me there—she knew I wasn't a threat to her relationship. It was more that I didn't belong. The only other time I'd dined with Gabe, it had been a pleasant evening, not at all awkward. The presence of Alex's down-to-earth family had made me feel as though I wasn't out of place. But Ivy's family would be different. If they were anything like her, they'd be elegant and aristocratic. Those were not words anyone would use to describe me.

THE EVENING BEGAN with cocktails in the drawing room. Going by the pinched lips of Mrs. Hobson as she accepted a martini from the footman's tray, the modern habit of drinking before dinner was not to her taste. Like her daughter, she was tall and willowy. The new fashion for slim-fitting dresses would suit her, but as with most women her age, she preferred the pre-war style with a corset that exaggerated her figure into an unnatural S shape, and layers of fabric arranged in drapes, with an abundance of lace.

Ivy inherited her sleek, dark beauty from her mother, but her golden eyes came from her father, as did her magical ability, apparently. Along with her brother, Bertie, the three of them were leather magicians. After magicians emerged from the shadows almost thirty years ago, thanks to the efforts of

Gabe's parents, Mr. Hobson had expanded his boot business. His footwear was known for their quality and longevity, and the military contracted him to make boots for the army at the outbreak of the war. It had made them extraordinarily wealthy, the results of which could be seen in the exquisite jewelry Ivy and Mrs. Hobson wore, as well as the latest fashion gracing Ivy's tall frame.

She looked even more beautiful than the last time I dined there. Her lavender silk dress was trimmed with seed pearls and white beads across a daringly low-cut bodice. Together with the diamonds and amethyst necklace covering her decolletage and skimming the swell of her breasts, she dazzled and shimmered as she crossed the floor to me.

With cocktail glass held away from her body, Ivy bent to kiss my cheek. "You look lovely tonight, Sylvia."

I bit my tongue and forced a smile. She probably hadn't meant to imply that I didn't look lovely last time we met. "Thank you. My dress is new."

Daisy had taken me shopping after I sold the painting. I'd spent far more than I intended on the outfit, but I was now glad that I had. At the time, I'd thought the deep blue dress with chiffon sleeves and elaborate embroidery in midnight-blue thread extravagant, but it was appropriate for dinner in Mayfair. Ivy would have coupled it with a necklace, but I didn't own one. Next time I'd borrow something from Daisy.

Mrs. Hobson had been watching me surreptitiously ever since we were introduced, but now she came to stand by her daughter's side. "And how are you connected to the Glass family?" she asked me.

"I work in the Glass Library."

"You're on the committee?"

"I'm assistant librarian to Professor Nash." I indicated the professor, talking with Gabe, Alex, and both Hobson men. Willie was nowhere to be seen.

"How…interesting." She sipped her cocktail.

Ivy touched my arm. "Sylvia is very smart. She used to be a journalist."

Mrs. Hobson's nostrils flared. "So Gabriel's dislike of journalists doesn't extend to former ones?"

Ivy's smile stiffened. "My family also has a dislike of newspapermen," she told me.

"For any particular reason?" I asked.

Ivy opened her mouth to speak, but Willie chose that moment to enter the drawing room. "You started cocktails without me!" She signaled to the footman who brought over the tray. She plucked off a glass, leaned closer to him and whispered something in his ear that made him laugh. "Go and get some more drinks," she added.

"Right you are, ma'am," he said with a wink.

Mrs. Hobson sighed as she watched him limp out of the room.

"The footman is new," Ivy explained to her mother. "You know how difficult it is to find good staff since the war."

"Indeed."

I sipped my cocktail, wondering if it was too soon for a second. I was beginning to think I might need fortifying to get through the evening.

As if he guessed I needed rescuing, Gabe excused himself and joined us. "What are you ladies discussing?"

"Sylvia's work," Ivy said. "I was telling Mother that she was a journalist but had to give it up. I was just about to ask her if she would return to it if she had the opportunity."

"I enjoy working in the Glass Library," I said.

She winked theatrically at me and gave me a sly smile, as if we were sharing a joke. "Of course you have to say that in front of your employer."

Gabe tensed.

"Professor Nash is my employer," I pointed out.

Ivy fell silent.

Her mother forged on, however. "Gabe's family pay your wage, Miss Ashe. That makes *him* your employer."

"The library's money comes from donations," Gabe said stiffly.

"Of which your family is a major contributor."

"Let's not talk about work and business," Ivy cut in. "It's all quite dull."

"The library work isn't dull at all," Gabe said. "Just today Sylvia found an old book which was once owned by the Medici family."

Mr. Hobson overheard from the other side of the room and joined us. "Medici, eh? How extraordinary. Tell us about the book, Nash."

The professor gave a brief account of the manuscript but didn't mention my personal reasons for wanting to learn more about its origins. "Miss Ashe is spearheading the research in the hope of tracing the silver magician who created the clasps."

At the mention of magic, Mr. Hobson's face lit up. "Silver magic? Now that would be a valuable craft. Pity one of those magicians can't be dug up somewhere. Not as important as time magicians, of course, but probably the next best thing, considering there's no gold magicians anymore. If you happen to rustle up a female one of marriageable age in your research, Miss Ashe, be sure to send her Bertie's way."

He laughed. Nobody else did, not even Willie. Bertie flushed scarlet while Mrs. Hobson drained her glass.

"Watch magic, not time," Gabe corrected.

"Come now, we both know Lady Rycroft can make the magic of others last longer. If we don't call it time magic, what can we call it?"

Gabe's thumb tapped furiously against his thigh.

It was a relief when the footman returned with more cocktails. Despite his limp, the liquid in the glasses hardly rippled. Several of the guests pounced on his tray, exchanging empty glasses for full ones. I was one of them.

Ivy remained with Gabe. She took his hand, forcing the thumb-tapping to stop. She said something quietly to him, but he didn't respond. He looked like he was regretting this evening as his guests waited somewhat impatiently for the dinner gong.

Mrs. Hobson sidled up to me. "Ivy tells me you're not a magician, Miss Ashe. Is there *any* magic in your family?"

"No."

She seemed pleased with my answer.

I thought it best to keep the conversation going. It would be a long night if the awkwardness was allowed to continue. "Your husband and both children are leather magicians, isn't that so?"

"They are."

"And you?"

"I'm sure there's magic in my ancestry."

"What makes you think that?"

She waved a hand. The large golden citrine ring dazzled in the light. "It's just a feeling."

Willie burst out laughing at something the footman said to her. When he realized everyone was looking, he dipped his head and left. Willie wiped her nose with the back of her hand and downed her drink.

"What a zoo my future son-in-law keeps," Mrs. Hobson said. "It's a wonder his mother put up with that one for so many years. And Detective Bailey, too," she added with a nod in Alex's direction.

"Detective Bailey and his son have always been gentlemanly and kind to me."

"Gentlemen indeed."

It was an enormous relief to hear the dinner gong, until I

realized I would be seated next to the same two people for the next little while. Fortunately I ended up with Alex on one side and Bertie on the other. Gabe sat at the far end of the table, Ivy to his right and Mrs. Hobson on his left. I certainly got the better deal.

As the footman and butler brought in the first course, Mrs. Hobson's voice rang clear around the room, as if she'd raised it so we all could hear. "Do you still have that Chinese cook, Gabriel?"

"Mrs. Ling is still in my employ, yes. I asked her to cook English food tonight, just for you."

Alex leaned down to my level. "Last time they were here, it was a disaster. Mrs. Ling served some traditional dishes from her homeland. Mrs. Hobson refused to eat any of it. She wouldn't even try. Poor Mrs. Ling had to quickly make something else just for her."

"What did Ivy say?"

"Nothing. I think she was too embarrassed."

"Do *you* like her cooking, Alex?"

He flashed a grin. "I love it. Mrs. Ling complains about the lack of authentic ingredients, which is why she rarely makes her traditional dishes, but when she does, every bowl and plate is licked clean."

"And Willie?"

"After some initial reticence, she has come to love it more than English cooking. She considers herself a worldly gourmand now." His voice softened and he even cast a fond look at Gabe's cousin. "She praises Mrs. Ling's cooking to anyone who'll listen, and takes great offence on her behalf when someone speaks against Chinese food." His gaze wandered to Mrs. Hobson. "After the Hobsons left, Willie was...loud in her objections."

"Oh dear. Poor Gabe, being caught in the middle." I accepted the bowl of mock turtle soup from Bristow. It was the most English of soups. "It seems Willie's offence doesn't extend to Ivy. She's always praising her."

He responded with a non-committal huff.

"Do be careful!" Ivy snapped at the footman. "You almost spilled it in my lap."

The footman picked up Ivy's napkin and dabbed the tablecloth to mop up the spilled soup. She snatched it off him and he straightened.

"Why can't I use it?" he said with a shrug.

Mrs. Hobson clicked her tongue and muttered something to her husband on her other side.

Bristow swooped in and ordered the footman out of the room. I'd never seen a man his age move so quickly. He apologized profusely to the Hobsons and vowed never to let the footman serve soup again until he'd had lessons.

The footman rolled his eyes, tucked the tray under his arm and limped out. Bristow followed him, looking like a thunder cloud about to burst over the poor fellow's head.

Willie sat through the entire incident with a smile on her face. I was beginning to think she didn't particularly like Ivy, after all. Yet she always spoke so well of her. Her smile vanished when Mrs. Hobson spoke again.

"You ought to replace him, Gabriel."

"He's a good worker," Gabe said. "He just needs some practice."

"But his attitude is deplorable! I know you believe you're doing the right thing by employing a damaged former soldier, but he's far too informal to be a footman in a house such as this."

"Thank you for your advice, Mrs. Hobson, but my staff are my concern." He spoke far less tersely than I would have.

She picked up her spoon and dipped it into her soup. "Then you'll be pleased when Ivy takes over the duties of running the household. She'll have the staff in ship-shape condition in no time."

Ivy looked utterly humiliated at her mother's crassness. Bertie had also gone very still and quiet beside me.

"Speaking of the wedding," Mr. Hobson said, "when will your parents be returning, Glass? Ivy says they didn't give a date, but I find that hard to believe. Surely they want to see you settled as soon as possible."

"They don't know how long they'll be gone," Gabe said.

Mr. Hobson accepted that answer for only a moment before he pressed the point again. "But why not set the date before they left? If I were them, I'd insist on it." He smiled at his daughter. "You don't want to let a pearl like Ivy slip through your fingers."

"Father," she ground out.

Willie swiped up her wine glass. "Matt and India aren't going to miss their only child's wedding," she snapped. "Anyone who knows Gabe knows how important it is for them to be there."

Ivy picked up her glass and saluted Willie with it. "Quite right." She placed her hand on Gabe's arm and bestowed a sweet smile on him. "Besides, Gabe is worth the wait."

After what felt like an agonizingly long silence, Gabe finally responded, "As are you."

The rest of the dinner was pleasant enough. Bertie was a nice fellow, albeit somewhat shy. The only way I could get him to talk was to ask him questions. He didn't ask me anything. If it wasn't for their similar looks, I'd never guess he was related to Ivy. With his insipid nature, he must be completely overwhelmed by her and their parents at home.

He explained that he'd not gone to war as his work in his father's factory was considered too important for the war effort. He told me how his magic worked but seemed somewhat embarrassed to admit that his father's and sister's was stronger. I joked that he was one-up on his mother, but he didn't see the funny side.

I was grateful to return to the drawing room briefly after dinner, to acquire a different companion. I gravitated toward the professor, but he was soon waylaid by Mr. Hobson, who wanted to talk about magic. I looked around to join another party, and spotted Gabe with Mrs. Hobson and Ivy. Mother and daughter were in a discussion that appeared to include Gabe. But one look at his eyes proved he wasn't listening. He might physically be in the room, but his mind was elsewhere.

He suddenly glanced at me. He didn't look away, didn't blink, or attempt a smile. He simply stared.

And I stared back. I was acutely aware that I'd not been alone with him all night, and in that moment, I would have given anything to leave the room with him at my side. Not because I needed his company, but because I sensed he needed mine.

In a room full of people he knew better than I did, *he* was the lonely one.

Four years of war changed everyone. Young women left at home became more confident and capable after doing jobs usually reserved for men. Parents of soldiers became fearful when their sons departed for the front and immeasurably sad when they didn't return. The men who did return were altered in all sorts of ways. Some were left too traumatized to function in society. Some came back reserved, unable to talk about their experiences. Others were more carefree, determined to live every day to its fullest. Some returned angry, and others were filled with guilt at having survived when their friends had not. Most had difficulty adjusting to the new world that war ushered in.

I suspected Gabe was still trying to discover who he was now. He couldn't go back to being the reckless fellow his friends claimed he was before the war. He'd been ripped out of that phase before he was truly ready. Yet he hadn't settled into the next phase of life yet. Perhaps the memories of the battlefields still haunted him, rendering him unable to move forward. It must be difficult to find his true nature when it was buried beneath so much sorrow and pain.

It was a good thing his wedding wasn't too soon. He needed to rediscover himself before he became a husband and father.

Gabe took a step in my direction, and I felt myself being pulled toward him too. Then he stopped. With a slight shake of his head, he turned back to Ivy and Mrs. Hobson. The connection between us snapped.

For the next ten minutes, I pretended to listen as Willie and the professor reminisced about the past. He then made his excuses, and I made mine too so we could depart together. Gabe's driver took Professor Nash home first then me.

I couldn't sleep. I lay awake for hours, staring into the darkness, trying to get Gabe's haunted gaze out of my mind.

CHAPTER 4

Gabe and Alex collected me from the library the following morning and we drove to Mr. Trevelyan's studio. When I commented on Willie's absence, Gabe told me she had gone to Scarrow's newspaper office to discreetly find out more about him.

I arched my brows. "Discreetly?"

He grinned. "As much as a woman wearing buckskins and a cowboy hat can be."

I was pleased to see he was smiling again. I wasn't sure what to expect after last night.

It was as if mentioning Albert Scarrow conjured him up. He left the photographer's studio as we pulled up to the curb. He didn't see us, and we waited until he was out of sight before alighting from the motorcar.

Upstairs, Mr. Trevelyan greeted us with simple nods and invited us to view the photographs. He laid them out side by side on the desk near the book itself. Increasing the size of the marks made them much clearer. They were indeed a series of letters.

"The writing is old-fashioned," I said.

Mr. Trevelyan agreed. "I'm not a handwriting expert, but to me, the style aligns with the era the Medicis were in power."

Gabe looked up sharply and studied the photographer before returning to the images. "It's a name. Some of it is still a little faint, but I think it reads Andrew Sidwell."

"It's probably the scribe's signature," Alex said. "Didn't they note their names on their work?"

"Some, yes," I said. "But usually at the back, not the front. The front is an important position and reserved for the client who commissioned the work. That's if this is a copy of another work, and a scribe was commissioned at all. If the manuscript is an original, then the author of the document most likely made it himself." They looked rather impressed with my knowledge, so I admitted it was something I'd learned from Professor Nash. He was the expert on old documents, not me.

"Wasn't Medici the owner?" Mr. Trevelyan asked.

"At some point. He might not have commissioned it, but perhaps acquired it after it was written. It could have been years later."

Gabe regarded him. "We never mentioned the Medicis to you."

Mr. Trevelyan flipped open the book to the first page. "I recognized their family symbol."

"Why so much interest in them?"

"I don't know much about rare books, but I'd wager a manuscript with a connection to the Medicis is rare. If word got out, you'd have a lot of interested parties attempting to buy it."

"It's not for sale."

Mr. Trevelyan leveled his gaze with Gabe's. It was like watching two prize fighters before they engaged, each sizing the other up. Mr. Trevelyan broke the stand-off and reached for his cigarette tin. He offered it to each of us then took a cigarette himself.

"Don't mention the manuscript to your journalist friend, Scarrow," Gabe said.

Mr. Trevelyan lit the cigarette dangling between his lips and shook the match to extinguish it. "He's not my friend." He plucked the cigarette from his mouth between thumb and forefinger and blew a coil of smoke into the air. "We work for the same newspaper. He asked me to work with him. We've been trying to find you, Gabriel Glass."

He must have guessed who Gabe really was. Considering there were photographs of Gabe in the newspaper recently, it wasn't surprising.

Gabe took it in his stride. "Why you? There must be several photographers employed by the paper, so why did he want you?"

Mr. Trevelyan shrugged. "I have a reputation for being tenacious. Maybe he wanted someone like me on this job. Someone who won't be intimidated by your friends." He jutted his chin in Alex's direction.

Alex crossed his arms, emphasizing the size of his muscles as they strained the sleeves of his jacket. "What do you know about the kidnapping attempt on Gabe?"

"Nothing that isn't written in every newspaper article about him." He drew on his cigarette and blew smoke out of the corner of his mouth. "The interest in your life is understandable, Glass. You never spent a day in hospital in four years."

"I'm just lucky."

"I was at the front on and off for two and a half years, and from what I saw, no one is that lucky."

Gabe extended his arms from his sides. "And yet here I am."

Mr. Trevelyan watched Gabe from beneath lowered lids. "And you, Mr. Bailey? Were you lucky too?"

Alex seemed taken aback at being addressed. "I wasn't there as long. I only signed up in Sixteen and I spent over a month convalescing after shrapnel was removed from my back. But you're right. I'm luckier than most. I'm still here."

It was impossible to tell what Mr. Trevelyan thought of Alex's war experience. He simply continued to smoke his cigarette. His features remained set in a bland expression and his eyes remained hooded by his heavy lids.

I gathered up the photographs and the book, eager to get away before the tension got worse. "How much do we owe you, Mr. Trevelyan?"

"No charge, Miss Ashe." He took a few steps closer. "May I take you out to dinner tonight?"

The request caught me off guard. Coming immediately after telling me there was no charge for the photographs made it seem as though there was a connection, and that the price was my acceptance. I didn't know how to answer.

Gabe slammed a bank note on the desk.

Mr. Trevelyan's lips twitched in what seemed to be the closest thing to a smile he could muster. He picked up the note and pocketed it. We made to leave. "Be careful of Scarrow. He might appear innocuous, but he's ambitious. He thinks one good story will make his career."

"He's probably right," Gabe said. "But he won't get a story from me. There's nothing worth writing about."

Mr. Trevelyan gave Gabe a lazy salute as he opened the door for me. "I hope we see one another again, Miss Ashe."

"Yes." Hearing how that sounded, I quickly added, "If our paths happen to cross, another meeting will be unavoidable." I cleared my throat. "Thank you for your time."

He gave me one of his half-smiles, but this time it was neither humorless nor sad.

Downstairs on the pavement near the motor, I said, "That was interesting."

Gabe opened the Prince Henry's door for me. "Was it?"

I showed him the photographs. "We now have a name connected to the manuscript. Other than Medici, I mean."

Gabe removed his hat, dragged a hand through his hair, and slapped it back on. He seemed to need the moment to collect himself. "He may be the magician who made the clasps."

"Andrew Sidwell sounds English to me. It'll make him easier to research."

"Excellent point. I can begin by checking to see if his name is on our magicians' list."

Alex smacked his arm with the back of his hand and glanced pointedly at me.

Gabe rolled his eyes. "She already knows about it." At Alex's loaded silence, he added, "We can trust her." He almost seemed angry with his friend.

Considering Alex had no reason to trust me, I wanted to reassure him. "I won't tell a soul, I promise. Gabe's secrets are safe with me." I hadn't meant to imply the other secrets Gabe kept, not simply the one about the list of magicians. Yet both men clearly thought that's what I meant, going by the way they looked at one another.

Whatever Gabe's secrets were, Alex knew about them. When the topic of Gabe's amazing feat of survival had been raised during the investigation into the stolen painting, I'd been quite sure Alex was in the dark as much as everyone else. Clearly they'd had a conversation in the meantime.

I was glad Gabe had confided in his closest friend. Perhaps sharing his secret would help him cope with his wartime experiences.

Alex cranked the engine while Gabe and I waited in the motor. Once the Prince Henry roared to life, Alex joined us, frowning. "There's a teashop down the street." He nodded at a bay window with cheerful yellow curtains. "Ivy and Mrs. Hobson are occupying the table in the window."

"And you're suggesting it would be rude of us not to drop in and say hello?" Gabe asked.

"No. I don't think they saw us."

"Then why do you look like you're about to receive a scolding?"

"They were with Lady Stanhope."

Gabe twisted in the seat to regard him properly. "Lady Stanhope from the Royal Academy?"

Alex nodded.

I'd had a number of encounters with Lady Stanhope while assisting Gabe with the art heist investigation during the Academy's summer exhibition. As the wife of a member, an organizer of the exhibition, and a collector of magical art, Lady Stanhope had even been a suspect. She'd disliked me from the start. As a temporary employee, I'd been beneath her notice, which is where I would have happily remained if it weren't for my association with Gabe, someone she considered to be far above me. It hadn't helped that I'd uncovered her scheme to buy art cheaply from paint magicians before they knew the worth of their work.

I leaned forward as Gabe drove away from the curb so that I could be heard above the engine. "Are the Hobsons friends of Lady Stanhope's?"

"It would seem so, but I wasn't aware they knew each other. But I don't know much about Ivy's family or their connections, so..." He shrugged.

I sat back, wondering how he could be engaged to someone for almost three years without knowing the family well.

Gabe and Alex stayed at the library only long enough to drop me off. They were going to return home to check their list of magicians for Sidwell and telephone their mathematician friend.

Meanwhile, Professor Nash and I searched the library's collection for any mention of Andrew Sidwell. "The name rings a bell," the professor said as he studied the photographs.

"We think the writing style is contemporary with the Medicis. Would you agree?"

"Perhaps. It's difficult to tell."

He wagged a finger in the air and strode off. I gathered up the photographs and followed him to the bank of small drawers housing the library's catalog. Within each drawer were dozens of cards organized alphabetically by subject. Each one sported the professor's neat, precise handwriting. No one else had ever written on them. He'd never employed an assistant before me.

Every book in the library had at least one card entry in the catalog, and the cards covered all magical disciplines, as well as places, dates, tribe or culture, and various other topics that may be of interest to the researcher. Professor Nash opened up the first drawer of cards labeled with an S and rifled through them.

"I knew it!" He pulled out a card and waved it like a flag. "'Sidwell, Sir Andrew.'"

"Sir?"

He showed me the card. "Apparently so, if it's the same fellow."

I studied the card. It contained only one reference, to a book written a hundred years ago about sixteenth century mathematics, astrology and the occult. "What a strange combination of topics to find in a single volume."

"Not necessarily." Professor Nash headed for the spiral staircase. "In medieval and Renaissance times, science and magic were often conflated. They didn't know how things worked so attributed natural phenomena to magic. The changing of the seasons, a lunar eclipse, and even long-distance exploration...all were considered to be a result of magic." He paused on the top step and smiled down at me, a few steps behind. "Of course, some of their theories probably *are* the result of magic. But some are certainly due to science. They just couldn't tell the difference." He continued on, into the stacks on the first floor. "Have you heard of Dr. John Dee?"

"Wasn't he an advisor to Queen Elizabeth in the sixteenth century?"

"Your history is very good."

"The sixteenth century is a little late for Cosimo de' Medici," I pointed out. "He was around in the early fifteenth."

"If my theory is correct, then our manuscript probably belonged to both men at different points in its history. Medici first, and then somehow, Sir Andrew Sidwell got his hands on it and wrote his own name on the second page. Unfortunately the ink he used has faded." He clicked his tongue as he entered one of the aisles. "Magical ink made by a strong magician would have ensured it was still visible today."

"But the paper on which the Medici family symbol appears looks to have been a *later* addition. The ink is in better condition than that on the other pages. If Cosimo owned it first, how can that be? Shouldn't it have faded too?"

He scanned the spines of the books at eye level. "If it was added later then the manuscript is even older than Cosimo de' Medici. Ah!" He pulled out a book by its spine. "Here it is."

He took the book to the desk where he drew over a second chair for me. I laid the photographs down as he flipped to the index. He found only one reference to Sir Andrew Sidwell.

We both leaned forward to read. According to the single

paragraph in which he was mentioned, Sir Andrew Sidwell did indeed live in the sixteenth century. The English ambassador to Florence was a prolific collector of scientific and medical books, including books on the occult and phenomena both natural and supernatural. He'd amassed a large collection at his country estate in Wiltshire by the time of his death.

"He must have been wealthy," the professor said. "Books were exceedingly expensive back then. Expensive to make, expensive to copy, and expensive to buy, even if they'd been written a century or two earlier." He tapped his finger on the photographs of the manuscript's second page and the name written in faded ink. "Collectors were rich men."

The manuscript's unpretentious wooden cover disguised its value. If it wasn't for the silver clasps, it would have looked ordinary indeed, but inside was a secret treasure that sixteenth century collectors valued.

I recalled what Mr. Trevelyan had said. "Collectors would pay a lot for the book now, given the Medici connection."

"And the silver magic one."

I pointed to Sidwell's name. "I wonder if *he* added the Medici page and the silver clasps after acquiring the manuscript. They don't seem to go with the plain cover."

"That's a good point. All we know for certain is that he's not the author, merely a later owner."

He sat back and stroked his chin. "How are you at science, Miss Ashe?"

"Not very good. Do you think the symbols in the manuscript have a scientific meaning?"

"My scientific knowledge is rudimentary too. Perhaps some of the symbols represent particular disciplines. It could be a discipline that has been forgotten over time."

"Or they could be occult in nature."

He agreed it was a possibility. "Whatever they may be, *Sidwell* knew this book fitted into his occult and scientific collection, so either he could read those symbols or someone advised him of the book's contents."

Whether he could or couldn't read them himself, I wanted to know more about Sir Andrew Sidwell. Not only could he be a direct link to the silver magician who'd made the clasps, he was also a link to the book's contents. Finding out more about him might help us find out more about the manuscript. I realized I wanted to decode the text as much as I wanted to find a silver magician.

Professor Nash's thoughts followed a similar path to mine. "If Sidwell possessed the Medici Manuscript, perhaps he also possessed the key to breaking the code."

"We need to find out where his collection ended up," I said.

He sighed. "He lived over three hundred years ago. It was probably sold off after his death and scattered to the four corners of the Earth. It could take us the rest of our lives to find all the books he once owned."

"Or we could begin with his heirs. The collection could very well have been handed down the family line. And if it hasn't, perhaps they have a bill of sale in their archives."

Professor Nash smiled. "You have a great deal of energy, Sylvia. I envy you."

"My energy pales in comparison to yours, Professor." I clasped his hand. "You spent decades traveling the world hunting for books like the Medici Manuscript."

His smile turned wistful. "Oscar was the one with the energy. If it weren't for him, I'd never have set foot out of the country."

The idea of chasing down Sir Andrew Sidwell's descendants was rather thrilling, yet daunting too. I had no idea where to start.

Perhaps Gabe would know after he checked his family's catalog of magicians.

I continued with my work while I waited for his return, all the while thinking about the Medici Manuscript. The book intrigued me. The more I contemplated its secrets, the more secrets I found worth uncovering.

Like the ink, for example. Andrew Sidwell's name had faded, yet the rest of the manuscript was clear, despite being written more than a hundred years before Sidwell acquired it. I would have assumed the author used ink that held magic, but Oscar Barratt had been an ink magician. He would have detected a spell if any had been put into it.

I raised the idea with the professor. He didn't seem surprised. He'd clearly already considered the possibility.

"The ink is certainly vibrant, even now, but some inks from those days were better than others. Its ability to last down the centuries could be due to the quality of ink used rather than magic." He pushed his glasses up his nose. "It's also a possibility that it was made by an ink magician but no spell was spoken into it."

"Because magician-made things are naturally superior, spell or no spell."

"Precisely. In fact, the only ink spell Oscar knew had nothing to do with improving its quality or longevity. It simply made his ink float." He absently stroked his hand across the book he'd been reading. "But I wonder if the magical sensation he felt in the silver clasps masked the magic in the ink, if there was any."

"Surely he could tell his own discipline's magic from another."

"I would have thought so, but Oscar's magic wasn't particularly strong." He reached for the telephone. "But I know an ink magician whose is."

I waited as he politely spoke to the telephone operator. After a brief conversation with someone who must be a relative of Oscar's, he hung up. He wrote down an address on a notepad and tore out the page.

He handed it to me. "When Gabe returns, you should pay a visit to Huon Barratt. This is his home address."

"Oscar's brother?"

"Nephew. His father—Oscar's brother—lives up north where the family has manufactured ink for years. Huon moved to London as soon as he came of age. He has a rebellious spirit and doesn't get along well with his father. Oscar was something of a mentor to him, but he wasn't in London much, so Huon was left to his own devices."

"You sound as though you don't approve."

He pushed his glasses up his nose. "Before war broke out, he seemed to be settling down and was even thinking of returning home to learn the family business. But after the war...he hasn't found anything with which to occupy himself. Unless one counts drinking and carousing, that is." He sighed. "I wish I could help him, but he doesn't want my help. I'm not Oscar, you see."

I touched his hand. "I'm sure you've done your best."

The door opened and Gabe entered, followed by Alex. "There are no Sidwells on our list," Gabe announced. "Have you had any luck here?"

I showed them the book mentioning Sir Andrew Sidwell and his interest in collecting books about science and the occult. "We wondered if the code's key was once also owned by him, but got separated from the manuscript at some point. If we can locate part or all of his collection, that would be a good place to start. It's possible the books are still owned by his descendants, if there are any."

Gabe checked the paragraph in the book that mentioned Sidwell. "Sidwell House is in Marlborough, Wiltshire, according to this. That's only a two or three hour drive from

London. We could be there and back in a day. What do you say, Sylvia? Fancy a drive?"

"Me?" I glanced at the professor. He nodded. "Oh. All right, then."

Alex glared at his friend, but Gabe pretended not to notice.

"But only if it's all right with Ivy," I added.

Gabe agreed. "I'll telephone her later."

"His heirs may not still live on the same estate," Alex pointed out. "Family fortunes change."

"True, but it's worth a try." Gabe turned to the professor. "May I have the Medici book? I'll take it to my mathematician friend."

"There's one other stop we think you should make first." The professor told him about Oscar's nephew, the ink magician. "He will know for certain whether the ink's vibrancy is a result of magic. I've already telephoned. He's expecting you."

We took the manuscript and drove to Marylebone where Huon Barratt lived in a handsome townhouse that looked too large for a bachelor. Perhaps, as with Gabe, it was a family home and he lived there with other relatives.

The butler who answered the door was expecting us and invited us into the drawing room. The gentleman lounging on the sofa with his eyes closed and an arm flung over his forehead didn't move. He must have heard us enter, but it wasn't until the butler announced us that the fellow moved. He sat up with a groan and swung his bare feet to the ground. He cracked open bloodshot eyes and squinted at each of us in turn.

"You must be the prof's friends." He pushed himself to his feet and shook Gabe and Alex's hands. "You look familiar," he said to Alex. "I think I've seen you out and about at clubs."

"Probably," Alex said.

"It must have been Rector's on Tottenham Court Road or the Buttonhole. Not Grafton Galleries, obviously."

Alex bristled. "Why not the Grafton?"

"Because they wouldn't let in that odd little woman you associate with. Grafton Galleries is for a more fashionable set. It has to be exclusive. It's an art gallery by day. Can't have the riff raff walking off with expensive pieces. The prince goes, sometimes. But like you, I prefer Rector's and the Buttonhole. The music's better, the crowd freer. Anyway, it's a pleasure to meet you, Mr. Bailey." He was about to shake my hand too, but stopped himself. His eyes flared and his gaze skimmed over me. He smiled. "And you must be the new librarian. It's a pleasure to meet *you*, Miss Ashe." He took my hand and bowed over it.

I was surprised he remembered my name from the professor's telephone call. He didn't seem in a fit state to remember much at all. At first I thought he was drunk, but I couldn't smell alcohol on his breath and there were no glasses nearby. He must simply be tired.

Indeed, he looked as though he'd just dragged himself out of bed, although it was mid-afternoon. His light brown hair was uncombed and stubble shadowed a square jaw. He wore a blue housecoat over trousers and an undershirt. I was used to seeing gentlemen in suits, not in casual attire. I kept my gaze on his face to avoid looking at the patch of chest hair protruding from the top of his undershirt.

He invited us to sit. I was about to, but Gabe spoke. "We're not staying long." His tone was brisk and cool, although he'd never met Huon before. "If you would take a look at the manuscript now, we'd appreciate it. We're very busy."

Huon dismissed his butler with a nod. He accepted the manuscript from me but didn't even look at it. He regarded Gabe. "Your mother is the watchmaker magician, isn't she?"

"Yes."

"Did you inherit it?"

"No."

Huon grunted. "Lucky you."

Gabe didn't react. In fact, he stood very still, not even blinking. Alex was the opposite. He glanced sharply at Gabe before looking down at the floor. He shifted his stance from one foot to the other.

Huon noted both of their reactions with a smile before he turned his attention to the book. He stroked the wooden cover. "The prof told me over the telephone that my uncle detected magic in this silver." He fingered the clasps then opened them. "I agree with his assessment."

"And the ink?"

Huon turned the page. He studied the Medici symbol without comment then turned the next two pages. He followed the pen strokes with his finger, carefully tracing the loops and patterns. He repeated the action on the next page and the next, until he'd tested several pages. Then he finally closed the book.

"There's no ink magic in it. Sorry, Miss Ashe."

"It's all right," I said. "It was simply an idea."

He folded the book against his chest. "Have you deciphered those symbols?"

"Not yet, but we're trying."

Gabe held out his hand, but Huon held onto the book. "If you please." Gabe's words were polite, but his tone was edged with steel.

Huon hesitated then handed the book over. "Did you know that Uncle Oscar died without a will?"

Gabe's jaw firmed. "Your point?"

"I don't really have one." He nodded at the book in Gabe's hands. "Dusty old tomes don't interest me, and they certainly don't interest my father. Of course, if he was interested, as Uncle Oscar's next of kin, he would have every right to stake a claim to the Glass Library's collection."

"No, he wouldn't. The books were purchased with the library's funds. They never belonged to your uncle."

Huon smiled brightly. "Silly me. No head for law." He rapped his knuckles on his temple. "No head for business either, much to my father's frustration. Hence my desire to stay here in London, out of his way."

"Thank you for your time," Gabe said stiffly.

"Thank you, Glass. It was a pleasure to finally meet you. Although, I must admit, the pleasure is entirely due to Miss Ashe's presence." He bestowed an easy smile on me. "It's been years since I've been to the library but I have a sudden interest to see the professor again, and hear his stories about my uncle. They used to thrill me when I was younger."

"I think the professor would like that," I said. "He misses your uncle terribly."

Huon's smile faded and his gaze turned serious. "I miss him too." He took my hand and kissed the back. "Good day, Miss Ashe."

"Good day, Mr. Barratt."

"Perhaps I'll see you out with Mr. Bailey one evening. Do save a dance or three for me."

"I don't go to dance clubs."

"You should. I think you'll find you won't be short of partners."

In the motor, as we waited for Alex to crank the engine, Gabe stretched his arm across the back of the seat. His thumb tapped the burgundy leather, over and over. He seemed unaware he was doing it.

"Is something the matter?" I asked.

He turned to me, sitting in the back seat. "No. Nothing."

The silence stretched, finally broken by the rumble of the engine. Alex slipped into the front passenger seat and closed the door. "He wasn't what I was expecting. Oscar was full of energy and ambition, but his nephew looks like he enjoys the nightlife more than I do."

Gabe grabbed hold of the brake lever. "He was too interested in the book."

Alex shot me a smile over his shoulder. "That wasn't the only thing he was interested in."

Gabe pressed the accelerator so hard we shot forward at speed, narrowly missing another motorcar. The driver shouted something that we couldn't hear over the roar of the engine.

We drove to Gabe's mathematician friend's residence then he took me back to the library. I considered asking Alex if he was going to a nightclub that evening but decided against it. I'd ask Daisy if I could go out with her tonight. She was always asking me to a dance or nightclub, but I usually declined. But I was suddenly in the mood for enjoying myself. I hadn't felt this way in a long time. Indeed, perhaps never.

London was beginning to agree with me. Or perhaps I was agreeing with it.

CHAPTER 5

*D*aisy wanted to try Rector's dance club on Tottenham Court Road. After hearing Huon mention it, I expected to see him there, but if he was, he was near the back, behind the throng of dancers.

The evening was like nothing I'd experienced. In low lighting that provided ample shadowy corners for amorous couples, a jazz band played the latest tunes, much to the delight of the patrons. The bright blare of the trumpet punctuated the music, its chaotic rhythm matching the twirls and kicks of the girls in heeled shoes and beaded dresses.

Unlike the dance halls of my youth, skirts were above ankle-length, and there wasn't a chaperone in sight. My mother would have been horrified by this desire for freedom and fun, but there was no denying the deep urge within people my age to dance the night away in an effort to forget. I was more conservative than Daisy, but after my initial hesitation faded away following two martinis, I joined her on the dance floor, laughing as I attempted to copy her dance steps.

When one of the tunes came to an end and some of the dancers left the floor, we both finally looked up.

And met the twin stares of Alex and Willie. They both leaned back against the bar, Alex with his elbow resting on it, looking very suave in his tuxedo with black tie. Willie wore trousers instead of her usual buckskins, and a gentleman's top hat with a shirt, waistcoat and tie. In the dim light, it would be easy to mistake her for a small man.

Alex nodded a greeting.

Daisy gripped my hand. "We should say hello." She didn't move. "You go first."

"I don't want to speak to Willie. But you should go and talk to Alex."

She made a scoffing sound. "Don't be silly. Why would I want to speak to him? He has been rude and condescending. He thinks I'm a silly flibberty-gibbet. I have no interest in extending our acquaintance further. Besides, there are dozens of other tall, handsome men here."

"Yes, but none quite so tall or so handsome."

She sighed. "True. But he knows it. Look at him preening as the women ogle him."

I didn't think he was preening at all. He didn't seem to notice the attention he garnered. After his initial stare, he now looked away from us as he spoke to Willie. She, however, continued to stare, her eyes narrowed. A leaden weight settled in the pit of my stomach.

I tightened my grip on Daisy's hand. "Save me from Willie."

"Why? I like her. She seems like fun. Perhaps I'll go and speak to her. I'll ignore Alex, of course. I do *not* wish to speak to him." She went to walk off in their direction, but I held her back.

"She hates me," I whined.

"That's because you're a threat to Gabe's relationship with Ivy."

"I am not! I do think he's handsome and wonderful, but I wouldn't dream of coming between them."

"I know that. But I don't think she does."

"She ought to know Gabe wouldn't hurt his fiancée. He's not like that. In fact, it's a little disappointing she doesn't realize it, considering how close they are."

Two women who'd been eyeing off Willie and Alex from the other end of the bar finally found enough courage to approach. The taller of the two smiled at Alex and put out her hand to him. He took it gingerly and leaned down to hear her over the music. The smaller woman said something to Willie.

When Willie turned to face her, the woman's mouth dropped open. Willie touched a finger to her chin to close it. Before withdrawing her hand, she stroked the woman's jawline with her thumb.

The woman continued to stare.

Before I knew what was happening, Daisy was dragging me toward them. She deposited me in front of Willie while she loudly greeted Alex as if he were an old friend. The woman he'd been talking to glanced between them, sighed, and walked away. Her friend trotted after her, glancing over her shoulder at Willie.

Alex arched his brows at Daisy. "What are you doing here?"

"What does it look like?" She twirled, showing off her figure in the slim-fitting green and black dress to perfection. "Dancing, of course. What about you? Wait, let me guess. You're determined to look sour and not have fun."

Alex's nostrils flared. "I am having fun."

Daisy snorted.

Willie poked me in the arm. "You scared away the fun. They were pretty."

"So are we," Daisy said with a little shake of her bare shoulders. "Prettier, in fact."

"But you ain't my type, Honey."

Daisy grinned. "Good point." She kissed Willie on the temple, making Willie blush. She turned away and ordered a drink from the barman.

With Daisy and Alex in the mood for flirting with each other, I suspected we were in for a long night. I decided to try to hurry it along. If they were going to kiss, they could do both Willie and me the courtesy of getting it over with earlier rather than later.

"Is Daisy your type, Alex?" I asked.

He grunted. "Pampered princesses aren't for me."

She straightened and thrust a hand on her hip. "You don't know a thing about me."

He shrugged. "You have no source of income so someone somewhere must be supporting you, probably your parents. I can tell by your accent and your carefree manner that you've had very few difficulties in your life."

"Not all difficulties are financial," she ground out.

"I didn't say they were."

Willie accepted the glass from the barman and offered it to Daisy. "Want to throw this in his face? Waste of good liquor if you ask me, but it might make you feel better."

Alex's jaw firmed. "Why did I invite you?" he muttered.

"Because Gabe wouldn't come." Willie circled her finger around the rim of the glass as she watched me closely. "He's dining at the Hobsons' tonight with Lady Stanhope."

"That's nice," I said.

"Ivy called at the house personally to invite him. He wasn't there when she arrived. He was with you."

"And Alex," I reminded her. "We're investigating the book's origins."

"You shouldn't be encouraging him to go out and about."

"It's his choice." At her troubled frown, I leaned in. "You

67

don't have anything to worry about, Willie. His relationship with Ivy is quite safe."

"I wasn't talking about their relationship. It's Gabe who's not safe going out and about. Someone's tried to kidnap him twice, and I don't think you can save him if they try a third time."

"I'm quite sure Gabe can save himself. He has so far. He also has Alex with him, most of the time."

We both looked to Alex, but he failed to notice. He was too intent on pretending not to watch Daisy dancing a mere two feet away. For her part, she was pretending she didn't know he wasn't watching as she shimmied to the music with her partner.

Willie suddenly clicked her tongue. "I shouldn't have let him go alone to the Hobsons."

"Did you have a choice in the matter?" I asked.

"No. Neither Alex nor me were invited. She doesn't like us."

"Ivy?"

"Mrs. Hobson." She drained her glass and asked the barman for another. "What about you, Sylvia? What are you drinking?"

"Martinis, but I've had enough."

She ordered me a martini. When she finally looked at me again, she narrowed her eyes. "Why are you smiling at me like that?"

"You like me, don't you?"

"I never disliked you. I just don't like you being around Gabe so much. He's engaged. It ain't right for another woman to spend so much time with an engaged man."

"I see your point."

"Ivy is a good match for him."

"They make a beautiful couple. They'll have beautiful children," I added in a mutter.

"Gabe wants to settle down, and I got to accept that. His days going out all night and drinking with me are over."

I tried to follow her train of thought, but couldn't connect her last statement to the ones about Ivy. I suspected the earlier martinis were catching up to me and addling my brain.

She accepted the drinks from the barman and handed the martini to me. "He doesn't want to have fun no more."

"He doesn't have fun with Ivy?"

She grunted.

I put down my drink. "I don't understand. Ivy doesn't make him happy?"

"Course she makes him happy. He wouldn't marry her if she didn't. I wouldn't let him." She picked up my glass and handed it back to me. "Like I said, he wants to settle down now, and Ivy's a good choice. She's level-headed and smart. She's not interested in dancing the night away like a lot of the girls nowadays." She nodded at Daisy, gyrating to the music. "That's what Gabe needs. I see that now. You know, I didn't like Ivy much at first. She seemed a bit too hoity toity for Gabe. You'd think she was a society lady, the way she talks to folk. But I got to admit, ever since they got engaged, he's been…settled."

"And settled is good?"

"It's what he needs."

I sipped my martini. It didn't help my suddenly dry throat.

"So you see why I don't want anything to jeopardize their relationship," Willie went on.

"I'm not a threat to it, Willie. The idea that I am is absurd." When she didn't respond, I clinked my glass against hers. "Now, what do you think about those two? Should we try to get them together or let them fumble their way through on their own?"

She leaned back, both elbows resting on the bar, the glass dangling from her fingertips. "It's a lot more fun watching from a distance."

A slim woman with short dark hair slicked back off her forehead approached. Willie dismissed me with a flick of her wrist and a smile for her new admirer. It was then that I realized I hadn't asked her what she'd learned about Scarrow after visiting the newspaper where he worked.

I joined Daisy on the dance floor and danced for another two hours before I declared I was ready to go home. Daisy looked around, most likely searching for Alex. But he'd gone, and so had Willie.

"My feet ache and my ears are ringing," I said as we left. "But I feel wonderful."

She nudged me with her elbow. "Glad you had a good time."

"I did. Let's do it again next week."

"Why not tomorrow night?"

I laughed. "Once a week is enough for me. I have to work most days." Thankfully I had the day off tomorrow. There was no way I could get out of bed at seven and work all day.

The crisp night air skimmed my cheeks, cooling me down after the vigorous dancing. Even so, I didn't need my wrap yet. "If clubs like that existed in Birmingham before I left, I certainly didn't know about them."

She hooked her arm through mine, laughing. "I can tell you for certain there was nothing like it in Marlborough."

I stopped and turned to her. "Marlborough, Wiltshire?

"Yes. Why?"

I knew she was from Wiltshire, but I didn't know which part until now. "How well do you know the prominent families of the area?"

She walked on. "Well enough."

"What about the Sidwells? It's possible they no longer live there, but they used to."

"I know them. They're one of the oldest families. They've lived in the area for centuries."

"Can you give me directions to their estate?"

"Yes. Why?"

* * *

I DID NOT SLEEP AS LATE as I thought I would. Although still a little tired, I couldn't get back to sleep so decided to see what was on offer for breakfast. I found the landlady in the kitchen, vigorously stirring a bowl of pancake batter tucked into the circle of her arm while reading a cookery book on the table. The page was open to a recipe written in an Asian language.

"Can you read that, Mrs. Parry?"

She chuckled, making her double chins jiggle and her eyes twinkle. "I'm trying to work out what the ingredients are from the pictures. I used to eat at a Chinese restaurant called the Cathay before the war but haven't had a single Chinese dish since." Her beating slowed as she stared into the distance. "The flavors in the food were extraordinary. There are such tastes in this world that we English have never known."

"And you're trying to replicate them for tonight's dinner?"

"I want to try one dish, and this one has the fewest steps." She sighed. "But I can't make head nor tails of it."

"I might be able to get it translated for you. Would you like that?"

She stopped beating. "Oh, would you? How good of you, Sylvia. Do you know a Chinaman?"

"Woman." I dipped my finger into the bowl and licked it. "She's my friend's cook. I'll call on them this morning. But you'll probably need to source the ingredients. Apparently authentic ones aren't easy to come by in London."

"I'll save it for another night then." She resumed her frenzied attack on the batter so I kept my fingers away. "So where did you go last night?"

It was said so sweetly that it took me a moment to realize I was in trouble. I thought I'd gotten away with sneaking out last night after curfew. I'd removed my shoes, avoided all the creaking floorboards, and quietly closed the front door, the key safely in my pocket. It would seem I wasn't as discreet as I thought.

"I, uh..."

Her wooden spoon stilled. She tilted her head and regarded me with the sternest look I'd ever seen her give. It was hardly the sort that made me quiver in my boots, however. With her apple cheeks and warm brown eyes, Mrs. Parry was motherly and gentle, even now. "At least you're not trying to lie."

"I went dancing with my friend Daisy. You remember her. She's a good girl."

Her lips flattened.

I chewed the inside of my cheek. "I'm sorry, Mrs. Parry, it won't happen again. Please don't throw me out. I have nowhere else to go."

She set the bowl down and wiped her palms on her apron. "I won't throw you out, Sylvia, but next time, tell me where you're going. I sleep better knowing where my girls are."

"Next time?" I echoed. "You'll let me go out again?"

"Times have changed, in case you haven't noticed. Young people want to dance and have fun. It would be wrong of people my age to deny you that, considering what your generation have been through." She picked up an egg in each hand and held them over an empty bowl. "I always tell the new girls there's a curfew, but most know I don't enforce it anymore. There's no point. You sneak out anyway." She cracked the eggs into the bowl then handed it to me. "Add another six and stir."

I smiled and did as she asked.

*　*　*

To say I was glad for an excuse to call on Gabe wasn't entirely correct. I already had an excuse—I knew where to find the Sidwell family in Wiltshire. But it was a fair assessment to say that I was glad for a second excuse. I could have given him directions to the Sidwell estate over the telephone, but speaking to his cook required a personal visit.

Bristow greeted me at the door without a wrinkle of surprise on his face. "If you'd be so kind as to wait in the drawing room, I'll inform Mr. Glass."

"Actually, I'd like to speak to Mrs. Ling first. Is she in?"

A rapid series of blinks was the only indication that he found my request curious. "She's in the kitchen. I'll fetch her."

"I'll go to the kitchen. I don't want her to go out of her way."

He regarded me down his nose. "The kitchen isn't a suitable place for a guest of Mr. Glass's."

"I'll be very quick and promise not to get in the way."

"If you insist, Miss Ashe." He opened the door wider. "My wife would like to see you again, too."

"Oh? How lovely. I'd like to see her, and I'm very much looking forward to meeting Mrs. Ling."

"Of course. But I will apologize in advance for Murray. The footman," he clarified at my arched brow.

He led me through a door hidden by the wall paneling and the shadows at the back of the entrance hall. The ebony and brass clock on the hall table chimed ten o'clock as the door closed behind us. We descended the narrow stairs to the basement, only to bypass the kitchen. It was empty and tidy, with only a large pot on the stove. The delicious smell of stock followed us to the adjoining staff dining room.

The five seated occupants looked up from their cups of tea. Four of them hurriedly stood. The fifth, Murray the footman, took a little longer. He was the first to greet me, however, extending his hand.

"You were here the other night," he said cheerfully. "Miss Ashe, isn't it?"

I smiled. "That's right."

Bristow ordered him to sit down. "Miss Ashe isn't here to see you. She wishes to speak to Mrs. Ling."

Murray rolled his eyes, but dutifully sat. "I'm ordered around here more than in the army," he muttered.

Aside from Murray and Mrs. Ling, I recognized Mrs. Bristow, the housekeeper and wife of the butler, and Dodson the chauffeur. The young girl seated between them must be the maid, Sally.

Mrs. Ling rounded the table and bowed to me. "Good morning, Miss Ashe. It's a pleasure to meet you." She had a soft voice with an accent and spoke carefully, as if she put thought into every word.

"And you, Mrs. Ling. I'd like to compliment you on the meal the other night. It was delicious."

Mrs. Ling bowed again and thanked me. She was a small, slim woman with high cheekbones and straight dark hair arranged into a long plait down her back. She smiled shyly at my praise. "I'm glad you liked it."

"I have a request from my landlady." I handed her the cookbook I'd brought with me. "She'd like to try a Chinese recipe and has found some. But they're not in English. Can you translate one or two for her?"

Mrs. Ling beamed. "Yes. Yes, of course. I will be happy to." She returned to her seat and opened the book.

Murray drew out the chair beside him and patted the seat. "Tea, Miss Ashe?"

"Murray," Mrs. Bristow scolded. "Miss Ashe will be having tea upstairs with Mr. Glass."

He crossed his arms and regarded her with a smirk. "She might prefer to have it down here with us. She's not like Mr. Glass."

"I'll have you know, Mr. Glass used to come down here all the time before. He liked the company."

"Before what?"

Sally leaned forward and lowered her voice. "Before Ivy Hobson got her claws into him."

"That's enough," Mrs. Bristow chided them both. "She's going to be our new mistress. The sooner we get used to it, the better off we'll be."

Murray crossed his arms. "If she speaks to me again the way she spoke to me the other night, I'm not staying. I don't care how good an employer Mr. Glass is, I won't be spoken to like I'm an idiot."

Sally reached across the table and patted his hand. "We know it's not your fault, and Mr. Glass said he spoke to Miss Hobson."

"Murray's foot was giving him all sorts of trouble that night," Mrs. Bristow explained to me. "It's not his fault he stumbled."

Murray lifted his trouser leg and lowered his sock, revealing a wooden leg disappearing into his shoe. He knocked on it. "What Mrs. Bristow is trying to say is that it wasn't my foot that gave me trouble. It was my lack of one." He chuckled and tugged his sock back up. "Anyway, Mr. Glass may have spoken to her, but did she come and apologize? No, she did not."

"*He* did, on her behalf."

"That ain't the same thing, Mrs. B, and you know it."

The servants on the other side of the table suddenly stood. Murray and I turned to see Gabe in the doorway. Murray swallowed audibly.

Gabe couldn't have failed to overhear the exchange.

CHAPTER 6

"*S*ylvia! This is a nice surprise." Gabe smiled disarmingly, and I couldn't help smiling in return. "Is everything all right or are you trying to steal my staff on behalf of your landlady?"

"I *am* here on behalf of Mrs. Parry, but I won't steal anyone from you. I hoped Mrs. Ling could translate a recipe for her."

Mrs. Ling turned the book around to show me a page she'd found. "This is Mr. Glass's favorite. Mrs. Parry should start with this one. I will translate it for you." She slipped past Gabe, out of the kitchen.

"Would you like tea while you wait?" Gabe asked me.

We headed back up the stairs and made our way to the drawing room.

"There's another reason I came, actually," I said. "Last night I discovered that Daisy comes from Marlborough, Wiltshire." I frowned. "Or perhaps on a property nearby. She could be from a well-off family; I'm not entirely sure. Anyway, the point is, she knew of the Sidwell family. A descendent, Lazarus Sidwell, still lives in the area. She gave me directions to the estate."

"Daisy is turning into an intriguing mystery." He glanced at the doorway then leaned closer to me. "One that Alex will enjoy unraveling. Just don't tell him I said that."

"You ought to have seen them last night, flirting with each other but pretending not to."

"Alex didn't tell me he was meeting you two."

"It wasn't planned. He and Willie happened to be at the same place as us."

He winced. "Did she behave herself?"

I smiled. "She didn't cause a scene, if that's what you mean."

"She didn't offend you again, did she? Or threaten you? If she did, I'll have another word with her."

"We talked. I won't say it was nice, but it helped clear the air. I think."

Bristow brought in tea and set the tray down in front of Gabe.

"Ask Dodson to prepare the Vauxhall for a country drive," Gabe said.

"Would you like Mrs. Ling to pack a picnic, sir?"

"Good idea. Thank you." Once Bristow had left, Gabe poured the tea. "I wish I'd been there last night to mediate." His lips twitched with his smile. "And enjoy a dance or two. It's been a while."

I was curious as to why he wanted to go out when his friends claimed he'd settled down after the war and was no longer interested in the excesses of his youth. I didn't probe further, however. It could lead to a sensitive topic that might cause awkwardness between us. Being with him was pleasant, and I didn't want to change that.

"You had other plans last night," I reminded him.

He heaved a sigh. "They told you I was roped into a dinner with Ivy's parents?"

"Willie mentioned it. She also said Lady Stanhope was there."

He handed me a cup and saucer. "According to Ivy, she recently introduced herself to Mrs. Hobson at a garden party. Yesterday, she somehow managed to invite herself to dinner."

"How odd."

"That's not the oddest part. Apparently she asked for me to attend. She said she wanted to get to know the son of the great magician, Lady Rycroft, after having met me at the exhibition."

"Was Mrs. Hobson upset that you were the object of Lady Stanhope's interest, rather than her?"

"I don't think she minded why an introduction came about, just that it did. Ivy says her mother was thrilled to make Lady Stanhope's acquaintance. She'd been trying to break into that set for some time, but they'd always snubbed her. Apparently the nobility don't like the women who come from new money, or some such nonsense."

It struck me as rather exhausting trying to be invited to the right parties and be recognized by the right people. I was glad I didn't have to join in. I was quite content with my life, I suddenly realized. There may be questions over my family's origins, but whatever I discovered, that was in the past now.

"What did Ivy think?" I asked. "Was *she* keen to make Lady Stanhope's acquaintance?"

"She didn't say."

"What did Lady Stanhope say to you?" The moment I asked, I regretted it. His evening was none of my affair. I was being far too nosy. "Sorry. That was rude of me."

"Not at all. I'd be curious too, considering our recent dealings with her. Besides, it's a question I'd expect my friends to ask, and we're friends."

I nodded politely, not quite sure how to respond. We weren't friends. We didn't know one another very well. Yet we were more than acquaintances.

"She asked a lot of questions about my maternal family," he went on. "My mother's parents were magicians, and their parents, and their parents. You get the idea. Lady Stanhope then asked if I was sure I hadn't inherited magic, and when I said I hadn't, she gave me a pitying look and said she hoped my children took after my mother."

"Not *their* mother?"

He frowned.

"Ivy," I said matter-of-factly. "She's a magician too."

"She is." He sipped his tea.

"Was she upset at Lady Stanhope's slight?"

"Nothing upsets Ivy. She's very agreeable, especially in company."

"Except when someone spills soup on her dress. It was a beautiful dress," I quickly added, lest he think I was disparaging her. "I hope it wasn't ruined."

"Nothing a good clean won't fix." His coolness came as a surprise. According to the servants, he'd apologized to Murray on Ivy's behalf. I wondered if it troubled him that she hadn't apologized to the footman herself.

Bristow re-entered the drawing room. "Dodson will bring the motorcar around in ten minutes, sir. Shall I wake Mr. Bailey and Willie?"

"Let them sleep. They came home late."

"But, sir—"

"Thank you, Bristow." Gabe's gaze scanned over me. "Bristow, can you see if there are any head scarves of my mother's here? Sylvia might need one if we drive with the top down."

"You want me to come with you?" I asked.

"Of course. It's your investigation. I'm merely the assistant this time."

"But I'm not dressed for a day in the country."

His gaze raked over me again, warmer this time. "You look fine to me. That dress is very fetching. But your hat won't stay on." He looked out of the window. "And it seems like a pleasant day for driving in the countryside in an open vehicle. Is that all right with you?"

"Yes." I sounded rather breathy, but I'd never driven through the countryside in a private motor before. I'd hardly been in the country at all. We'd always lived in cities, where it was easier for my mother to find work. Sometimes I wondered if she chose larger centers so we could be more anonymous. "Shouldn't we take Alex with us in case there's another kidnapping attempt?"

"There won't be. The kidnappers don't know where I live or they would make their attempts here. We won't be followed. You're in no danger."

"It's you I'm concerned about. Nobody has any interest in me."

He smiled into his teacup. "I can take care of myself, Sylvia."

Ten minutes later, with one of Lady Rycroft's scarves covering my hair and secured under my chin, driving goggles in place and a lightweight coat to keep the dust off my clothes, we drove out of the city. It took a little while to reach the edge of London, but once we left the crowded streets behind, the Vauxhall Prince Henry picked up speed. I turned my face toward the sun and breathed the fresh air into my lungs. I was so used to London's smoke that I'd forgotten what clean air smelled and tasted like. And the colors! The grassy verge and the leaves on the trees were bright green, the fields beyond sprinkled with yellow wildflowers. Even the buildings in the villages we passed through didn't seem as gray as those in London.

I caught Gabe glancing at me out of the corner of my eye, smiling. With the wind whipping past our ears, talking was impossible. I didn't feel like talking anyway. I wanted to take in every exhilarating moment of our journey.

As we drew closer to Marlborough, I had to direct Gabe off the main roads using the map. The route became narrower, lined with stone walls or hedges, making it difficult for two vehicles to pass. He did well to dodge most of the holes and the roughest sections. There were no signposts, but with Daisy's directions and the map to guide us, we only had to backtrack once.

The rusty iron gates marking the entrance to the Sidwell estate were open part way so I got out to widen the gap so the motorcar could fit through. I thought it would be easy, but the rust and vines made them stick. Gabe had to help me.

The view from the top of the long, straight drive was like a postcard. The grand manor stood proudly at the end of an avenue of plane trees, with a fountain in the front forecourt and dozens of chimneys reaching into the sky.

But the grandness was an illusion. As we drew closer, it became clear the manor was in disrepair. Some of the upper floor windows were boarded up, the window frames rotting. Vines crept up the wall of one wing, and weeds infested the lawn. A puddle of green-black water pooled in the bottom of the fountain. The building looked early eighteenth century to me, with its extravagant Italianate design. It wouldn't have been built by our Sir Andrew Sidwell. His house would have been in an Elizabethan or Medieval style that had probably once stood on the same spot.

We climbed the front steps, careful to avoid the loose and broken tiles. Gabe knocked on the door. A swallow nesting above the lintel took flight, frightening the life out of me. I sprang toward Gabe. He settled a steadying arm around my shoulders, drawing me close. It was warm in the circle of his arm, and safe. I didn't want to move away.

He released me and stepped back. "I don't think anyone lives here anymore."

I trotted back down the stairs and peered through a window.

Something inside moved.

I gasped and hurried back to the porch. "Either someone is home or there's a ghost wandering about."

"Ghosts aren't real."

"Most people didn't know magic was real until thirty years ago, so I'll keep an open mind."

He laughed softly and knocked again.

The door opened a crack and a pale face peered through. I couldn't tell if it belonged to a man or woman. "What do you want?"

"My name is Gabriel Glass and this is Miss Sylvia Ashe. Are you Lazarus Sidwell?"

"I am." The voice was male and reedy. Although I could see little more than one light blue eye and the side of his face, I guessed him to be late middle-aged. "I'm not selling."

"Selling what?" Gabe asked.

"My house. The only way you'll get me to leave is if you carry me out in a casket, and that'll be a long way off. You can report back that I'm as fit as a fiddle."

"We're not interested in your house. We want to ask you about a collection of books once owned by your ancestor, Sir Andrew Sidwell, in the sixteenth century."

"Sir Andrew's books?" The eye blinked slowly. "You weren't sent here by my pus-filled boil of a nephew?"

"No. We don't know your nephew. Is this Sidwell House?"

"It says so on the sign on the gate, doesn't it?"

"We didn't see a sign on the gate, but these were the directions we were given to Sidwell House."

"It may have fallen off or been covered by the vines. Last time I saw it, it was a little rusty." The eye narrowed. "Who gave you directions?"

"My friend, Daisy Carmichael," I said.

"Daisy!"

The door was flung open, revealing a small man with slightly protruding front teeth and thinning blond hair. He was younger than I first thought, perhaps aged only in his early forties. His skin was remarkably smooth and there was a youthful excitability about him.

"Why didn't you say you knew Daisy?" He stepped aside and beckoned us in. "You must tell me how you know her. Is she well?"

"She's very well," I said. "She loves London."

"I'm so pleased she's having an adventure. She always wanted to leave here and go to London. Fortunately, her grandmother died."

I glanced at Gabe, but he merely shrugged. "I don't follow," I said.

Mr. Sidwell pressed his fingertips to his lips, covering his laugh. "I am sorry. I've forgotten how to hold a proper conversation. I simply meant that it's good of Daisy's grandmother to remember her in her will and leave the dear girl something so she could have an adventure. She probably told you her parents were against her leaving home. If it wasn't for the money, she'd still be there, moldering away in that big old house."

I bit my lip to stop my retort.

He noticed, however. "Yes, the irony of my statement isn't lost on me, Miss Ashe." He chuckled. "But the difference is, I don't wish to leave and have an adventure. Daisy did."

"You're close to her family?"

"Their land abuts mine." He waved a hand in the general direction of a distant row of trees. He closed the door. "Come in, come in."

The entrance hall alone was larger than my entire room, although it was difficult to estimate its scale without a single piece of furniture in it. My eye was drawn up the sweeping staircase to the domed ceiling far above us. Its paintwork had faded but it must have once been beautiful. Whoever built the manor had been wealthy indeed. The current owner was not, going by his worn shoes and patched-up jacket.

Like many country houses built over the centuries, Sidwell House was decaying. The cost of maintaining such beautiful, grand structures was enormous, and their owners no longer had the means to fix their mounting problems. They hadn't inherited a treasure, they'd inherited a burden in the form of bricks and debt. One day, if Sidwell House wasn't torn down, the vines and weeds would consume it altogether, and its walls would crumble into the earth.

Mr. Sidwell led us into a reception room. Unlike the entrance hall, this room contained signs that it was regularly used. A sheet had been thrown over a lumpy sofa, the middle of which dipped from overuse. Other dust sheets covered what I guessed to be armchairs, and a book sat open on one of the many occasional tables. A sideboard was bare except for a decanter half-filled with a reddish-brown liquid and a dirty glass. Above the sideboard was a deer's head, complete with antlers, although the tip of one was missing. A large birdcage housed what I thought was a pet, but it turned out to be a stuffed kestrel. It was missing several feathers on both wings and its glass eyes made the poor creature look cross-eyed.

Mr. Sidwell picked up a chipped china cup from the table nearest the sofa. "I'll make some tea and you can tell me all about Daisy's new life in London. Please, sit down." He indicated the sofa.

I sat and resisted the urge to cover my nose. I wasn't sure if the moldy smell came from the furniture or the man.

"I wonder why Daisy didn't warn me about him," I whispered after he'd gone.

Gabe leaned down to regard the kestrel. "Perhaps she didn't think she needed to. He seems harmless."

"I suppose."

He joined me on the sofa. "I forgot, you're not from the country. You don't know how some of these old families are." His lips twitched with his smile. "For centuries, they didn't move outside their local area, and since important families wanted to marry their children into other important families, they ended up breeding with one another, over and over."

"You know a great deal about inbred families, do you?" I teased.

"Believe me, you don't want to look into the Glass side too closely. My father's uncle was a bully with a poor heart, and his cousins are mad. Well, one is nice. Believe me, it's fortunate my grandfather married my grandmother, and my father married my mother, to bring fresh blood into the line."

"Wait a moment. By calling your Glass cousins mad, are you implying that Willie is not?"

He grinned. "Her madness is self-inflicted, not inherited." He nodded at the door through which Mr. Sidwell had exited. "I like him and I like this house." He nudged me with his elbow. "Ghosts and all."

Mr. Sidwell returned with the tea and we chatted about Daisy. She seemed to be one of the few friends he had, and I could tell he missed her company. Apparently she used to visit him weekly. Since she left, her parents came regularly, bringing food and other necessities as he rarely left the house, but he claimed it wasn't the same. She'd been a bright spot in his otherwise dull life.

We told him that I worked for the Glass Library and had found a book we couldn't read, except for the faint signature of Sir Andrew Sidwell on the second page. "There is also a Medici family symbol on the first page, and we believe Sir Andrew owned it after Cosimo de' Medici."

"The Glass Library?" Mr. Sidwell asked. "I'm afraid I don't know it. Is it your library, Mr. Glass?"

"It was named after my parents," Gabe said. "The collection contains books about magic, but since we can't read this one, Miss Ashe doesn't know where to shelve it."

"Intriguing. I do enjoy a good mystery."

With tea completed, he led us to the library. It was much larger than the one in Gabe's Park Street house, yet it felt cozy. I turned around on the spot to grasp the scale of it, breathing in the smell of leather and old paper. The bookshelves were almost entirely filled with books, but there were gaps here and there. Most of the gaps were occupied by a vase or other object, but some were empty. The bare spaces saddened me. This library ought to be bursting with books. But like the building itself, the library was neglected, its glory days long past.

Aside from the bookshelves, there was also a glass-fronted display cabinet. Inside were artefacts I wouldn't expect to see in a library. The saws, pliers, drills and clamps could be builders' tools, but the rest were odd indeed. There was a metal structure that looked as though it was designed to fit over a face and head, and a leather mask with a long beaked nose, and several sharp looking instruments whose function I couldn't determine.

Gabe knew, however. "They're all old surgical tools."

I shuddered. I didn't want to know more details.

The library may have been neglected, but it wasn't

unloved. Mr. Sidwell introduced us to his collection with pride. "About half of these books date from Sir Andrew's time." He indicated the side of the library housing the oldest books. "And the rest have been added over the years by various ancestors. The knowledge held within these walls is remarkable, and many of these are irreplaceable. You won't find copies anywhere in the world."

"Have you read them all?" Gabe asked.

"Lord, no. Most are either in a foreign language or the English is too old fashioned. I prefer modern novels. Daisy's mother shares hers with me." He indicated a large portrait of a bearded gentleman hanging over the fireplace. "That's Sir Andrew. Since he started this collection it's only fair he watches over it."

"Have you ever come across a book with strange symbols in it?" I asked. "A little like Egyptian hieroglyphics."

"I'm afraid I'm not familiar with the texts. Do you have the Medici Manuscript with you?"

Gabe shook his head as he studied the spines. "It's with a mathematician friend who's good at puzzles and codes. If he can't break it, no one can."

Mr. Sidwell frowned. "I do hope he'll treat it carefully. These old books are quite fragile."

"He will and it's only until tomorrow. He promised he'll return it to the library then."

Mr. Sidwell regarded the collection with hands on hips. "Hopefully we can find the key amongst these to assist him."

I glanced over the spines of Sir Andrew's collection. Several covers looked newer than sixteenth century. Someone must have re-covered them in the last century or so.

I began at the beginning. The leather cover of the first book was decorated with an elegant border that had almost worn smooth. I could just make out the flowers the bookbinder had carefully stamped into it many centuries ago. In the middle, the title was clearer, but I didn't recognize the language. I showed it to Gabe and Mr. Sidwell.

"It's German," Gabe said. "I think it means 'reader beware.'"

"How thrilling," Mr. Sidwell said. "Beware of what?"

Gabe carefully turned the pages. "I know very little German, but some of these words are religious." He pointed out the name of Martin Luther, the religious reformer. "It doesn't have any symbols like the Medici Manuscript."

I slotted it back onto the shelf and pulled out the next one. This was going to take some time. "Do you have a catalog of the books anywhere? It will help focus our search."

"There are some old ledgers and papers dating back to Sir Andrew's time in the attic," Mr. Sidwell said. "Perhaps one of them lists the books in his collection."

Gabe accompanied Mr. Sidwell to the attic while I continued to look through the texts. The men returned a mere fifteen minutes later with a plain wooden casket. Gabe set it on the table by the window.

Mr. Sidwell wiggled his fingers, as if he couldn't wait to get his hands on the contents. He opened the box. Dust drifted off and joined the film of dust already covering the desk surface. Aside from a cobweb on the hinges, it was clean inside.

Gabe picked up one of the ledgers on top and Mr. Sidwell removed another, revealing bundles of loose sheets of paper underneath. I pulled them out and untied the twine around them. We sat and read in silence.

Twenty minutes later, Gabe announced he'd found something. "This ledger is a list of accounts covering the years 1560-1569. There are no entries for bookbinders or book-shops." He pointed out some of the lines, each listing an object purchased in Florence—art, furniture, cloth. Considering Sir Andrew was an ambassador to the city state, it wasn't a surprise to see the Florentine entries. "But look at this entry here."

"One-hundred and eighty-five books," I said on a breath. "That is a lot to buy at once. But not from a shop. How odd."

Gabe pointed to the seller's name. "He bought them all from Dr. Thomas Adams."

"There's no figure in the amount column. Were they a donation from the doctor perhaps?"

Mr. Sidwell squinted at the page. "What does it say on the second line?"

"'For monies owing,'" Gabe read. "Dr. Adams must have owed Sir Andrew money and given him his collection in exchange for wiping the debt."

"That must have been quite a large debt," I said. "Professor Nash told me how expensive it was to make or buy books back then."

Gabe looked across the room to the cabinet. "I'm not entirely sure the collection included only books. It probably included Dr. Adams's medical instruments too."

"He wouldn't have been able to continue to practice without his tools."

We continued to search through the books and documents for more information about Dr. Adams. Since the book with the silver clasps was most likely older than the sixteenth century, and the doctor was a contemporary of Sir Andrew, it couldn't have been written by Adams himself. He had to have acquired it from another source. Hopefully the papers from the attic could shed more light.

But after another two hours, we came to the end of the casket's contents. Gabe had found more entries alluding to Dr. Adams in the accounts, some where the doctor was being paid for his services, and others where he borrowed enormous sums from Sir Andrew. After the transfer of the books and instruments to Sir Andrew, there were no more entries for Dr. Adams. Our specific book wasn't mentioned.

"At least we can assume it's a medical text if it was owned by a doctor," Mr. Sidwell said, once again perusing the library shelves. "It probably doesn't belong in a library about magic, Miss Ashe."

"Not necessarily." I told him what Professor Nash had told me, that the disciplines of medicine, astrology, and the occult were intertwined. "Dr. Adams may have acquired the book because he had an interest in the occult, or magic, and how he thought it related to medicine. But how he pried it out of Medici hands is anyone's guess."

With so many books to look through, Gabe suggested we come back another day.

Mr. Sidwell had a better idea. "Why don't I continue the search. I'll set aside anything that looks relevant and you can check next time you come. Perhaps bring the book with you. I'll write to you when I've completed the task."

Gabe took the casket back up to the attic while Mr. Sidwell and I waited in the entrance hall at the base of the staircase.

"I want to apologize again for earlier," he said. "I should have been more welcoming."

"We ought to apologize too. We should have given advanced warning of our arrival. Thank you again for letting us see Sir Andrew's collection. It's truly marvelous."

"I'm glad we learned a little more about it today. Before I begin looking through the books, I think I'll take another rummage through the attic and see if I can find a catalog of the items that came from Dr. Adams. It's possible more than the Medici Manuscript is missing."

"Hopefully you can find out how Dr. Adams acquired it in the first place. We're very interested in its origins, not just what it's about."

"Ah yes, the Medici connection. If you prove the provenance, it will be even more valuable."

I didn't tell him about the magic in the silver clasps. It was the only detail we'd not mentioned. I wasn't entirely sure why, except that it simply never came up.

Gabe returned and shook Mr. Sidwell's hand. "You have an interesting home. These walls must have some tales to tell."

"They certainly do. There are secret passages, curious carvings, and even a door that leads nowhere. I also have a ghost for company." He chuckled.

Gabe shot me a mischievous smile. "If it's Sir Andrew, please ask him about the Medici Manuscript."

We thanked him for his time, and he asked me to pass on his regards to Daisy. Then Gabe and I put on our motoring accessories and climbed into the Vauxhall.

"Hungry?" he asked me over the rumble of the engine.

"Very."

He drove until we came across a pretty meadow, accessed via a wooden gate. He carried the picnic basket packed by Mrs. Ling then helped me lay the blanket out under a shady tree. The blue country sky stretched endlessly above, broken only by the occasional fluffy cloud floating idly past.

Gabe handed a small chicken pie to me. "I can't imagine Daisy being friendly with Lazarus. They seem like an odd couple."

"I can. They're both eccentric. Kind, too, once you get to know them. But heaven help it if they take a disliking to you."

He laughed softly. "Is it just me, or are there more eccentric people now than before the war?"

"I've noticed it too. It's as if people were hiding their true selves, but can no longer keep up the pretense. Or they simply don't want to. I like it this way. I like seeing people as they truly are."

"As do I." He huffed at a thought.

"What is it?" I prompted.

His lips tilted crookedly. "It has only taken a year and a half, but you've made me see that something positive came out of the war."

"It wasn't me. You pointed it out."

"Even so." He smiled. "It's a start and I'm an optimist. Perhaps there are more positives that I'll soon see."

"Of course there will be. Your wedding, for one thing, and after that, children."

Gabe's smile vanished. He stared off into the distance until I offered him one of Mrs. Ling's jam-filled pastries. I wanted to apologize for dampening his good mood, but apologizing for mentioning his upcoming nuptials seemed like an odd thing to be sorry about.

So I said nothing.

We ate in a silence that was heavy to begin with but quickly lightened. It was easy to be with Gabe. I was comfortable in his presence. I used to be shy around men, and still was with some, but I'd never felt awkward with him. From the moment we'd met, I'd felt as though I was in the presence of a friend.

I should have felt self-conscious with him. He was good looking, charming and possessed an abundance of natural gifts, yet I never felt inferior, and certainly never afraid.

My mother would have been horrified to see us like this, together in the middle of a meadow with no one else around. She would want me to be more cautious. She'd told me the only man I could trust was my brother, and had even taught me some self-defense moves to protect myself against unwanted attention. I appreciated her for that caution after having used those moves recently during the investigation into the stolen painting.

Yet I was mature enough now to know she was not altogether right. Not all men wanted to hurt me. Some men could be trusted.

I wondered what she would have made of Gabe.

After eating the rest of our picnic lunch, I leaned back against the tree and sighed. The day was turning out so differently to the way it had begun. Sidwell House had been gloomy and dusty, but here, seated on a bed of wildflowers beneath leaves whispering in the breeze, I felt as though I was a world away, not mere miles.

I found I didn't want to talk about the manuscript or Sir Andrew Sidwell or Dr. Adams. I simply wanted to breathe. I wanted to enjoy this moment for as long as possible.

Gabe seemed to want that too. After finishing the food, he lay on his back and closed his eyes. His chest rose and fell with his steady breaths, and I thought he was asleep. But then he spoke.

"Ever since I returned, I feel like I've been treading water."

I blinked at him, a little disoriented by his confession.

"I knew there'd be a period of readjustment. I know I can't expect things to be the way they were. And I don't want them to be. But..." He heaved a sigh. "I don't know what I'm trying to say." He rubbed his forehead. "Sorry, Sylvia."

"It's all right. I think I understand. It's as though you're walking along a foggy path in winter and you can't see more than a few feet ahead. I've felt like that ever since my brother died and then my mother. No matter how much I tried to pull myself out of the fog, I couldn't. It's only recently that I've felt as though it has lifted."

He suddenly sat up. "Yes, that's it! Everything is foggy

and I can't see through it or move out of it. How did it lift for you?"

"Actually I have you to thank for that."

His lips curved with his smile. "Me?"

"The investigation," I said quickly. "It gave me a purpose as well as a new job that I adore. And I've met new friends because of it, and my friendship with Daisy has deepened. I miss my mother and James terribly, but...I no longer feel lonely."

His hand suddenly covered mine. The move was an instinctive one.

And I instinctively responded, by turning my hand over and grasping his in return. Our gazes met. My pulse quickened yet time slowed, or so it seemed.

Then he broke the connection and collected the plates, dusting the crumbs off. "It's getting late and there's something I need to do before the day is out."

With my blood still thrumming in my veins and my brain not fully functioning, I helped him pack up the picnic. He strapped the basket to the back of the Vauxhall then cranked the engine. I settled my driving goggles in place and tied the scarf under my chin, all the while trying not to think about how the touch of his hand wasn't enough.

It wasn't nearly enough.

CHAPTER 7

*O*ur arrival at the Park Street house was met with disapproving scowls. Alex's was directed at Gabe, but Willie's was for me.

"You should have woken one of us," Alex said.

"What good would that have been?" Gabe said, handing his driving coat to Bristow. "A sleepy bodyguard can't act quickly. Besides, I was in no danger. The kidnappers don't know where I live."

Willie pointed the cigarette she was holding at him. "You can't be sure of that."

Gabe nodded at the cigarette. "I thought you'd given up."

"It ain't lit. I just need to hold it. For my nerves."

"Your nerves are made of iron."

"Not when it comes to your safety, Gabe. Alex is right. You should have woken one of us." She pointed the cigarette at me. "Before *she* came along, you wouldn't have cut us out like this."

"Don't blame Sylvia. This is her investigation. If anything, I foisted myself on her."

She stuck the cigarette tip into her mouth, only to

remember it wasn't lit. "Damn it." She handed it to Bristow. "Take it away."

He clasped it between thumb and forefinger and held it at arm's length. "Yes, madam."

"We've been through this. Don't call me madam. Or ma'am."

Bristow kept his features schooled and regarded her with mild amusement. "M'lady?"

Willie made a sound of disgust in her throat.

Bristow dipped his head in what was the closest thing to a bow the elderly butler could manage. He turned to me. "Miss Ashe, Mrs. Ling's translation is complete. I'll fetch the cookbook for you."

"I'd like to thank her in person, if that's all right with you, Bristow."

"That is perfectly all right, Miss Ashe. Come with me."

I followed him, and Gabe followed us both. Alex and Willie didn't want to be left out again so they came with us to the kitchen. When she saw me, Mrs. Ling wiped her hands on her apron and smiled.

"Did you enjoy the picnic?" she asked.

"It was delicious," I said.

She beamed.

Bristow handed the cigarette to Mrs. Bristow. She pulled a face at it. "Lady Rycroft wouldn't be pleased," she said.

Willie threw her hands in the air. "She ain't here, and it ain't lit. I didn't smoke it."

Mrs. Bristow dropped it into a bucket of water by the stove.

Willie sank into a morose silence in the background.

Mrs. Ling picked up the book and showed me which recipes she'd translated. Each translation included some suggestions to make the process easier, or a note on whether an ingredient substitution would work if the original couldn't be sourced. Finally, she gave me a separate sheet, torn from a notebook, with a name and address on it.

"He is my supplier," she said. "He is also my brother. If your landlady mentions me, he will be good to her."

"Thank you, Mrs. Ling. Mrs. Parry will be pleased. I can't wait to taste these."

"I have some samples for you and Mrs. Parry to try." She opened the lid of a wooden toolbox on the table and showed me the four bowls inside, each covered with paper tied down with string. "I made a little for you and your landlady to see which one you like best. When you come here next, tell me which is your favorite."

I hesitated, not sure if it was polite to invite myself back. "If I can't manage to come, I'll send you a message."

Gabe had been watching Murray, Alex and Willie, having a quiet conversation. Murray sat at the end of the table, fixing the handle on the sugar barrel, but he put it down to talk to them. He looked a little sad.

I thanked Mrs. Ling and tucked the recipe book under my arm. Gabe picked up the toolbox with the Chinese food inside. We passed Dodson the chauffeur in the corridor. Gabe asked him to take me home in the Hudson, and to leave the Vauxhall where it was, still parked out the front.

"I'll be heading out again shortly," he added.

"Very good, Sir."

Willie waited for Dodson to leave then, hands on hips, confronted Gabe. "Where are you going now?"

Gabe gestured for me to walk ahead of him up the stairs. "Out."

"You ain't going without one of us this time."

"You can come if you want, but stay in the car. What I need to do must be done alone."

"Why?"

"I'll tell you when we get there."

"Where?"

"Actually, I'll tell you afterwards."

She huffed out a breath as we reached the entrance hall. "You're being difficult."

Gabe gave her a challenging look while Bristow, who'd followed us, sported a small smile. Willie pretended not to notice.

Bristow opened the front door to watch for Dodson while Gabe handed me the hat I'd left behind at the house when I put on the scarf for the drive. Willie fell into a silent strop, but nobody seemed to care.

"Is Murray all right?" Gabe asked Alex.

"He's still settling in. Give him time. He'll get used to how Bristow likes things done."

"I don't care about that. Not even Bristow cares about the way things used to be."

"Amen," Willie muttered so the butler couldn't hear. "Ever since the war, he's let his standards fall. And he's more high-and-mighty than he used to be."

"Murray's grateful for employment," Alex went on. "But he's bored."

"That's to be expected." To me, Gabe added, "Alex and Murray used to work together at the Met before the war."

"He was a constable." Alex shook his head slowly. "But he couldn't return there. They claimed they had nothing for him to do."

It was a similar story for many men who'd been disabled in the war. Those whose work was physical in nature found they weren't suited to return to it, but they weren't trained for administrative roles either. The government issued them with a pension, but for men used to being useful and still capable of working, it wasn't what they wanted. For their own self-respect, they needed to work.

Going from an active role as constable for the

Metropolitan Police to a footman in a Mayfair household must be difficult indeed, particularly when that household ran quite well without a footman.

"I'll keep giving him repairs to do, but I don't think he finds it satisfying work," Alex said.

Bristow announced that Dodson had arrived with the motorcar to take me home. Gabe escorted me outside, carrying the toolbox. Dodson got out of the car and switched on the headlamps before standing by the door, ready to open it for me.

I turned on the front porch to say farewell to Gabe when another motorcar pulled up behind the Hudson. Alex and Willie thrust me aside and stood in front of Gabe. Willie reached into her inside jacket pocket but thankfully didn't pull out her gun. She glared at the new arrival.

The driver got out and opened the rear passenger door. I blew out a steadying breath. This wasn't another kidnapping attempt.

It *was* an ambush, however. Lady Stanhope emerged. She was all smiles as she extended her hand to Gabe. He shook it, although I suspected she expected him to kiss the back of it. Her smile tightened ever so slightly before softening again.

"I'm so pleased I caught you, Mr. Glass," she cooed. Considering our former interactions with her had been strained, her cheerful manner grated.

Gabe was polite, however. "I'm sorry, I'm on my way out. You should have telephoned beforehand to save yourself the journey. Perhaps I can call on you tomorrow?"

"This won't take long." She stepped onto the next porch step, heading to the front door, but when Gabe didn't follow her, she stopped.

He smiled mildly back at her. "Shall we say three o'clock tomorrow?"

Her polite façade didn't falter. "I simply wanted to discuss with you the matter of your engagement to Ivy Hobson."

"Forgive me, but I don't see how that is any of your concern, madam."

"Oh, but it is. You see, I don't think you realize how it is for us ladies." At his blank look, she continued. "As you know, I have taken an interest in Ivy. It's my observation that she's much too polite to tell you how she truly feels."

"About what?"

"About waiting indefinitely for your parents to return so you can marry."

"Ah."

"Can you not see how upsetting the delay is for your fiancée?"

"I do see that, yes."

"She can have her pick of gentlemen, you know. She doesn't need to wait for you, yet she chooses to."

"You are right. Thank you for coming here and telling me. Now, if you don't mind, I have somewhere I need to be."

Lady Stanhope didn't move. She appeared to be planted on the pavement, her feet slightly apart. "Perhaps I can wait here for your return. I would like to get to know you better, Mr. Glass, since you are going to be Ivy's husband and Ivy has become dear to me. I can wait with Lady Farnsworth in the drawing room."

Who was Lady Farnsworth?

Willie's eyes widened so much I worried she might strain them. "I can't entertain you! I have to go with Gabe!"

I frowned. *She* was Lady Farnsworth? One of her husbands had been a lord?

I pressed my lips together to stop myself laughing at the image of Willie hosting a country house party. It was absurd. She was the least ladylike woman I knew.

"I can't keep you company either, I'm afraid," Alex said in a sarcastic tone.

Lady Stanhope's smile finally faded. She cleared her throat and stared at Gabe.

Gabe looked longingly at his motorcar.

"Do you have the time, Mr. Glass?"

Since he was holding onto the toolbox with both hands to keep it level, he couldn't reach for his pocket watch. Considering she could clearly see his hands were full, it was an odd request to make.

He looked to Alex. Alex checked his wristwatch. "Six thirty-five," he said.

Lady Stanhope ignored him. "You don't wear a wristwatch, Mr. Glass."

"I prefer my pocket watch."

"Is it magical?"

"It was given to me by my parents."

"Of course, and it *must* be magical." She laid a hand on his arm. "Considering what your mother is."

He remained silent.

"You're so fortunate to be the son of such a powerful magician. I'm sure all of your clocks run on time and never have to be wound up."

Gabe gave her a thin smile.

Willie crossed her arms. "He ain't selling you one of India's clocks."

Lady Stanhope pressed a hand to her chest, offended. "I have no need of more clocks, Lady Farnsworth. It was simply idle chatter with a friend."

Willie's top lip curled into a sneer at being called by her proper title. The sneer deepened when Lady Stanhope called Gabe a friend.

Lady Stanhope once again lay her hand on Gabe's arm. "Do consider poor Ivy's feelings and don't delay the wedding any longer. She will make you an excellent wife. And your children will be..." She fluttered her gloved fingers in the air, leaving the rest of the sentence to our imaginations.

"Magical?" Willie snapped.

"I was going to say beautiful. You do seem rather captivated by magic and magicians, Lady Farnsworth. I hope you won't be disappointed if their children are born artless, like their father."

Alex stilled. He didn't even blink and he certainly didn't look in Gabe's direction. Lady Stanhope watched Gabe intently, however.

Willie huffed and Gabe's only reaction was to smile and apologize for not inviting Lady Stanhope inside.

She climbed back into the passenger seat of her motorcar. Bristow closed the door and it drove away.

We all watched until it rounded the corner.

"What was that about?" Willie blurted out. "She doesn't care about Ivy's happiness."

"She probably did want one of my mother's clocks." Gabe nodded at Bristow who opened the Hudson's passenger door for me.

His answer didn't satisfy any of us. Willie looked confused, while Alex and Gabe were too quiet. They were keeping something from Gabe's cousin. From everyone. And it had something to do with him being artless.

Gabe leaned in and placed the toolbox on my lap. "Thank you for an enjoyable day out, Sylvia."

"It's me who should be thanking you. It was pleasant." Pleasant? It was far more than that. It had been the best day I'd had in years. But I couldn't say that to him. It wasn't appropriate, and his friend and cousin were looking on, scowling at us again.

Gabe straightened. Before the door closed, I heard Willie

say she despised being called Lady Farnsworth. "She was only calling me that to rile me."

"It could have been worse," Alex said smugly.

"How?"

"She could have accused you of murdering him."

* * *

THE FOLLOWING MORNING, I told Professor Nash all about Lazarus Sidwell and his ancestor's book collection. "It didn't consist of just books. There were surgical instruments as well. They were rather gruesome."

"Medicine was little better than butchery back then."

We sat on the sofa in the ground floor reading nook where we could hear anyone entering through the front door. He'd made coffee in his upstairs flat and brought it down on a tray. The coffee pot was an exquisite antique made of copper, and intricately engraved with foliage from the top of its hinged dome cover to its base. He told me he'd bought it at a souk in Fez, Morocco, many years ago, believing it was magician-made only to be informed by Oscar Barratt that it wasn't.

"Unfortunately we didn't find the key to deciphering the manuscript," I went on. "Although Mr. Sidwell said he'd keep looking. Perhaps something will turn up in his attic."

He adjusted his spectacles. "You had quite a day, driving to Marlborough and back. Fortunately the weather was good. The roads can be quite treacherous in the rain."

"How was your day off, Professor?"

"Informative, as it happens. I learned something that may be pertinent to our manuscript."

I lowered my coffee cup to look at him properly. "You worked on your day off?"

"It's not work when you enjoy it. Anyway, you worked too."

"Yes, but the book may be a link to my family. I don't consider it work."

We exchanged smiles. It would seem neither of us disliked our jobs.

He set the cup down and picked up a book from the table. "I borrowed this from a former colleague at the university. He's a professor of history. I wanted his opinion on books from the era of our Medici Manuscript. He told me to read this." He showed me the cover. It was a book about books, antique ones, to be exact. "Do you recall what I told you about books being expensive back then?"

"Expensive to make and purchase," I said.

He raised a finger to indicate I'd made a good point. "Expensive to purchase also means profitable to sell. And where money can be made, someone unscrupulous can be found peddling fakes."

"You think the Medici Manuscript is a fake?"

"It's a possibility."

"But it looks old to me."

"It is. But is it as old as we believe it to be? Perhaps it was made in the sixteenth or seventeenth century, after all, not the fifteenth. Books on science and magic were incredibly popular then and would have sold for very high prices. My point is, if it is a fake, perhaps the author simply wrote those symbols to make it more intriguing to earn a higher price."

"You mean they may not be a code at all, but random doodles of a greedy forger?"

He nodded gravely. "It pains me to say it, but we must consider the text has no meaning at all." He pushed his glasses up his nose. "There are still the magical clasps, however, and it's still worth finding out who the author is, to see if that brings up a name for the silver magician who made them."

But deciphering the symbols may not lead us to the silver magician. It may lead us nowhere.

"We can be almost certain it came into Sir Andrew Sidwell's possession," I said. "Otherwise his name wouldn't be on page two. And we also know he purchased a large collection of books from Dr. Adams. So if it is a fake, either Dr. Adams made it to dupe Sir Andrew, or Dr. Adams himself was duped by the forger."

He pointed his finger again. "The problem is, how do we know if it's a fake?"

I wanted to see it again and look for clues. We suspected the page with the Medici symbol was added later than the rest, so that page could have been forged to increase its value. As to the rest, I wanted to touch it again. Perhaps feeling the pages would give me a clue where simply looking hadn't.

The front door opened and a man called out. "Hello? Is anyone here?"

The professor asked me to see to the newcomer while he took the coffee cups and pot upstairs. I greeted the man standing by the front desk with a welcoming smile.

"You must be Gabe's mathematician friend," I said, nodding at the Medici Manuscript held carefully in both hands.

His round eyes stared at me for a long moment. "You're a woman."

"My name is Sylvia Ashe." I held out my hand.

He continued to stare as if not quite sure what he was supposed to do. Then, as if a switch was flipped, he put the book down on the desk and shook my hand. "It's nice to meet you, Miss Ashe. I was expecting a man."

"Professor Nash. Yes, I'm sure you were."

"I am sorry. That was impolite of me. It's just that your presence took me by surprise. Gabriel knows I don't like surprises, so I don't know why he didn't tell me about you.

Perhaps he didn't know I would come here. Yes, that's probably it. He told me to telephone him when I was finished with the book, but I decided to come in person. I wanted to see the library. I haven't been here before."

"You know Gabe doesn't work here, Mr....?"

"Stray. My name is Francis Stray."

Mr. Stray was a rather non-descript man with brown hair and eyes, neither tall nor short, fat nor thin. He had no distinguishing features, not even an oddly placed freckle on his nose, and no facial hair. His suit was well-made if unremarkable, and his shoes polished to a sheen, and his hair was tidy. Not a strand of it was out of place. I guessed him to be the same age as Gabe, late twenties.

To that end, I asked, "How do you know Gabe?"

"We went to school together."

"And you've remained friends ever since? That's nice."

"I suppose it is."

He *supposed* it was nice? What an odd response.

I invited him into the library proper seeing as he'd come especially to see it. He picked up the book again and carried it gingerly. I invited him to set it down on the desk in the reading nook while I showed him around.

He was reluctant to let it go. "It shouldn't be left lying about out here with no one to guard it."

"You're right. I'll hold it." I took the book from him and immediately felt relief wash over me. I hadn't realized how much I'd worried about losing it. I caressed one of the silver clasps with my thumbs. "It is a valuable thing," I murmured.

"Indeed."

I looked up sharply. "You've managed to decipher it?"

"I'm afraid not."

My heart sank. "Oh. You were referring to the Medici connection."

"I was."

"So the code is too complex?"

"I tried all of the ciphers I know. None worked. I'm afraid that without something to start with, it's impossible to decode."

I sighed. "Thank you for trying. You must have worked on it all day yesterday."

"And much of the night."

"Oh dear, I am sorry. You could have kept it longer."

"There's no need to be sorry, Miss Ashe. I enjoyed the challenge. I feel invigorated for seeing it and honored to have been the one Gabriel came to."

He didn't look invigorated. Indeed, his expression hadn't changed from the moment he entered the library.

"Would you like the tour now?" I asked.

"Yes, please. I've been looking forward to this."

"So I see." Well, not quite.

His face remained blank as I showed him our collection, even taking him upstairs where we met Professor Nash. The professor took over the tour while I returned downstairs with the manuscript.

I sat at the front desk and opened it, skipping past the first and second pages. I carefully inspected the remaining pages, using the desk lamp to improve the lighting and even taking out a magnifying glass from the top drawer. I felt the pages, too. Except for the first one, the others were thick and coarse, their quality inferior to modern day paper. I glanced around. Seeing no one nearby, I leaned down and smelled it. It was musty with a kind of tang that I couldn't quite place.

It *had* to be old.

The men joined me twenty minutes later. "What will you do with it now?" Mr. Stray asked.

"Catalog it." The professor pointed to the card drawers. "Without knowing the title, we'll simply call it the Medici

Manuscript and shelve it with other books on the occult that date to the Middle Ages."

We would also note that the clasps held silver magic, but neither of us mentioned that.

"It was kind of you to show me the library, Miss Ashe, Professor Nash."

Professor Nash shook Mr. Stray's hand. "Not at all. It's the least we can do in exchange for your efforts. The time you spent on the manuscript is very much appreciated."

Mr. Stray nodded.

I held out my hand too.

This time he didn't hesitate to shake it. "It was a pleasure to meet you, Miss Ashe. Once again, I apologize if I was impolite earlier."

"It's quite all right."

He watched me for a moment before shaking his head. "I feel as though I ought to explain myself. You being a woman doesn't preclude you from being a good librarian."

"Er, thank you."

"In my estimation, it's a job eminently suited to the gentler nature of females. My surprise was simply in finding a woman in a library. All librarians I know are men. It's all about the odds, you see."

"Thank you for clarifying. And thank you for your efforts with the manuscript."

He opened the door and touched the brim of his hat in farewell. Then he was gone and I was left staring at the door in much the same way as he'd stared at me upon his arrival.

"What a curious man," I said.

Professor Nash chuckled. "I think he likes you."

"How can you tell?"

"I've known men like him my entire life. Learned, intelligent, yet socially stunted. I suppose I've become used to deciphering them."

"Like a code." I tapped the cover of the Medici Manuscript. "If Mr. Stray becomes a regular fixture here, I may have to ask you for clues to help me decipher him. I was at quite a loss just now."

The professor asked me to create a catalog card for the book then shelve it. I was in the middle of writing up the card when he joined me and peered over my shoulder.

"I have an idea," he said. "The Medici connection makes the book valuable and the code makes it mysterious. That's an enticing combination. I think the public will be interested in it, and perhaps there is someone out there who'll come and look at it and be able to decode it."

"You want to put it on display?"

"Yes, and notify the newspapers of our plan. It'll promote the library and perhaps even bring in some donations. I will have to pass it by the committee first, of course."

"And get a display cabinet that locks securely."

"I'll commission the same cabinet maker who built the others, and have the glass magician fit it with magical glass."

The most valuable books in the library's collection were kept behind locked glass doors in cabinets on the first floor. A magician had cast a spell on the glass to make it unbreakable.

It was in one of those cabinets that we temporarily stored the Medici Manuscript, until a special display cabinet could be made.

Professor Nash pocketed the key. "You ought to telephone Gabriel about Mr. Stray's visit. He'll want to know. And what about calling on Huon Barratt and asking him if his magic can verify the age of the ink?"

I made my way downstairs to the front desk and reached for the telephone. My hand recoiled when the front door burst open. Willie stood on the threshold, glowering. She shook her finger at me.

"You! It's all your fault!"

CHAPTER 8

"What did I do?" I asked. "What's happened? Is Gabe all right?" Oh God. What if there'd been another kidnapping attempt, this time a successful one? Although I failed to see how I could be blamed for it, I had no doubt that Willie would find a way.

"He ain't all right." She slammed the door behind her with such vigor that her hat slipped down over her forehead. She pressed her knuckles on the desk and leaned in. "His life is falling apart, and *you're* to blame."

I leaned back, out of her reach. "Please calm down and start at the beginning. What are you accusing me of doing?"

"Encouraging him to break off his engagement to Ivy."

She couldn't have surprised me more if she'd slapped me. I shook my head, over and over, and stared at her. I may have attempted to speak, but no words came out. I couldn't even form a coherent thought.

The professor's heavy step on the staircase echoed in the silence. "Willie! This is a library. What is the meaning of this racket?"

"You've got to dismiss her, Prof. She's trying to hurt Gabe."

Something switched on inside my head, banishing the confusion. I shot to my feet. "I am not!"

Professor Nash put up his hands. "I won't be dismissing anyone until I know what is going on. Willie?"

I pressed my knuckles on the desk and leaned forward too. I wasn't going to let her intimidate me and make wild accusations. Not in my place of work, and certainly not about something I didn't do.

Willie and I glared at one another, our faces mere inches apart. "Gabe tried to end his engagement to Ivy last night," she said.

It would seem I'd heard her correctly the first time. "I don't understand."

"Luckily she didn't accept it and is giving him a second chance."

"She didn't accept it?" I echoed. "But if it's what he wants—"

"It ain't. I know him better than you. I know him better than himself, and I can see it's the wrong decision." She wagged her finger at me again. "And it's your fault because he told me and Alex that you advised him to end it."

"That is not what I said, and I'm quite sure that's not what he claims I said either. What were his exact words?"

"That after speaking to you, it became clear he needed to end it."

"That is not the same thing as me advising him to end it." I blew out a breath in an attempt to steady my racing pulse. But it was no use. Blood thumped through my veins in time to a wild drumbeat. "Yesterday he told me he wasn't ready to marry, that he hadn't fully emerged from the foggy state the war had plunged him into. I suggested he discuss it with Ivy as it concerned her. That's all. If he decided to end it with her based on that, well…that's his decision."

Willie continued to scowl at me, but at least she didn't continue to argue her point or round the desk and challenge me to a duel.

Professor Nash cleared his throat. "Forgive me, Willie, but I fail to understand your fury. Why do you want Gabriel to remain engaged to Ivy if he wants to end it? Do you not want what he wants?"

She stepped back and poked the brim of her hat with her finger to raise it. "He doesn't really know what he wants."

"He's a grown man, and intelligent, too."

She shook her head. "He ain't thinking straight. Ivy's right. Gabe needs time. He needs to consider his future carefully, not act on a whim after spending the day with a pretty woman who looks at him with cow eyes."

"I do not!" I cried. "What are cow eyes, anyway?"

She ignored me and addressed Professor Nash. "He needs to think about why he chose Ivy in the first place."

"And why did he?" he asked.

"Because he needs her. She helped him after the war. She's been good for him."

The professor pushed his glasses up his nose. "Has she?"

Willie seemed surprised by his challenge. "He's better than he was."

"That could be attributed to time passing, not Ivy. Willie," he said gently, "have you considered that Gabriel *has* thought this through carefully?"

"How can he? He decided only yesterday, after he'd been with *her*."

I sighed. Nothing I could say would change her mind.

The professor didn't give up quite so easily. "Gabriel is a gentleman. He'd keep his word if he could. For him to end it, he must know it's what he wants. He wouldn't make the decision lightly. I suspect he was thinking about ending the engagement well before yesterday."

He was right and Willie knew it. She suddenly looked deflated, as if someone had let the air out of her. She leaned against the desk and lowered her head.

"You say Ivy didn't accept his decision," Professor Nash went on. "What did Gabriel say to that?"

"Nothing. We overheard her telling him on the Hobsons' front porch as he was leaving. The only thing he said to us when he got in the motor was that he ended it with her but is going to tell everyone that she ended it with him."

The professor nodded wisely, as if he'd given advice on such matters for years. "It's the honorable thing to do."

I stared at the telephone, wanting to speak to Gabe and yet not daring to make the call. What would I say? Would I even succeed in reaching him? I suspected Willie wouldn't allow it. She'd want me to stay well away.

"Will you telephone Gabe about Mr. Stray's visit?" I asked the professor. "Then perhaps we can call on Huon Barratt, as you suggested."

"You go. I ought to stay here and man the ship."

He handed me the key to the cabinet, and I went to fetch the book. My thoughts were not entirely on the manuscript, however.

When I returned, Willie was still there, listening as the professor spoke into the telephone. I kept my distance until he hung up the receiver.

"Are you sure you can't come?" I asked him.

He frowned. "Is something the matter? Is it Huon? He's something of a cad, it's true. Perhaps you can ask Gabriel to go with you." He picked up the receiver again.

Willie plucked it out of his hand and hung it up. "I'll go with you."

My eyes widened. "I couldn't ask you to do that. You must have better things to do."

"Nope."

The door opened and Daisy breezed in. Dressed in a yellow dress with a black sash tied at the waist and a black hat with a large yellow bow, she looked striking and modern. She also looked like my savior.

I embraced her as if I hadn't seen her for weeks. "Say yes," I whispered in her ear. I drew back and said in a louder voice, "We're about to call on an ink magician, the nephew of the professor's friend, Oscar Barratt. Would you like to come?"

"Is he handsome?"

I glared at her. "Yes," I said tightly.

She grinned. "Then yes I will. Who else is coming?"

Willie pointed her thumb at her chest. "Me." As we headed along Crooked Lane, she wanted to know why the professor called Huon Barratt a cad.

"He's something of a womanizer," I said.

"Is that all?"

Daisy took my hand. "Sylvia doesn't like men."

"That's not true!"

"They make her feel uncomfortable."

"Not all men," I muttered.

"Just the cads."

Willie adjusted her hat, tugged on her jacket, and quickened her pace. "Then you're about to get a lesson in how to deal with them."

Willie drove us to Huon's house in Marylebone in the motorcar she'd borrowed from Gabe. When she got out, she tipped her head back and whistled quietly. "Nice place. Barratt's doing well for himself."

"His father is," I said. "Huon is not inclined to join the family business at this point. That's why he's here in London, far from his parents."

We found Huon dressed in the same blue house coat as the last time, his feet bare once again. His chest was also bare. He wore no shirt or undershirt, and the coat gaped. He didn't bother trying to cover himself. Neither of my companions minded. While I didn't dare lower my gaze below his chin, they both openly stared. Huon strutted like a peacock.

Willie indicated his chest with a wave. "You're missing something."

"Would you like me to put on a shirt?" He asked it with the confidence of a man sure the answer would be no.

"It ain't a shirt you're missing. It's chest hair."

Huon tugged the edges of his coat together. "Tea, ladies?" He smiled oh-so sweetly at Willie. "And...sir?"

She sat on the sofa, stretched out her legs and crossed them at the ankles. "Why not? We've got time."

Huon nodded at his butler then invited Daisy and me to sit too.

He lounged in an armchair and regarded Daisy through half-lowered lids. She bore it well, pretending not to notice. She didn't so much as blush either. "Miss Carmichael, was it? Or may I call you Daisy?"

"You may. And I shall call you Huon."

He smiled.

She indicated the room. "You have a lovely home, Huon. It's in a very smart part of town."

"Thank you. Perhaps you'd like a tour?"

She looked to me. "I'm not sure we have the time."

"You're welcome to come back whenever you like. I'll give you my telephone number before you leave. You may call me at any time, night or day, and I shall oblige you with a personal tour."

Daisy was a rather forward girl, but even she was shocked by his boldness.

"Thanks for the invitation." Willie stretched her arm

along the back of the sofa, behind Daisy. "But I reckon we'll wait for your parents to come to London. It's their place and it wouldn't be right to accept a tour from their boarder."

Huon huffed a laugh. "I see how it is." He looked pointedly at Willie's arm resting on the back of the sofa. "My apologies. I misread the situation."

Daisy emitted a small gasp, but before she could tell him that she and Willie weren't together, I came to the point of our visit. "Is it possible for you to tell how old ink is?"

"It is." He nodded at the Medici Manuscript. "You want to know if it's as old as you think it is?"

I passed the book to him. "Apparently many fakes were made at a later date. We're almost certain the first page was added later, but we're not sure of the rest."

He lightly touched the balls of the Medici symbol then turned the page without comment. He didn't see the faint mark of Sir Andrew Sidwell until I asked him to touch that too. He then continued to turn pages and caress several of the letters and symbols.

"Well?" I asked.

The butler entered with a tray which he set down on the table. He poured while Huon continued to study the book. Once the butler left again, Huon rose. He stood by the window, angling the book to the light. Then he lifted it to his nose and sniffed.

We sipped our tea and watched.

He returned to the armchair and opened the book to the page with Sir Andrew's signature. "The ink used here is from the early sixteenth century and is of inferior quality. That's why it hasn't lasted." He turned back one page. "The ink on these balls and *fleur de lis* is earlier, mid fifteenth century. The quality is excellent. The rest of the book was written approximately one hundred years earlier again, in the fourteenth century. The quality of the ink is superior. It would have been expensive to make and purchase."

"How can you tell?" I asked.

"I'm a bloody good ink magician."

"Humble, too," Willie muttered.

"Humility is for the artless. We magicians have finely tuned senses when it comes to our own craft. My father taught me at an early age how to analyze what I sensed, how to identify the individual ingredients in all kinds of inks. Since the ingredients used to create inks have changed over the centuries, I can pinpoint an ink's age to a certain period of ink history."

"That's interesting," I said. It was also just what I hoped he could do. "So that's why the text has lasted so long in such good condition."

He studied the book again. "I'm glad you brought it back, Sylvia. It allows me to admire it more. I didn't appreciate it as much last time."

I suspected that was because he was still drunk from the night before, but I didn't say so. I reached out to accept the book from him, but he didn't pass it over.

"Have you managed to decipher any of it?" he asked.

"Not yet."

He pointed to one of the symbols. "I think I've seen this before."

I stood and peered over his shoulder. He indicated one of the symbols I'd taken particular notice of. The others were generic symbols—an eye, a rabbit, a sun, wavy lines, et cetera. But this one looked like a complicated knot within a circle. It was difficult to see where the knot started and finished.

"Where have you seen it?" I asked.

"After university and before war broke out, I traveled across Europe." He tapped his finger on the page as he thought. "I recall seeing it on several buildings in the Catalonia region."

"Perhaps it's the crest of a wealthy family from the area." Much like the Medici symbol appeared on many Florentine buildings from the time, this symbol could also represent an important patron. "But why does it appear in this book?"

It was a question none of us could answer.

Huon continued to look through the book as we drank our tea, only to get to the end and shake his head. "That's all I can contribute to solving the mystery, I'm afraid."

I rose. "Thank you, Huon. You've been helpful."

He passed me the book. When his fingers touched mine, he smiled. "It has been a pleasure, Sylvia. I hope I'll see you again soon." He drew my hand to his lips. "Very soon."

I almost dropped the Medici Manuscript in my haste to withdraw my hand. Huon grabbed the book to steady it and we clashed fingers again. My face heated, which only made him smile. It wasn't conceited, however. It was almost sweet.

He escorted us to the motorcar, but Willie wouldn't let him crank the engine. She insisted on doing it herself. After we drove away from the curb, she glanced over her shoulder at Daisy, seated in the back.

"I see what you mean. She's real awkward around men."

"I am not," I protested. "Not with all men. Anyway, I thought you came to protect me from Huon. You did a poor job. Why did you let him think Daisy was your lover, but not me?"

"You ain't my type."

I suspected she hadn't intervened because she saw me as a threat to Gabe's relationship with Ivy, and hoped I would give Huon a chance.

Daisy leaned forward from the back seat. "So I am your type? How flattering. I suppose I'll forgive you if you're going to say such nice things."

"Forgive me for what?" Willie asked.

"Ruining any chance I had with Huon. I was going to telephone him and ask him to meet us at a club tonight."

Willie screwed up her nose. "You don't want to do that. He's a cad. I reckon he's got a different girl every week."

"I don't think he's as bad as he makes out," I said. "I think it's an act. Willie, watch out!"

She swerved to miss a motorcar as it roared through an intersection. "I saw it." She was an erratic driver, preferring to dart in and out of the traffic instead of pulling on the brake lever. She did it with a look of determination, too, as if she were in a race.

"*You* should telephone him, Sylvia," she said to me.

"You just called him a cad, and advised Daisy *not* to telephone him."

"I reckon you could change him. You said yourself he's probably acting."

Now I was certain she was foisting me in Huon's direction and away from Gabe. "Are you still blaming me for Gabe's decision?"

"You ain't off the hook yet."

I turned to her fully. "Look. I may not know Gabe as well as you do—"

She grunted.

"But the professor does, and if he thinks Gabe would never hurt Ivy based on something I said, then that's good enough for me."

She grunted again, but if I was reading her noises correctly, she wasn't quite as angry with me anymore. Perhaps she didn't even blame me now. That grunt was probably the closest thing to an apology I'd get.

Daisy leaned forward again. "What's going on?"

"Gabe has broken off his engagement to Ivy," I said.

She gasped.

"Based on Sylvia's advice," Willie said over her shoulder.

I rolled my eyes. "I did not advise him to end it. Anyway, it's not very clear what's happening, yet. Apparently Ivy refused to accept it was ending and told him to think about it."

Daisy pulled a face. "That's very mature of her. If it were me, I'd have called him names, threatened to ruin his reputation, and thrown a glass of wine in his face."

Willie grinned. "That's why I like you."

"Ivy's temperament is somewhat cooler than yours," I told Daisy. "And positively icy compared to yours," I said to Willie.

She thought that was a compliment and grinned.

* * *

I AWOKE EARLY the following morning and enjoyed a leisurely breakfast with Mrs. Parry and two of the other lodgers who also woke early. One of the girls had already been out to buy a newspaper and she shared the pages around. A brief article on the second page caught my eye.

"Disturbance at Army Boot Supplier Hobson and Son", the headline read.

Hobson and Son was Ivy's family-run boot manufacturing business. According to the article, three people had been arrested outside the factory, one of them a former soldier who'd lost both his legs in the war. The reason for the disturbance wasn't reported.

The article played on my mind all the way to Crooked Lane. Or, rather, how Gabe would feel about ending his relationship with Ivy now that her family was experiencing some difficulty. While she didn't work for the company, it was part of the fabric of her family. Magicians and their craft were intwined in ways that couldn't be separated. As a magician herself, she might feel the trouble keenly.

As a gentleman with a kind heart, Gabe wouldn't want to cause her or her family any more difficulty at this time.

All thoughts of the Hobsons' problems vanished when I reached the library. The front door was ajar. I always let myself in with my own key of a morning. My arrival signaled the library was open for the day.

I pushed the door open further and peered inside. Nothing was amiss. Perhaps a patron had come early, knocked, and been let in by the professor.

But the professor was usually still in his flat at this time, and with the false door in the bookshelves closed, as well as the vestibule door, his flat acted like a bubble in which the outside world couldn't be seen or heard.

Then I noticed the broken window.

"Professor!" I raced up the stairs, taking two at a time. "Professor! Are you all right?"

Silence.

I opened the hidden door in the bookshelves and banged on the vestibule door. No answer. I tried the handle, but it was locked. I went to bang on it again when it suddenly opened.

The professor squinted at me. "Sylvia? Whatever's the matter?"

I threw my arms around him. "Thank goodness you're all right. I was so worried."

He put on his glasses and peered past me. "Why? What's wrong?"

"There's been a break-in."

"Has anything been taken?"

"I don't know. I came up here immediately."

He followed me through the stacks. We glanced along each row until we reached the end. But I knew the thief hadn't taken anything from the regular shelves. They would have tried the locked cabinets where the valuable books were kept.

Where we'd stored the Medici Manuscript after returning from Huon's place.

Thank goodness for the magical glass fronting the cabinets. Unlike the window, it couldn't be broken. The thief could still force the lock, but it would require strength.

Professor Nash had the same thought as me. We both strode to the cabinet containing the Medici Manuscript. My heart sank when I saw it.

Shattered glass littered the floor, and the book was missing.

I picked up a large shard. "I thought the magic in this made it unbreakable."

The professor sighed. "Magic doesn't last." He sighed again as he surveyed the damage. "I suppose it was due to have the spell put into it again. I'm not very good at keeping track of these things."

We both stood in front of the cabinet and stared at the empty space where the book had been displayed, unable to comprehend the loss. The positivity I'd felt over the last few days vanished. All I wanted to do was sit among the broken glass and cry.

CHAPTER 9

*C*yclops decided soon after arriving at the library that Gabe should be hired for the investigation since he'd been helping me trace the Medici Manuscript's origins. The fact that its silver clasps contained magic confirmed that Gabe was the right choice. All Scotland Yard investigations with a magical element employed Gabe as consultant.

Gabe arrived a short while later with Alex, who'd be assisting him on the investigation. Willie merely came along because she loathed being left out.

She drew me aside after I had my fingerprints taken. "Do not tell Gabe that I came here yesterday."

I accepted the cloth from the constable and wiped my hand. "Why not?"

She glanced around to make sure no one was listening. "Because I don't want him to know I told you about him and Ivy."

"I won't lie to him."

"I ain't asking you to lie. I just don't want you bringing it up." She frowned at the cloth as I handed it back to the constable. "They found fingerprints?"

"Two sets on the wooden frame of the cabinet. They probably belong to the professor and me, which means the thief wore gloves." I waggled my ink-stained fingers at her. "Cyclops wanted to check our prints to eliminate us."

Gabe and Alex joined us after being briefed by Cyclops and the professor. "What are you two whispering about?" Alex asked.

"We ain't whispering." Willie held up my hand. "She was telling me about being fingerprinted. What'd your pa say?"

"It seems the thief looked through the card catalog first to find the record for the book then went straight to the cabinet. The drawer wasn't closed properly. He's sending men out to question the neighbors now."

I didn't think he'd have much luck there. Most of the neighboring buildings housed offices that were only occupied in the daytime.

Alex looked to Gabe. When Gabe didn't speak, Alex nudged him with his elbow. "You were going to ask Sylvia to join us with the professor."

Gabe nodded. "Right. Sylvia, come and take a seat on the sofa. The professor is making tea."

I led the way to the sofa in the reading nook, only to realize Gabe hadn't followed. He walked slowly behind me, listening to Alex who spoke with some earnestness. The only word I caught was Alex's final one.

"Agreed?"

Gabe nodded.

Alex clapped him on the back and told him to sit.

Gabe sat. "Sorry, Sylvia. I'm a little distracted today."

"Oh?" I hoped he'd tell me about his engagement ending, but he did not.

"But he's going to give this investigation his full attention." Alex glared at his friend. "Right?"

Gabe tugged on his shirt cuff. "I certainly will. Are you all right, Sylvia? Are you shaken?"

"Not really. I'm...sad, I suppose. Sad at the loss of the manuscript. I was enjoying our investigation and felt as though we had our first breakthrough yesterday in decoding the text."

"Go on."

Professor Nash and Cyclops arrived. The professor carried a tray of tea things while Cyclops carried a tray with plates and a cake. He sliced it up and handed them out while the professor poured.

"Sylvia was going to tell us she learned something about the manuscript yesterday," Gabe told them. "Where did you go?"

"And why did you go without us?" Alex asked.

"I called on Huon Barratt," I said.

Gabe paused, the teacup halfway to his mouth. "Alone?"

"He's quite harmless."

"I know, but...never mind. You're right. He's indolent and egotistical but I don't think he could harm a fly." He sipped.

The professor lifted his cup and pointed it in the direction of Willie, chatting to one of the constables. "Anyway, Sylvia wasn't alone. Willie and Daisy joined her."

Gabe swung around to look at Willie. She suddenly stopped what she was saying and marched over to us. "Why's everyone looking at me? You all miss me, eh?" She chuckled, somewhat nervously.

Cyclops rolled his eyes. "Why are you here? Don't you have husband number three to woo?"

She pulled back her jacket to expose the gun strapped to her hip. "I'm keeping Gabe safe, but if you keep talking about me marrying again, I might accidentally miss the kidnapper and shoot you instead."

Cyclops muttered something I couldn't quite hear into his

teacup. He cradled it in his palm since his finger was too large to fit through the handle. He sipped thoughtfully then spoke to Gabe. "The offer for police protection is still open."

Gabe thanked him but refused. "I'm going to maintain a low profile. Tonight I have a dinner to attend, but it's only with a small group. It's a casual affair and won't be written up in the papers."

"That seems to have been the link so far," Alex told his father. "An event which Gabe will likely attend is written up in the newspapers, then there's a kidnapping attempt. It's too coincidental for there not to be a link."

Cyclops frowned. "You said 'So far?' Are you expecting that to change?"

Alex's gaze drilled into Gabe, but Gabe pretended not to notice.

He put down his cup. "I want to get moving on this investigation before the trail goes cold. The longer we wait, the more time the thief has to sell the manuscript."

"It may already be sold," the professor said heavily. "Now the war is over, I suspect the market for old and valuable books will reactivate after a period of hibernation."

"Aside from the people sitting here, there are only four others who knew about the Medici Manuscript." Gabe removed a pencil and notepad from his pocket and began writing names. "Carl Trevelyan, the photographer. Huon Barratt, the ink magician."

The professor pushed his glasses up his nose. "It's not him."

We all looked at him.

"It's not. He's Oscar's nephew."

Gabe moved on. "Lazarus Sidwell, the descendent of Sir Andrew, and Francis Stray, my friend the mathematician."

"And Daisy." Alex pointed to the next line. When Gabe

didn't write it down, he added, "She knew so she's a suspect. We should investigate her."

"We should," Willie said idly. "I want to speak to her anyway. I want to find out if she telephoned Huon and met him at a club last night."

Alex swiveled to get a better look at her. "She was going out with a man she hardly knows? Not to mention you all think he's an indolent cad?"

"But he's handsome, in a way. Ain't that right, Sylvia?"

I saw no reason not to join in the teasing. "Very handsome. I'm not entirely sure he is a cad or indolent. I think he's covering up the fact he's quite intelligent and sensitive."

Alex and Gabe both slumped into the sofa.

Willie took the notepad and pencil from Gabe and wrote down Daisy's name. "We'll start with her."

Gabe took the notepad and pencil back. "Daisy's not a suspect."

Cyclops cleared his throat to get our attention. "The perpetrator is someone who didn't know the professor lived upstairs. Even though we now know his flat is sound proof, it's unlikely anyone else knows. So I suspect the thief wasn't aware he was even here. The methods employed didn't require strength or any particular intelligence. We're not dealing with criminal masterminds, necessarily. They smashed the window and cabinet, grabbed the book, and left through the front door. That doesn't mean they're stupid, just that they saw no need to over complicate things."

Gabe made a few notes on his pad. "We'll start with Trevelyan."

After our tea was finished and the police had left, Willie and Alex walked ahead of Gabe and me out of Crooked Lane. Gabe had suggested I join them since the manuscript was my interest. It was an odd request, but a welcome one. I jumped at the opportunity. I did notice that he waited until Cyclops left before suggesting it. I suspected my presence wouldn't meet with Scotland Yard's approval.

Gabe indicated we should slow our pace and let the other two go on ahead. I thought it was so they could check the coast was clear before Gabe exited the lane, but then I realized he wanted to say something to me without being overheard.

"I know why Willie was here yesterday," he said. "I know she told you about my decision to end things with Ivy, and I know she blamed you for it." He stopped altogether, so I stopped too. He leveled his gaze with mine until I broke the connection and looked away. "I'm sorry, Sylvia. I should have realized she'd ignore my directive to stay away. I hope she wasn't too much of a bully."

"Actually, we came to an understanding. Professor Nash is a good mediator and explained that you're not the sort of person to make rash decisions, that it must have been something you'd been thinking about for some time."

"I tried telling her that, but she wouldn't listen."

"She probably didn't hear anything you said over the noise of her anger. She was in quite a state when she got here." I started walking again, before the others noticed we'd dropped back. "Don't blame Willie for being Willie. She's protective of you because she loves you. You're very lucky to have her."

"I know. Usually she's not too bad—she leads a busy life of her own—but with the kidnapping attempts, she's been around more."

Willie and Alex had exited the lane through the narrow entrance but didn't climb into the motorcar. They both stood there, blocking the entryway, surveying their surroundings.

"Are *you* all right?" I asked Gabe.

He blinked in surprise. "No one else has asked me that. Thank you. And yes, I will be all right once the dust settles.

Until then..." He gave me a grim smile. "I'll concentrate on getting the manuscript back."

"I read about a disturbance outside the Hobson and Son factory in this morning's newspaper. I hope everything is all right there."

"So do I. Alex and I were just discussing it in the library. He thinks I shouldn't call on them anymore, but I thought I ought to see if Ivy was affected. I feel guilty for adding to their burdens, but he thinks a clean break is best for everyone."

I thought Alex had a point, but I also suspected Gabe was trying to be as gentlemanly about the situation as possible. "Do you know what the commotion outside the factory was about?"

"No."

Alex ushered us through the lane entrance to the parked motorcar. He stood on one side of Gabe while Willie stood on the other, her hand tucked into her jacket. I suspected it was resting on her gun, ready to whip it out at any moment. Ever since the first kidnapping attempt, they'd been cautious and protective, but it had waned over time. These efforts were new.

When he saw me following the gazes of his companions as they swept up and down the street, Gabe explained why. "Someone followed us from home this morning, but they seem to have left."

Willie opened the front passenger door of Gabe's parents' Hudson Super Six. "Could be just around the corner, waiting for you to leave. Go on, get in." She pointed to the passenger seat. "I'll drive."

Alex had been about to crank the engine, but suddenly straightened. "No, you will not! You drive like there's no one else on the road."

"It's the only way to earn the respect of the other drivers."

"Get in the back seat. I'll take the wheel."

As Alex jerked the handle, Gabe climbed into the front seat and I climbed into the back. Willie waited by Gabe's door until Alex was ready, then she slid in beside me.

"Is it that journalist again?" I asked as we drove off. During the last investigation, there'd been a reporter watching Gabe's house and following him. Albert Scarrow wasn't the only journalist interested in finding out more about Gabe's so-called luck, but it wasn't him. He didn't know where Gabe lived.

"No," Alex said. "Gabe confronted that fellow last week. He hasn't returned."

Willie cracked her knuckles.

I stared at her. "I see," I murmured.

Gabe turned around to glare at his cousin. "I threatened to call the police. The confrontation wasn't violent, no matter what Willie likes to think."

She peered through the rear window and watched the vehicles. Clearly they were all assuming the person following was the kidnapper, not a journalist.

"Could it be Scarrow?" I asked. "Perhaps he finally learned where you live." Indeed, it was odd that Albert Scarrow hadn't returned to the library to wait for Gabe. I doubted he'd given up so easily. So where was he?

"I'm not sure Scarrow is intelligent enough to unearth that information," Gabe said. "His photographer, however, is another matter. He has a sharp mind."

I watched Willie as she watched the vehicles behind us. "You told Cyclops there was a link between the newspapers reporting you attending events and the kidnappings, but now it seems someone is following you from home." I eyed Gabe in profile. "Did you lie to a Scotland Yard detective?"

"I didn't want him worrying," Gabe said.

Alex grunted. "You realize he knows we lied."

"It's back!" Willie cried. "The same Ford."

"Everyone hold on!"

Alex increased the speed and darted around the slower vehicle in front. He wove between motorcars and horse drawn carts, and turned into streets that took us away from Mr. Trevelyan's studio instead of toward it. He was an excellent driver. Unlike when Willie drove, I never felt as though we would collide with another vehicle, although I would have liked to have been strapped into place. If I hadn't held onto the seat in front of me, I would have tumbled all over the place.

Willie let out a whoop. "Lost 'em!"

We slowed and turned a few more corners until we found ourselves driving down the street on which Mr. Trevelyan's studio was located. Alex pulled the motorcar to the curb and parked.

Gabe picked up Alex's hat, which had come off during the drive. "If you'd just let me confront him, we wouldn't have had to do that."

Willie clapped Alex on the shoulder. "But it was more fun."

Alex remained with the motorcar but Willie got out to come up with Gabe and me to the studio. He had another idea, however.

"Find out where the nearest public call office is and telephone home. Ask Murray to go to Barratt's house and watch him all day. If he's the thief, he might be meeting a buyer."

"Murray'll like getting out of the house," she said, nodding.

"Then I want you to stay here after we leave and follow Trevelyan around."

"What about Francis Stray?" I asked. Our fourth suspect, Lazarus Sidwell lived outside London so it wouldn't be feasible to assign someone to watch him. Considering he was a recluse, I couldn't imagine he was the thief anyway.

"Francis is my friend. We'll talk to him, but I doubt he's the thief."

Willie left with a spring in her step while Gabe and I entered the building and headed up to Mr. Trevelyan's studio. He did not let us in straight away. He blocked the doorway with one forearm leaning against the edge of the door at shoulder height, a cigarette dangling between his fingers.

His gaze flicked over Gabe and lingered on me. "This is a surprise. To what do I owe the pleasure?"

"May we come in?" Gabe asked with uncharacteristic gruffness.

Mr. Trevelyan hesitated a moment then stepped aside. "Please do." He plugged the cigarette into his mouth and quickly tidied up the desk, gathering loose photographs together and slipping them into a drawer.

From the glimpses I'd seen, each photograph showed the same woman, a pretty girl about my age, staring seductively back at the camera. She was fully clothed in all the images, although her skirt was short and her shoulders bare. She must be a private customer. I thought he only took photographs for newspapers, but it appeared I was mistaken.

He tapped the ash off the end of his cigarette into a tray at the corner of the desk. "You haven't brought the book, so I assume you're not here to ask me to photograph another mark."

"The manuscript was stolen from the Glass Library last night," Gabe said.

Mr. Trevelyan didn't miss a beat as he drew on the cigarette and blew smoke toward the ceiling. "And you think I did it."

"Did you?"

Mr. Trevelyan shook his head. "No, but I don't expect you

to believe me." He swept his hand in an arc. "Take a look around. I'm not developing anything right now so you can check in there too."

I searched the development room while Gabe looked through the front office. I could hear him interrogating Mr. Trevelyan while he searched.

"Where were you last night?"

"Here until one in the morning, then I went home. I live in a flat down the road."

"Did anyone see you leave here and arrive there?"

"I didn't speak to anyone or see anyone I knew. It was late."

"Do you always work that late?"

"Sometimes."

"Did anyone call on you either here or at your flat during the night?"

There was a slight hesitation before Mr. Trevelyan answered. "No."

"Did you mention the book to anyone?"

"No."

I finished my search and joined the men. I shook my head at Gabe. If Mr. Trevelyan had stolen the book, he'd either hidden it elsewhere or already sold it. If he'd had a buyer lined up, it was possible he'd got rid of it last night or early this morning.

Downstairs, Gabe and I spoke to the shopkeepers whose shops were in the immediate vicinity. Two of them lived above their shops, their residences sharing walls with Mr. Trevelyan's studio. One claimed to have woken during the night to the sound of voices coming from the studio.

"There was a man and a woman speaking," he said.

"Shouting?" Gabe asked.

"Just talking. These walls are thin and sound travels, but not enough that I could make out what they were saying. I stayed awake for a while, then when I heard the door close, I looked out the window. I saw the woman leave."

"What time was it?"

"Almost three."

"Was she carrying anything?"

"A small bag." He indicated the size with his hands. It was large enough to contain the Medici Manuscript.

We returned to confront Mr. Trevelyan with this new information.

"You claimed no one was here last night," Gabe said. He remained by the door, blocking the exit. "We know you had a female visitor."

Mr. Trevelyan huffed a humorless laugh. "Very good, Detective."

"We also know she left carrying a bag."

Mr. Trevelyan stubbed his cigarette out in the ash tray and blew smoke from his nose. "Did your witness also tell you my visitor *arrived* with that object?"

Gabe stayed silent.

"If she arrived with it, how can it be the book, if you're assuming I stole it and gave it to her?" He reached for the top drawer of the desk.

"Keep your hands where I can see them," Gabe snapped.

Mr. Trevelyan put his hands in the air. "Miss Ashe, would you be so good as to remove the photographs."

I opened the top drawer and pulled out the photographs showing the pretty woman with the seductive stare. She posed a little differently in each. In one, she was looking over her shoulder. In another, she propped her chin up with her hand. Sometimes she stood and her entire length was visible, while others just showed her face. I handed them all to Gabe.

"It was her my neighbor overheard speaking to me last night," Mr. Trevelyan said. "I developed those early this morning. She'll be collecting them at two this afternoon if you want to ask her any questions."

"Why was she here so late?" Gabe asked.

"She wants to be a star. Stage or screen, she doesn't mind which." Mr. Trevelyan removed his cigarette tin from his inside jacket pocket and removed one. He didn't offer it to us again. "For that she needs professional photographs. Since she's a hard-working girl with two jobs, she couldn't come at any other time. During the day, she works in the perfume section of a department store then at night, she's a waitress at a club. Her lunch break isn't long enough to get all the way here and back again, in addition to the time it takes to photograph her." He took the photographs back and pointed to the feathered head dress she wore in the top one. "She brought her own props. If your witness saw her when she arrived, he would have seen her carrying a bag *into* my studio."

"Why the secrecy?" Gabe asked. "Why didn't you tell us about her earlier?"

"Because I didn't think you'd believe it was an innocent arrangement and I didn't want Miss Ashe to think badly of me."

"Is that so?"

Mr. Trevelyan's gaze narrowed. "I charge everyone the same price, including those who come in the middle of the night." He sat on the edge of the desk and studied the top photograph. "Some of them are desperate to become famous. That desperation makes them vulnerable to unscrupulous men, from directors and producers at the end of the process all the way to the photographers at the start. I've heard some stories of girls who've been badly exploited. Sometimes they've simply been duped into handing over a lot of money, more than they can afford. Other times…well, let's just say those stories make me sick."

If we were to believe him, then he was a good man. I

really wanted to believe him, but I wasn't prepared to dismiss him as a suspect yet. Not without speaking to the woman in the photographs.

"What's her name?" I asked.

"Madge Dowd. As I said, you can meet her at two."

Gabe gave a curt nod and opened the door. "You can expect us. One more thing, have you seen Scarrow in the last few days?"

Mr. Trevelyan shook his head as he blew out a puff of smoke. "Not since that morning we spoke to Miss Ashe outside the library. I don't think you have much to worry about there." He tapped his temple. "He's not the smartest tool in the box. It's unlikely he'll work out where you live."

"He might get help."

"He won't get it from me. I don't believe in pestering a fellow at his home or interrogating his friends to get answers. Don't worry, Glass. Whatever your secret is, it's safe from the likes of Albert Scarrow."

We left him studying the photographs of Madge Dowd as he smoked, and headed down the stairs. I could tell from Gabe's purposeful steps that he'd thought of something and was eager to tell me.

He waited until after we'd apprised Alex of what we'd learned, however. "But what if he's lying?" he finished.

"About Madge?" I asked.

He nodded. "His story of an aspiring actress having photographs taken in the middle of the night is strange."

Alex agreed. "No self-respecting woman would visit a man alone at that time unless she's his mistress or he's taking advantage of her. If you believe he's honorable, and so is she, then you have to assume she *didn't* come last night."

Gabe looked triumphant, but I didn't quite follow. "So are you suggesting that the woman the witness overheard *wasn't* Madge Dowd?" I asked.

"I am," Gabe said. "I think it was a buyer for the manuscript."

"Then why did he suggest we return to speak to Madge? He's risking her telling us the truth."

He checked his pocket watch. "It's eleven now. That gives him plenty of time to telephone her and order her to lie and say she was here last night." He returned the watch to his waistcoat pocket. "Let's assume there was a woman here, but it wasn't Madge. That woman quite possibly bought the manuscript off Trevelyan after he stole it."

My mind immediately leapt to the only woman we knew who was interested in magical objects and was ruthless enough to obtain them by dubious methods.

I gasped. "Lady Stanhope!"

Gabe had come to the same conclusion before me. His smile didn't waver while he watched me reach it on my own. "I think we need to pay her a visit."

CHAPTER 10

$\mathcal{I}$ suspected most people felt honored when Lady
Stanhope smiled at them the way she smiled at
Gabe in the drawing room of her Mayfair townhouse. She
was, after all, socially important, wealthy and a viscountess.
The smile also lifted her features, reminding those around her
that she'd been a beauty in her youth.

Gabe was not one of those people, going by the coolness
of his greeting. Since Lady Stanhope didn't bestow her smile
on me, I was quite unaffected by it, too.

She looped her arm through Gabe's, even though he'd not
offered it, and steered him to the sofa. She sat beside him. I
could have sat beside her, but chose to occupy an armchair
opposite instead. It was easier to observe from a distance.

"I am so pleased to see you, Mr. Glass."

Gabe pointedly looked my way.

Lady Stanhope turned her smile on me for the first time,
although it visibly tightened. "You've brought your librarian,
I see. Are you interested in my husband's library, Miss...?"

"Ashe," I said. "Gabe and I are here about a book, yes,
although it doesn't belong to your husband."

"We're here in an official capacity," Gabe said. "I've been engaged by Scotland Yard to investigate the theft of a book from the Glass Library. Miss Ashe is assisting me."

"What an unusual arrangement. Does Ivy know?" It was said lightly, almost jokingly, but no one laughed.

Nor did Gabe inform her about the change in his relationship with Ivy. "Where were you last night, ma'am?"

Lady Stanhope took the question in her stride, and this time, she did laugh. "Good lord, you don't think I took the book? Why would I do that? I don't particularly like to read."

"It's a valuable book."

She looked offended. "Do you think we are poor?"

"This book has a magical connection."

"That would be why it was in the Glass Library, I assume."

"Please answer the question, Lady Stanhope. Where were you last night?"

"At Lord and Lady Presterton's ball. I was there all evening and arrived home at three-thirty."

I thought Gabe would leave the questioning there, but he pressed on. "May we speak to your chauffeur?"

She bristled. "You're taking it too far, Mr. Glass."

"You were caught attempting to swindle magician artists only recently. It appears to Scotland Yard that you covet magician-made pieces. Since the book wasn't for sale, perhaps you took it upon yourself to find another means to obtain it."

She spread out her fingers on her lap, as if searching for something to grip. The rest of her went quite still. "I'm neither a thief nor a swindler. In regard to the paintings, I was at the mercy of an unscrupulous fellow who took advantage of me."

The look Gabe gave her was filled with skepticism, but he

didn't tell her he didn't believe her. "We'll find the chauffeur in the garage, I assume."

Lady Stanhope's nod was curt. "Huggins will escort you." She tugged on the bell pull. "I will forgive you for this, Mr. Glass, but only because Ivy has become a dear friend to me. Next time I see her, I will of course have to tell her that you were here...with Miss Ashe."

"Feel free to do so. Ivy has broken off our engagement, so she won't mind who I partner with on an investigation."

"But...I only saw her yesterday! She didn't mention it."

He didn't respond.

She frowned. "You say *she* ended it?"

"You should speak to her if you want her side of the story."

The butler entered and she gave him instructions to take us to the chauffeur. Her mind wasn't on the task, however. She continued to frown. Before Gabe and I left, she stopped him with a hand on his arm. "The ending of your engagement to Ivy has come at a very difficult time for the Hobson family. Have you read the newspapers today?"

"I have. I'll help them if they need it, of course. Our engagement may have ended, but that doesn't mean I wish her or her family ill."

"I hope they throw those rioters in prison for a very long time."

"It was a protest, not a riot, and a peaceful one at that. I'm sure the reason for it will come to light soon."

"What reason could there be except jealousy that a hard-working family have gotten ahead?" She glanced at me from beneath lowered lids and stepped closer to Gabe. "I'll have a word with Ivy. You two will be together again soon, I'm sure. You are a perfect match."

Gabe extricated himself from her grasp and we followed Huggins. Gabe was quiet, and I wondered if he was contemplating the fault in his plan. By allowing Ivy to tell everyone that she ended the relationship, he was going to have to put up with people offering sympathy and suggesting ways he could win back her favor.

According to the chauffeur, he drove Lord and Lady Stanhope to the ball and brought them home at approximately three-thirty. There were no other visits in between. That didn't mean Lady Stanhope couldn't have taken a taxi to Mr. Trevelyan's studio. Indeed, she would be wise to travel anonymously if she planned to buy the book off him.

"We could ask the people who held the ball whether they saw her leave during the night," I said as we left the garage in the old mews.

Gabe shook his head. "They won't tell us, even if she did go and come back. These people look out for one another. They won't tattle to us."

"Even though you're the son of a lord?"

He smirked. "My parents didn't associate with many people from society, and they never forced me to, either."

"I suppose that must seem unconventional to the likes of Lady Stanhope."

"And the Hobsons. Balls and parties are just beginning to be held again, now that the war is behind us, but Mrs. Hobson didn't understand why I wouldn't go, even when I was invited."

"And Ivy? Did she understand?"

"She never said anything."

That wasn't the same thing as understanding, but I didn't point that out. I suspected he knew.

* * *

FRANCIS STRAY WORKED in the mathematics faculty of University College, located in Gower Street, Bloomsbury, not far from where I used to work at the London Philosophical Society library. He was between classes and invited us into his office. Although small, it was neat. Indeed, it was so neat, it looked like no one spent any time there. The pencils were lined up on one side of the desk, perfectly parallel, and the notepad was centered, its edge aligned with the pencils. The bookshelves were arranged by topic and sub-sorted by author name. Each one stood upright. Where there was a gap, a bookend had been placed to stop the books leaning.

Mr. Stray didn't smile upon greeting us, but it was clear from the way he heartily shook Gabe's hand that he was pleased to see him. Mr. Stray shook mine too and invited us to sit. "I wasn't expecting to see you again so soon, Gabe. Has there been a breakthrough with the book's code?"

"I'm afraid not." Gabe leaned forward and gave Mr. Stray an apologetic look. "I'm sorry but I have to ask you to detail your movements last night. You see, the Medici Manuscript was stolen from the library."

Mr. Stray's brows rose. It was the first real expression I'd seen him make. "That is terrible news." He fidgeted with a pencil, turning it one way then the other before straightening it again. He seemed unaware of his movements. "I understand why you have to ask me where I was last night. I must be one of the few people outside of the library who knew of its existence."

"Your understanding doesn't make it any easier for me to be here. In some ways, it makes it worse."

Mr. Stray frowned. "Now *that* I do not understand."

Gabe smiled. "Never mind. Your alibi?"

"I don't have one. I was in my rooms alone all evening." To me, he added, "I live on campus."

"Are you sure no one saw you?" I asked. "A neighbor or friend from the faculty? A maid, perhaps."

He shook his head. "I am sorry."

"There's no need to apologize. It's a shame no one saw you, but I'm sure it will be all right. As Gabe said, we're sure you didn't do it."

"But you must still consider me a suspect. I saw the Medici family crest in the book, and I know it must be valuable. Don't eliminate me yet. It wouldn't be prudent."

I would have laughed if he didn't look so serious.

Gabe continued to war with a smile. He seemed unsurprised by his friend's response to being a suspect. "Did you mention the book to anyone else, Francis?"

"No. You asked me not to, so I didn't." He sounded matter-of-fact rather than offended. I suspected Mr. Stray understood the need for that question to be asked, too, and would have been concerned if it wasn't.

Mr. Stray walked us to the door, but it was clear something troubled him. He wouldn't meet our gazes, nor would he open the door.

"Is something wrong, Francis?" Gabe finally asked.

Mr. Stray chewed the inside of his lower lip.

"Is it to do with the stolen book?"

Mr. Stray suddenly looked up. "No!"

"Then what is it? You can tell us. We're friends."

"Yes. Yes, we are. And friends should tell one another when a conversation concerns them, even when that conversation is supposed to be confidential." Mr. Stray wiped his palm down his trouser leg and looked away again. "I really shouldn't tell you, but…"

Gabe had enormous patience. I wanted to grab Mr. Stray by the shoulders and shake him until he talked, but Gabe simply waited until his friend was ready.

"Perhaps Miss Ashe should leave the room," Mr. Stray said.

"I'll tell her anyway so she might as well stay."

My heart swelled. "I won't repeat it to anyone," I assured them both.

Mr. Stray swallowed. "My commanding officer called on me yesterday."

"From your days in Military Intelligence?" Gabe asked.

Mr. Stray nodded.

"Francis was a codebreaker during the war," Gabe told me. "He cracked the code on the Zimmerman telegram."

"I was *one* of a team of codebreakers assigned to it," Mr. Stray clarified.

I remembered when the telegram was made public. Decoding and publishing the communication from Germany had ultimately drawn the United States into the war. It had been a significant breakthrough by British Military Intelligence. "That is impressive. It's no wonder Gabe wanted you to look at the Medici Manuscript."

Mr. Stray blushed. "I wish I could have helped."

"Does your C.O. want you to work with him again?" Gabe asked.

"No. He asked about you."

Gabe drew in a sharp breath then let it out slowly. "I see." He didn't seem altogether surprised. Perhaps he'd been expecting this, considering the interest in him lately. "What did he say, precisely?"

"He asked me how well I knew you. He said he'd looked into your background and discovered you went to the same school as one of his former codebreakers. That's me," he added for my benefit. "I told him we were friends. He then asked if I remembered anything about you that made me think you were a magician."

"And?"

"And I said you were the son of a well-known magician. He knew that, of course. Everyone does. But you'd never claimed to be a magician and never done anything magical in my presence."

"And then?" Gabe prompted.

"And then he asked if I was sure, and to think carefully. To which I replied that of course I was sure. I have a perfect memory. Gabe, why is he interested in you?"

"I suspect it's because some articles have recently been written about me, speculating on my luck."

"I don't understand. He's interested in probability?"

"I think he's more interested in me defying probability."

Mr. Stray nodded as if he understood then shook his head. "No one can defy probability. Certainly it can *appear* that someone beats the odds, or is lucky, but further experimentation always proves otherwise. The key is to do a lot of experimentation to increase the sample size."

"Did he say anything else?"

"No."

Gabe was satisfied with that response, but I wasn't. "How did he seem to you?"

"Seem?" Mr. Stray turned a blank look onto me. "I don't know."

Gabe placed his hand on my lower back which I took to mean not to ask again. I stayed silent.

"What's your C.O's name?" Gabe asked.

"Jakes."

As we trotted down the stairs of the mathematics faculty, Gabe glanced over his shoulder to make sure the door to Mr. Stray's office was closed. "Francis is very literal. He doesn't understand mood or tone. He seems unaware of how to interpret certain cues, like a silence or a speaking glance. He's all right with obvious facial expressions, but the commanding officer of the codebreaking division of Military Intelligence has probably learned to be guarded. It would be impossible for someone like Francis to read anything beyond what is said."

"How extraordinary. He becomes more and more interesting on every meeting."

"He's unique, I'll give him that. Unfortunately for him, uniqueness isn't a highly prized quality in school. He got into a lot of trouble."

"Trouble which you helped him out of?"

"I hate bullies."

He repeated what Mr. Stray had told us to Alex in the motorcar. Alex was more concerned about the Military Intelligence officer's interest in Gabe than Gabe seemed to be. He wanted to confront the man known as Jakes and assure him that the speculation in the newspaper articles was wild and baseless.

Gabe disagreed. "If we go in all guns blazing, he'll think there *is* something of interest. But if I act disinterested, he'll think there's no substance to the articles."

"You're a fool if you believe he'll leave you alone," Alex growled.

"There's no point worrying."

"He's Military Intelligence! Gabe, don't dismiss this like you've dismissed those articles. It's getting serious."

Gabe rested his arm on the back of the seat as Alex pulled the car into the traffic. His thumb tapped furiously. He was more worried than he was letting on.

Although I was incredibly curious about the speculation surrounding Gabe and the seemingly impossible feats he'd performed, I kept my mouth shut. I didn't want Alex to snap at me.

Gabe would confide in me if he truly felt he could trust me.

We ate a quick luncheon at Le Café De Paris, a thriving little restaurant tucked into the streets behind Leicester

Square. Afterwards, we checked in with the professor at the library before returning to Mr. Trevelyan's studio. We arrived early to be there when Madge Dowd showed up, but remained downstairs on the pavement. We didn't want to question her in front of Mr. Trevelyan.

Gabe had asked me to interview her as he thought a woman's touch might be best in this instance. I wasn't so sure but promised to try. If she seemed more likely to speak to him, I would let him take over.

The woman who went to push open the door to the studio wore the black uniform of a department store employee. She was extraordinarily pretty with wavy blonde hair and blue eyes framed by long lashes darkened with makeup. I suspected the rosy cheeks and lips were the result of cosmetics too.

She looked around upon hearing her name, a surprised arch on her brow. "Do I know you?"

I approached her. "No, but Mr. Trevelyan gave us your name."

She glanced at the door leading up to the studio. "Is something wrong with my photographs?"

"Not at all. They're quite beautiful. I've seen them myself."

The cosmetics didn't hide the real blush that infused her cheeks. "Thank you."

"My name is Sylvia Ashe and this is Gabriel Glass."

Her gaze widened as it fell on Gabe. She patted her hair and offered him a tentative smile.

"We're consultants for Scotland Yard," I went on.

Her hand fell to her breast. "Oh! Is something the matter? Of course it is, or you wouldn't be here." She glanced at the door again.

"No one is hurt, if that's what you mean. We're investigating the theft of a valuable book from a library."

"A valuable book?" From the way she wrinkled her nose, I suspected she considered it an oxymoron. "I didn't steal it. I've never even been in a library."

"We don't think you stole it, but you may be able to help us nevertheless. What time did you come here last night to have your photograph taken?"

She gasped. "Did Carl steal it?"

I was beginning to wish I hadn't mentioned the book at all and simply tried to establish Trevelyan's alibi first. "We're just trying to get to the truth. So what time were you here?"

"Two."

"And what time did you leave?"

"About three."

"Why so late?"

"I work during the day and most evenings. I'm on my lunch break now and don't have long." She nodded at the door. "May I go?"

"This won't take a moment. Were you carrying anything when you came here?"

"I had a small bag full of props. A hat, scarf, gloves, jewelry, that sort of thing."

"How large was the bag?"

She indicated the dimensions with her hands. It was approximately the size of the book, just as the witness had described. It was possible Mr. Trevelyan telephoned her after we left this morning and told her what to say, but I tended to believe her.

"Thank you, Miss Dowd," I said. "You can go."

"Just a moment." Gabe stepped forward, smiling that charming smile of his.

Madge smiled back. "Yes, Mr. Glass?" I suspected if I'd asked her to wait, she'd be annoyed. I completely understood why she responded to him, however, and wasn't in the least surprised. When Gabe gave someone his full attention, it was difficult to refuse him anything.

"Can I ask why you came to Mr. Trevelyan to get your photograph taken? Why him specifically, I mean. There are many photographers in the city, and most are probably cheaper too."

"He's not expensive. In fact, that's part of his appeal. Of course, his photographs are excellent, but the real draw is his character. He won't take advantage of us girls, you see. Others would, and not just in the financial sense, if you get my meaning."

"I think I do."

"He's got a reputation for being fair and honest, you see. He also keeps his hands to himself." She wiggled her fingers. "A friend of mine told me to come here. She said Carl likes to help out girls like me. Girls who want to be on stage."

Gabe and I exchanged glances.

"It's not what you're thinking! The photographs are tasteful, we keep our clothes on. Come up and see them if you like."

"We have seen them," I said. "And they are tasteful. Forgive us, but it seems unlikely for a man who made a reputation for himself as a war photographer to also take photographs of aspiring actresses. It just seems...unbelievable."

She gave me a sympathetic look. "You've been working for the police too long, Miss Ashe. You see everyone as a criminal. But some folk are just nice. Carl is nice, although it's a result of misfortune, so my friend told me."

"Go on," Gabe said.

"Apparently Carl had a sister." She frowned. "Maybe he still does. I'm not really sure. Anyway, this sister wanted to be on stage, but a producer took advantage of her naivety and, well, I'm not sure what happened to her exactly, but you can guess it didn't go well for her. Ever since then, Carl has vowed to help girls like her and do what he can. He knows there aren't just bad producers, but there are bad photographers as well. When he takes our photograph, he talks to us, makes sure we're not auditioning for someone with a reputation for treating girls poorly." She shrugged. "He just cares more than most men. So, I really hope he's not guilty of stealing that book, because London needs more men like him."

We thanked her and let her go. As the door closed behind her, I made up my mind to believe her. She seemed genuine, and quite without guile. Either she was telling the truth, or she was the best actress in London.

We headed back to where Alex was leaning against the motorcar's door, his arms and ankles crossed. Before climbing into the passenger seat, Gabe and I looked up at the studio window.

Mr. Trevelyan gave us a lazy salute with his forefinger to his temple then disappeared from view.

"Well?" Alex asked once we were inside the vehicle. "What did she say?"

"She confirmed that it was her leaving the studio at three," Gabe said. "And I believe her."

"So that means Lady Stanhope was also telling the truth. She didn't come here and buy the book."

"It doesn't get Trevelyan off the hook entirely. He could still have stolen the book before he met Madge." Gabe glanced over his shoulder at me. "What do you think, Sylvia?"

"I don't believe he stole it. I know he's prickly, but after hearing Madge speak about how he helps girls like her, I don't think he's a thief. The sort of man who doesn't fleece vulnerable, desperate women isn't the sort of man who'd steal a book."

Gabe regarded me silently for so long that I began to feel the heat rise in my cheeks. Then he turned away and didn't say a word until we reached Huon Barratt's home.

He opened the door for me and assisted me from the motorcar. "You did very well back there, Sylvia. For a first interrogation, I couldn't fault it."

"I shouldn't have told her about the book. I shouldn't have mentioned the crime at all. She put her guard up."

"We're supposed to tell witnesses why they're being questioned, so you did the right thing. But you're right. Sometimes doing the right thing doesn't get results." He winked. "Don't tell Cyclops I told you that. He's a by-the-book detective these days."

My gaze slid to Alex, sitting in the driver's seat.

"He doesn't tell his father everything, only what's important. You can trust him."

He remained by the motor. When I realized he wasn't following me, I doubled back.

"Speaking of trusting people…" he went on. "Why do you trust Trevelyan?"

I shrugged. "Instinct, I suppose."

"Is it because he's handsome, charming?"

I laughed softly. "Mr. Trevelyan is as charming as a hammer."

His lips flattened.

"I think it's more that Madge didn't accuse him of anything. If he was going to take advantage of her, he would have done so when he photographed her in the middle of the night. If I were her, I'd have brought a friend and met him during the day. I'm not sure if she was brave or foolish to meet him alone."

"Definitely foolish."

Thinking about it brought up all the old worries my mother had instilled in me about men.

Don't be alone with them.

Don't trust them.

According to her, they just wanted to hurt you, or control you or denigrate you. The accusation changed depending on her mood.

I'd broken so many of her rules since coming to London. Since meeting Gabe, actually. He made her warnings seem excessive.

"Don't trust Trevelyan yet," he said. "He may still turn out to be the thief. I don't want to see you get hurt."

He walked off, leaving me staring at his broad back. Did he expect me to start a relationship with Mr. Trevelyan? I wanted to tell him that I didn't trust the photographer *that* much, but I kept my mouth shut. It would reveal more about my insecurities than I was prepared for him to know.

For now, a small voice added.

CHAPTER 11

*W*e interrupted Huon Barratt's bath. He had no qualms telling us this when he joined us in the drawing room fifteen minutes after our arrival. His damp tousled hair made him look more slovenly than usual, but at least he didn't seem as though he needed to crawl back to bed.

"I know you must think me odd for bathing in the middle of the afternoon," he drawled. "I'm heading out to the Savoy's American Bar and want to look my best."

It was early for cocktails but neither I nor Gabe mentioned it.

"Have you been there, Sylvia?"

I shook my head.

Huon picked up the silver cigarette case and offered it to me then Gabe. "I've seen you there, Glass, but not since the war."

Gabe refused the offer. "I used to go frequently, before."

"Why not anymore?"

"I haven't been in the mood."

"Really?" Huon lit a cigarette and breathed in deeply, as if he'd been looking forward to it for some time. "I'm finding the mood of the city has changed this year. The new decade is making people restless. Everyone wants to go out and enjoy themselves. Bars, clubs, parties...every night there's something happening. You don't feel it, too, Glass, this restlessness?"

"I've noticed a sense of...change, I supposed you'd call it. No one wants to go back to the way things were. Personally, I'm not restless. I feel..." He shrugged. "I don't know."

Huon blew smoke into the air. "It's your fiancée, isn't it? She's forcing you to settle down and stopping you from going out."

"She didn't."

Huon didn't notice the past tense. "Can't say I blame her for not letting you off the leash."

Gabe's thumb tapped on the chair arm, but he remained silent. While he'd told Lady Stanhope that Ivy had ended their relationship, he seemed reluctant to tell Huon. Perhaps he thought it was none of Huon's business since he didn't know Ivy.

I couldn't let him get away with such an offensive comment, however. "He's nobody's pet, Mr. Barratt."

Huon put up his hands in surrender. "My apologies. You're right. Glass is his own man. I simply meant he would be popular with the fairer sex if he wasn't engaged to be married." He slotted the cigarette between his lips and smiled around it. "Thank God for the rest of us mere mortals that he's off the market."

"You know a great deal about my life, Barratt."

"I keep up with the gossip, it's true. It's only natural, considering our families are connected." He pointed the cigarette at himself then at Gabe. "Do you think it's destiny that we met?

"I don't believe in destiny. I don't believe our futures are set."

Huon's only response was to thoughtfully draw on his cigarette.

"Where were you last night, Barratt?"

"Here and there. Why?"

"The Medici Manuscript was stolen from the library. Only a few people knew of its existence."

"You think I took it?" He didn't seem offended. "I suppose you must consider me a suspect. With my father tightening my belt from afar, I'm in need of some ready, and that book would fetch quite a tidy sum, I'd wager. Unfortunately, I don't know anyone who dabbles in the black market for old books, so it would be pointless me stealing it. My conscience wouldn't allow it either, of course. That's if you believe I have one." He winked at me.

"Can you tell us the names of the places you frequented last night?" Gabe asked.

"All of them?"

"Yes."

Huon tugged the edges of his robe together and stood. "I'll write a list." With the cigarette dangling between his lips, he bent over the writing desk and wrote on a sheet of letterhead. He handed it to Gabe.

Gabe read the list. "We'll call on them now to see if the managers remember seeing you."

"And if they don't?"

"Then you're still a suspect."

Huon grunted. "That's fair, I suppose. Good luck. I hope you get your book back, Sylvia. In the meantime, if you feel like drowning your sorrows with a friend who isn't encumbered by a fiancée, you can find me at those places again tonight after I leave the Savoy." He waved at the list in Gabe's hand. "You're welcome too, Glass, of course, if you can manage to get away."

"I have plans tonight," was all Gabe said.

Huon didn't seem to hear him. He was once again sitting on the sofa, legs sprawled out in front of him, puffing thoughtfully on his cigarette as if it were his one true pleasure.

* * *

GABE and I spent the rest of the day visiting each bar and club on Huon's list. The staff were busy preparing for the evening and were brisk with their answers, but all remembered Huon being in their establishment the night before. They couldn't account for his movements the entire time, however, which meant he could have detoured to the library between clubs. We couldn't dismiss him as a suspect yet.

We didn't have time to discuss how to narrow down our suspect list. Gabe had a function to get to and it was growing late. Alex asked if he could drive me home after dropping Gabe at the pub first. I agreed, only to discover Gabe wanted to change before going out.

I waited in the drawing room of number sixteen Park Street, Mayfair, hoping Willie wouldn't wander in. Alex kept me company, regaling me with stories of the years before the war when he and Gabe traveled around the country together. Before that, Gabe had studied at university while Alex joined the police force as soon as he left school. After university, Gabe learned how to manage his father's business interests. He'd joined the army as soon as war broke out, much to his parents' distress, but Alex waited until 1916.

Alex's gaze turned distant. The jovial retelling of his travels had turned melancholy by the end of his story. I hoped he might tell me a little about Gabe's so-called luck, but he spoke no more about the war. It was probably too much to hope that he would confide in me when Gabe hadn't.

Gabe entered the drawing room dressed in a suit similar to the one he'd worn all day. I'd expected him to change into his officer's uniform or eveningwear. My surprise must have been written on my face, because his first words were an explanation for his civilian attire.

"The men from my company prefer to dress informally for our get-togethers."

Alex insisted on going too, even though he hadn't been part of Gabe's company and Dodson the chauffeur was driving. He didn't want Gabe out on his own, unprotected.

"I'll be with friends," Gabe chided. "No one will attempt a kidnapping. Besides, I haven't seen anyone watching the house, and tonight's event was moved to an out-of-the-way pub on purpose. I'll be safe."

Alex didn't seem to agree but remained silent.

Dodson drove us to a pub in Clerkenwell. The venue was about as far from being the Savoy cocktail bar as possible. The narrow timbered façade was bookended by classical columns, all painted black, although it was flaking off in parts. Large windows must let in an abundance of light during the day, but dusk had already fled from the streets of this working-class area. They'd certainly chosen a secluded place for their gathering.

Just as our motor pulled to the curb, two men who'd been about to enter the pub stopped. They greeted Gabe with hearty handshakes and smiles. They shook Alex's hand too, so they must know him even though he hadn't served in their company.

The gaze of one of the men fell on me, still seated in the back seat. He opened the motorcar's door, bowed, and insisted on an introduction. His charming manner was made even more intriguing by a Spanish accent.

Gabe introduced me as a friend and the man as Juan Martinez. He introduced the other fellow as Stanley Greville. Stanley's eyes were bloodshot, the puffy sacks below shadowed from lack of sleep. The hand that held his cigarette shook slightly. His war may not have left physical scars, but he'd been affected nevertheless. Although he nodded a greeting, he didn't meet my gaze. He stayed close to Gabe and folded his arms tightly, as if hugging himself. Every now and again he lifted a hand to smoke the cigarette, pinched firmly between his fingers.

"You are new to London?" Juan asked me.

"Yes. How do you know?"

"I have an instinct for these things. I am new to London, too."

Gabe rolled his eyes, but his small smile was good natured. "I mentioned you to Juan just a few days ago."

He'd mentioned me?

"And Juan isn't new to London. He arrived a few years before war broke out."

Juan shrugged, as if Gabe's explanation was close enough to his own that it didn't matter.

"You're originally from Spain?" I asked.

"Catalonia."

"Catalonia!"

He grinned. "This interests you?"

"Yes. Gabe, why didn't you say you knew someone from Catalonia?"

"I didn't realize it was relevant to anything," he said.

I'd forgotten to tell him that Huon Barratt recognized one of the book's symbols from the time he traveled around that region. Gabe hadn't been with Daisy, Willie and me when he'd mentioned it.

"Huon identified one of the symbols from the book," I told him. To Juan, I said, "Have you seen a symbol that looks like a complicated knot inside a circle? Apparently it appears on many buildings in Catalonia."

His face lit up. "Yes! You know of it?"

"I do. Which family did it belong to?"

"De la Riva, a very old family. They were once powerful and important, many, many years ago, but their fortune didn't last. They were like a raging fire—very bright and fierce but soon finished."

"Middle or late Medieval?"

"Eleventh or twelfth century, I think."

That didn't quite equate to our book's timeline. It wasn't that old. So why was the author using the De la Riva symbol?

Gabe must have been thinking the same thing. "Did the knot inside a circle come to represent something else in Catalonia?"

Juan made a fist. "It means power."

So the symbol in the book could represent a powerful person, not necessarily a member of the De la Riva family, who'd most likely lost their power by the time the book was written. It meant the author was familiar with Catalonia.

"Can you think of other symbols from your region?" I asked. At his blank look, I described some from the manuscript.

One was familiar to him, as were another two that Gabe remembered. Juan thought the symbol of a type of green onion popular in the region might represent harvest or wealth. He was sure another of the symbols depicted the fire-works lit by devils at a popular festival, and yet another was the wiggly tail of a pig. That one needed no interpretation. Disgusting men were called pigs in many cultures over many centuries.

I was impressed that we'd discovered four symbols from the Catalonia region, which had to mean the author was Catalonian or had spent some time there. But there was a fifth symbol we were able to interpret, but not with Juan's help. It was Stanley Greville who piped up with an answer when I described the snake entwining a stick.

"That's the rod of Asclepius," he said in a soft voice. "Asclepius is a Greek god of healing and medicine."

Juan clapped him on the shoulder, startling the smaller man. "Jolly good show, old chap!" He grinned at his own poor attempt at an English accent.

It was frustrating not to be able to sit with the book and begin transcribing the symbols we'd learned this evening. I wished I'd made a copy of the pages, but there'd been too many. Even so, when we got the book back, I would begin.

If we got the book back.

Another member of Gabe's company arrived. The sleeve that should have been filled by his left arm was pinned to the shoulder. Stanley and Juan followed him into the pub. Gabe told them he'd join them in a moment.

"Sylvia, promise me you won't investigate alone tonight," he said.

"The only other suspect we haven't questioned is Lazarus Sidwell, and I'm hardly about to order Dodson to drive me to Marlborough now. I think I'll see what Daisy is up to. Would you like to come, Alex? We can have dinner together."

"I'm busy this evening until Gabe returns home."

"Alex…" Gabe chided.

Alex turned to me. "Dodson will take you home."

The pub door opened a fraction and Stanley's face appeared in the gap. "Captain? You coming, sir?"

Gabe touched the brim of his hat in farewell, cast a final glare in Alex's direction, then followed Stanley inside.

"You're worried about him, even here where he is among friends?" I asked.

"He might try to tell you otherwise, but these men will do anything he asks of them. If he tells them he doesn't need escorting when he leaves, they'll obey and go their separate ways. We were mobilized to the same locations sometimes, but he wasn't my captain. I have no qualms ignoring his orders." He leaned against the lamppost and tipped his hat forward. "I've been ignoring him ever since he ordered me to stop throwing my toys out of the cradle."

I laughed and he flashed a grin. "You are a good friend to him." I nodded at the door. "Did those men fight alongside Gabe throughout the entire war?"

He watched me for a long moment. "They were together for some time, but not the entire war."

"Juan and Stanley appeared unharmed. Physically, at least."

He crossed his arms and pushed his hat even further forward. "Be careful, Sylvia, or I might think you've become a journalist again."

"If I were a journalist who wasn't getting answers from the source, I'd be asking the men in that pub, not you. You may be his closest friend, but they were on the battlefields with him. If there is more to his survival than mere luck can explain, they'll be able to shed light on it."

"You think like a journalist. You must have been good at your job."

"I was all right at some aspects but not others. I might *say* I'd interview the soldiers, but I would have done everything to avoid speaking to them. And if I did force myself to go through with it, my stomach would have been tied in knots for days beforehand and I would have fumbled my way through the questions, most likely forgetting some and writing down answers that made no sense when I read them back later."

He pushed the brim of his hat up with his finger and frowned at me.

"Anxiety," I said. "It rears its head from time to time, particularly in the presence of a group of men."

"You've never had a problem with Gabe or me. And you fought off a fellow a few weeks ago."

I smiled. "That was instinct. If I'd had time to think, I doubt I'd have been able to shout at him let alone defend myself. As for you and Gabe, I've always felt comfortable with you two. Besides, I'm better than I used to be. Time has seen to that."

He grunted. "They say time heals all things."

"You don't believe that?"

"Time hasn't healed Stanley's anxiety." He eyed the pub door. "Gabe says he's more nervous than ever."

"Perhaps some forms of anxiety take longer to heal, depending on the circumstances in which it was acquired." With the benefit of hindsight and maturity, I could see that my mistrust of men was a result of my mother telling me to fear them. Stanley's anxiety was clearly a result of his wartime experiences. He'd lived through something awful. I'd merely been warned about it.

"It's playing havoc with his life," Alex said. "Apparently he's finding it difficult to fit back in."

It was an awful thing to see a grown man reduced to a trembling shadow. The way he hovered near Gabe on the pavement, it was clear he didn't want to be too far away from him out here, where he was exposed to more dangers than inside. That was a sure sign Gabe had protected him on the battlefield. Perhaps Stanley had even benefited from Gabe's so-called good fortune.

Alex shifted his weight from one foot to the other. He was in for a long night alone if he waited out here until Gabe left.

"I'll telephone Willie when I get home," I said. "I'll ask her to relieve you here in a little while."

"Much appreciated." He cleared his throat. "And if you see Daisy tonight, give her my regards."

"The warmest."

"Not too warm. I don't want her reading more into it than there is. She's not my type."

"So I observed."

"At the club the other night?"

"Yes, and elsewhere."

He inspected his fingernails intently. "I think I'll go there again later."

"I'll be sure to tell Daisy."

He lifted one broad shoulder, as if he didn't care, but I saw the way his gaze heated.

* * *

I USED the telephone in the hallway of the lodging house to call Willie. To my surprise, she was polite to me. She even thanked me for telling her that Alex was still with Gabe. She was more than happy to join him to keep watch.

Since she seemed grateful, I thought it a good time to ask her a question. "The other day, you went to Albert Scarrow's newspaper office to find out more about him. What did you learn?"

"I didn't ask questions because I didn't want his colleagues knowing I was investigating him. Asking too many questions makes them curious, 'specially journalists. I reckon you know that already, Sylvia. You ain't too stupid."

"Thank you, I think. So you learned nothing?"

"I didn't say that, did I? I decided to wait for him to show up at the office and follow him."

"Where did you follow him to?"

"He didn't show up."

"Oh. Perhaps if you'd waited longer—"

"I waited all day! I went back there this afternoon, too, and asked to see him. They said he hadn't been in for days. They looked concerned. He missed a deadline."

"That is concerning, but at least he's no longer bothering Gabe."

"If he's dead, it ain't my fault."

"I didn't say it was, nor was I thinking it, but it's interesting that you *assume* that's what I thought. Do you have something to confess, Willie?"

"That ain't funny." There was a click then the line went dead.

I hung up the receiver, smiling. I rather enjoyed provoking her.

I ate dinner with the other boarders in the dining room and was settling into a quiet evening of reading in my room when Daisy arrived. Thankfully she caught a taxi instead of riding her bicycle in the dark. She wanted me to go out to a club with her, but I wasn't interested so we retired to my room with cups of tea. I sat on the chair at the small table while she reclined on the bed, my pillow at her back and the teacup resting on her bosom.

She regarded me with a pout. "Why won't you come out with me?"

"I have work tomorrow, and tonight I want to think."

She pulled a face. "Why would you do that? This is 1920, Sylvia. It's time for letting oneself go, for experiencing and feeling, not for thinking."

"I'm in the middle of an investigation. I have to think or we'll never get the book back."

"You poor thing. I know how much you want it back. You'll find it. You, Gabe and Alex."

"Speaking of Alex, he asked me to tell you that he's returning to Rector's again soon." It wasn't what he'd said, but it was what he wanted me to tell her, even if he wasn't able to admit it to himself.

Daisy sniffed. "I'll be sure to avoid it then."

I glanced at the clock on the shelf. It was only eight-thirty. The clubs didn't begin to thrive until eleven or twelve. "Will you go out with another friend?"

"I don't have other close friends. Not as close as you. I'd rather spend the night with you, Sylv." She batted her long eyelashes.

"That might work on the men, but not on me. I told you I have to work."

"And think, yes, I know. But you can think at a club, and the professor won't mind if you nap on the sofa tomorrow."

"That's not a good way to stay gainfully employed."

If I didn't know Daisy's story, I would have worried how she got on without wage-paying employment. But she'd been supported by her parents before moving to London, and now survived on a small inheritance from her grandmother. It allowed her to dabble in painting and acting without needing to find work. But unless she stopped dabbling and started taking her endeavors seriously, she wouldn't make a go of anything, and the money must run out eventually.

I suppressed my smile and asked her how her acting career was coming along. "Did Willie's producer friend have any work for you?"

"He auditioned me for a part in his upcoming production, but I haven't heard back. I don't think he was interested, but he did make some excellent suggestions."

"Such as?"

"Such as how to walk into a room." She lifted her chin and lowered her eyelashes so it appeared she was looking down her nose. "He told me to show disdain for everyone else. Act like you don't care if you get the part or not, and it will be their loss if they cast another actress."

"I'm not sure that's good advice."

"It's what all the stars do, even before they were stars. He says you ought to pretend as though the producers are fortunate you've deigned to show up to their audition. Oh, and I ought to get some professional photographs taken."

I straightened. "I know of someone who'll do it, but I insist on coming with you. I'm not sure he can be trusted."

"Do you mean that mysterious Trevelyan fellow? The one we met at the library? I had an appointment with him today."

"Today! Why didn't you tell me?"

She waved off my concern. "He wouldn't harm me if he was that way inclined. He knows I'm friends with you, and you're friends with Gabe, who has close ties to Scotland Yard. He's not a fool. Anyway, I felt perfectly safe with him." She sat up and tucked her bare feet under her. "He asked me about you."

"Oh?"

"He wanted to know if you were in a relationship with anyone."

"And what did you say?"

"That he should ask you himself."

I laughed. Daisy sipped her tea, giving me a sly look over the cup as if to say I ought to call on him again. Perhaps I should. If I were looking to be in a relationship with him, I ought to make a point of visiting him without Gabe. After all, the more I learned about him, the more I was inclined to think he was a good man.

But I still didn't know him very well, and I wasn't particularly inclined to learn more.

"So why did you want Trevelyan to take your photo?" I asked. "Why choose him in particular when there are so many other portrait photographers in London?"

"The producer recommended him, and then another girl waiting to be auditioned mentioned him, too. She said he was trustworthy and inexpensive." She put the cup down on the bedside table and scooted to the end of the bed. She set her feet on the floor but remained seated, and regarded me with as much sincerity as she ever had. "You two would make a good match."

"Daisy," I said on a heavy sigh.

"You'd soften him, Sylvia."

"And what could he do for me?"

"Take nice photographs of you?"

I chuckled into my teacup.

She placed her hands behind her on the bed and leaned back. "He mentioned that you think he's a suspect in the theft of the Medici Manuscript. Is that true?"

"It is. Everyone who knows about it is a suspect. Including you."

She made a scoffing noise. "No one would believe it was me. I have no interest in books, and I have an adorably innocent air about me. But what about Lazarus Sidwell? You don't think *he* took it, do you?"

"He saw it, so he's a suspect too."

"But he's a recluse! He wouldn't leave the house unless it was very important, and the only thing he finds important is that house and its history. Oh." She blinked at me then quickly looked away.

"What is it?"

She scooted back up the bed and picked the teacup up again. She shrugged as she sipped.

"Daisy, tell me. What is it?"

She studied her teacup then heaved another sigh. "I still don't think he's a thief, but...his interest in the house and its history extends to the contents. He loves it all, even the dusty old books his ancestor collected."

"And he believes the collection should stay together," I finished.

She winced. "I wish I hadn't said anything. Please don't mention it to Gabe or Alex. They might jump to the conclusion that Lazarus is the thief."

"Not without evidence they won't. Both men are honest and thorough, Daisy. I will have to say something. Indeed, we're going to speak to Lazarus tomorrow, so I can't guarantee Gabe won't ask some difficult questions. It is his job, after all."

She pulled her legs up and hugged her knees. "Poor, sweet man."

I remained silent. Daisy had been wrong about people in the past.

CHAPTER 12

*P*rofessor Nash was in a low mood when I arrived early at work the following morning. I found him staring at the cabinet that had briefly housed the Medici Manuscript, a cup of coffee clutched between both hands. The broken glass had been cleared away and the remaining contents of the cabinet moved to a safer location until the glass could be replaced. The magician was coming to the library later to replace it.

"Are you all right, Professor?" I asked gently.

He gave me a sad smile. "I feel as though I've lost a little piece of Oscar along with the book. He worked hard to acquire every single one in our collection." He sighed. "It's as if something of him is in each of them, so to lose one... It's a little painful."

I clasped his arm. "Come and sit down. Can I get you anything? More coffee?"

He showed me his cup. It was half-full. He allowed me to steer him to the study nook where I placed the blanket across his lap, even though it wasn't cold. "I have some news about the book, as it happens."

His head jerked up. "You have a chief suspect?"

"No. I didn't mean I had news about its theft. The news relates to the contents." I told him what Juan and Stanley had told us about each of the symbols they recognized. "There could be more, but without the book on hand, we were relying on our memories."

Discussing the book's contents seemed to distract the professor from its loss and cheer him a little. "Fascinating. Power, wealth, medicine, the devil and pigs. That's quite an eclectic combination."

"And for the symbols to be interspersed with letters...I feel as though that's important. Otherwise, why not just use letters to spell out everything? A cipher is almost impossible to decode without the key anyway, so why add the symbols?"

He pushed his glasses up his nose. His melancholia had vanished, replaced with the earnest, studious man I was familiar with. "You just gave the reason yourself. You said a cipher is *almost* impossible to decode. But being almost impossible might not have been good enough for our author. By adding symbols, he or she has added another layer to the code, making it even more difficult."

"But still not impossible."

He smiled. "You are determined to crack it, aren't you, Sylvia?"

"I am."

He patted my hand. "Hopefully you'll be rewarded and it points to a silver magician ancestor of yours."

"I don't mind if it doesn't. I simply don't want to be beaten by it." It was true, I realized. I'd almost forgotten that we'd started this investigation because the silver clasps might have a link to me. I wanted to solve the mystery of the book simply because the mystery existed, not because it might help me find out more about my family.

The professor shook his finger as a thought occurred to

him. "Did Gabriel's Catalonian friend say anything specifically about the power symbol?"

"The knot inside the circle? Only that it was associated with the De la Riva family whose influence had waned by the time the book was written. He said the symbol still represented power, even now, but wasn't specific to that family."

My answer excited him, but I couldn't grasp why. He put down the cup. "So we have symbols instead of letters to make the code more difficult to decipher, and we know one particular symbol represents power. What if it represents a powerful *person*?"

"That would be clever. Even if the rest of the code is cracked, no one can be certain who it was written about because all the people are represented by symbols. Their names aren't spelled out. But we still don't know who those people are."

"We can make an educated guess with the benefit of knowledge gained over the centuries. Tell me, Sylvia, who was the most powerful person in the fourteenth century?" From his smug look, I suspected I ought to know.

"I'm not familiar with Spanish or Catalonian history."

"Think larger than those countries. Think about Europe itself."

"The pope!"

He smiled. "Precisely. What if that knot symbol represents the pope?"

He threw off the lap blanket and moved to the desk. He plucked a fountain pen and notepad from the top drawer and sketched the five known symbols on the paper. Beside the knot symbol, he wrote Pope. His pen hovered over the page until he gave up and replaced the lid on the pen.

"I'm afraid I don't know who the devil could represent," he said. "Perhaps a king who disagreed with the pope, or a wealthy family who committed atrocities on their people."

My history was a little rusty, and I'd forgotten the powerful families of the age, except for the Medicis. "That onion symbol could represent the Medicis. Juan said the symbol means prosperity, not necessarily wealth gained from the land. The Medicis were bankers, so it could fit."

We both stared at the list for a while until we heard the front door open and close. He folded the paper and slipped it into the drawer.

Gabe entered the library. "Good morning. You both look eager. Have I missed something?"

Professor Nash retrieved the piece of paper and waved it in the air. "Thank your Catalonian friend for us. We think we've cracked the meaning of one of the symbols."

"The knot symbol," I clarified for Gabe. "Juan said it represents power and the most powerful person in Medieval Europe was the pope."

"That seems like a logical conclusion." Gabe looked over the list before handing it back. "No ideas for the others?"

The professor shook his head. "Perhaps a little research will throw up some names. Kings, queens, wealthy families of Europe... It's possible the author is widely traveled and knew many people across many countries."

"Very likely," Gabe said. "Juan only recognized those five symbols. Four, actually—Stanley knew the medical one. He didn't know the others we described, so I'd guess the author picked up a few here and a few there."

"Mixing them together would make it even harder for someone to decipher the code. They'd have to be well traveled too."

"Fortunately we know someone well-traveled," I said, smiling at the professor.

He pointed at his chest. "Do you mean me? But I didn't recognize any of the symbols, even the Catalonian ones and I've been there." His gaze drifted to the bookshelves. "Perhaps I wasn't the most observant traveler. Oscar was the observant one." He laughed softly. "He used to tell me if it weren't for him, I'd have become lost on the way from the front steps to the back door."

Gabe indicated the bookshelves with a sweep of his arm. "Could any of these tell you more about the symbols?"

"I've already looked and no, they can't." The professor glanced down at his list. "I think it's time I called on some acquaintances and ask to look through their books. What do you two have planned for today?"

"We'll be telephoning Mr. Sidwell to ask him his whereabouts on the night of the theft," I said.

Gabe shook his head. "He doesn't have a telephone. I asked him on our last visit when we were in the attic. We'll have to drive out."

"Oh," I murmured. "That's a shame. I can't go if the professor is out."

Professor Nash scoffed. "Nonsense. Of course you can. Just lock up when you leave here."

"But what if someone wants to look at the books?"

"They can return tomorrow."

It didn't seem like a very good solution to me, but I kept my mouth shut. I wanted to drive to Sidwell House with Gabe. It had been enjoyable last time, just the two of us in the motorcar. There would be no picnic in the meadow this time, but I wouldn't care if we drove all the way home without stopping. I wanted to be with him.

"No escort today?" I asked as we walked along Crooked Lane.

"I left before Alex and Willie were awake."

"They won't be happy that you left without protection."

"Then they ought to get out of bed earlier."

"Did anyone follow you?"

When he didn't immediately respond, I glanced sideways at him. His jaw was set firm. "Don't, Sylvia," he growled.

His strides lengthened and I had to quicken my steps to keep up. Perhaps the drive wouldn't be so pleasant after all.

He paused in the narrow entryway to the lane and scanned the street. He must have been satisfied that none of the vehicles or pedestrians looked suspicious because he signaled for me to follow. He opened the Vauxhall's passenger door and held out his hand to assist me inside.

His fingers tightened around mine. "I'm sorry for snapping at you. None of this is your fault."

"It's all right. You must be frustrated by all the fuss everyone is making. But it's only because we're worried about you."

"It's not that." He closed the door but didn't release it. "I'm just tired."

I watched him crank the engine. It was a physical task that required strength, but he made it look effortless. His hat hardly moved and he wasn't even flushed when he got into the driver's side.

But I suspected he hadn't been referring to being physically tired. He was emotionally drained. Although he'd told me the fog of war had begun to lift for him too, I wondered if ending his relationship with Ivy had seen it settle back over him again. Guilt must be weighing on him. Adding that to the guilt that many soldiers felt upon returning from the war with life and limbs when so many didn't...it was no wonder he was weighed down by it all.

* * *

WE WERE NOT FOLLOWED to Sidwell House. I was certain of that. I'd taken it upon myself to regularly check behind us, but the vehicles were always different ones. The closer we drew to the front gate, the less traffic there was anyway. We traveled for miles on narrow roads without seeing another motorized vehicle. The occasional horse-drawn cart moved aside to let us pass, but ours was the only motorcar in the vicinity.

Upon realizing it was us on his doorstep, Lazarus Sidwell flung the door wide and welcomed us inside. "I'm so glad to see you both! I was going to write today. I've discovered something, you see." He ushered us into the library, only to stop short. "My apologies. I haven't offered you refreshments! You've had a long journey." He glanced at my hair. "A windswept one, too, I see."

I patted my hair self-consciously. I'd not worn a scarf over it and what started as a neat arrangement suitable for a day's work at the library must now look like a bird's nest.

"Allow me to make the tea," Mr. Sidwell went on. "While you wait, cast your eye over this document." He retrieved several sheets of paper from the desk and handed it to me before leaving us in the library.

"Do I look that bad?" I asked Gabe.

"Let's just say you should avoid mirrors for the rest of the day."

I lightly thumped his arm and he laughed.

I waved the papers at him. They were thick and yellowed from age. Some sported tears or were missing corners, and the ink had faded, but was still legible. "It appears to be a list of books. It's hard to read; the handwriting is old fashioned."

Gabe peered over my shoulder. He stood close, his body warming my back. His hand brushed my arm as he lifted it to point to a line. It took me a moment to focus on what he was saying, and not on the way my insides leapt in response to him.

"I think it's a list of the books from Dr. Adams' collection, which he gave to Sir Andrew Sidwell." Gabe indicated one of several dates written with each entry. "1563, about two hundred years after the Medici Manuscript was written."

Gabe was right. The list took up all four pages. The writing was tightly packed and in a hand that was strange to our modern eye, but at least it was in English. Below each title and author's name was a physical description of the book, and below that was a description of its contents. Each entry also had a name and place associated with it, and a date. I quickly scanned through the pages to find something that might represent the Medici Manuscript.

We found it on the third page. The title was given as "Unknown" and it had no author associated with it. We knew it was our book from the physical description. The cover was written as "Wood Board" and it mentioned the silver clasps, although there was no hint that they held magic.

According to the description of the contents, the book contained "symbols of unknown purpose, perhaps alchemical." It then went on to say that one of the symbols depicted the devil and represented the Medicis, but the others were unknown.

"That's quite a statement," Gabe said.

"Do you think whoever wrote this list knew for certain or they were just guessing, like us? It was written many years after the book, and we know the Medici page was added later."

"Perhaps the author of this list added that page himself."

Mr. Sidwell entered carrying a tray with tea things. He asked me to hold it while he brushed a handkerchief over the table. The handkerchief, already discolored from age, came away filthy with dust. I set down the tray and took it upon myself to pour.

Mr. Sidwell picked up a book from the desk which we hadn't noticed. "The pages are in remarkably good condition for their age, don't you think? I found them inside the front of this book, which was stored in the bottom of a locked trunk in the attic. I had to pry the trunk open with one of the gardener's tools."

Mr. Sidwell's ancestors clearly lacked curiosity. If I lived in a house as old as this, in an attic full of locked chests, I wouldn't be able to rest until I'd discovered the treasures inside.

Mr. Sidwell opened the book to the first page and the name written there. "This belonged to Dr. Adams, the man who gave his collection to Sir Andrew in exchange for wiping his debt, so I think it's safe to assume the list belonged to him too."

I passed around the teacups then sat next to Gabe on the sofa. "The Medici Manuscript is listed on page three. Dr. Adams seemed to believe one of the symbols could be attributed to the Medicis themselves. The devil, he called it. We think we know which symbol he's referring to." I told him what we'd learned from Gabe's friends, Juan and Stanley, and how we'd subsequently guessed that the book was written by someone well-traveled.

"How intriguing," Mr. Sidwell said. "But unfortunately Dr. Adams doesn't even know who the author was. He does suggest the symbols may be alchemical in nature, but doesn't say why."

Gabe put down his teacup and asked to see the pages again. He pointed to one of the lines for the Medici Manuscript entry. "'Niccolo di Mario, doctor. Florence. May 1563.' There are a few other entries that also mention the same person, but not as the author. Those that also mention Niccolo di Mario have the same date, May 1563."

I pointed to two different entries. "The inks are a little different, too. The ones written with the same ink must have been made at the same time."

None of this came as a surprise to Mr. Sidwell. He seemed

pleased that we'd worked it out, too. "I think each entry was written as Dr. Adams acquired each book. The Medici Manuscript was bought along with three others in May 1563 from Dr. Niccolo di Mario of Florence."

"It's hardly surprising that he bought them from a doctor," I said.

"Nor is it surprising that he describes the contents as possibly alchemical," Gabe added. "Like most doctors of the time, Niccolo di Mario of Florence probably dabbled in alchemy, as Dr. Adams would have done."

"He didn't know for sure." I pointed to the line where Dr. Adams described the symbols as *possibly* alchemical. "Which means the man he bought it from probably didn't know either." I sighed. I felt sure we'd made some progress by discovering the list, but it turned out we hadn't.

Gabe seemed to share my dejection, but Mr. Sidwell's face was animated as he talked about discovering the origins of his library collection.

"Just think, all of these books were once handled by my ancestors." He gazed up at the dusty tomes housed on the shelves. They hadn't been touched in years, let alone opened and read. "They had a thirst for knowledge, particularly Sir Andrew. He must have been clever. He was wealthy, of course. He had to be to afford all of these books. Wealthy, influential, and handsome." He nodded at the portrait of his ancestor hanging above the fireplace. I didn't think him handsome, but I wasn't a sixteenth century woman. "He was a real paragon," Mr. Sidwell went on. "A man like that shouldn't be forgotten."

"It's fortunate you are the custodian of the Sidwell estate then," I said. "You seem to love every inch of this place."

"Oh, I do. I was born here and I'll die here. Sidwell House and everything in it is in my blood. Mind you, it hasn't been easy keeping it all together. Some of my ancestors sold off various pieces to make ends meet." He pointed at the ceiling. "That new roof was paid for by my father. He had to sell off some paintings to fund it. It was a difficult decision for him, but if he hadn't done it, all of this would have succumbed to the elements by now." He gazed around the library with a spark in his eye. He didn't see dust and decay. He saw history and achievement. He was proud of his ancestors. "Hopefully a future generation will be able to re-purchase the paintings one day. Not my revolting nephew." He pulled a face. "He hasn't got a brain, that one."

Gabe set down his teacup. He looked so serious that Mr. Sidwell's face fell. He slowly lowered his teacup to the saucer.

"I'm afraid the book has been stolen from the library," Gabe said.

Mr. Sidwell dropped the teacup and saucer on the floor. "My god!"

I collected the china and set them on the table. A puddle of tea collected in the most worn section of the carpet near Mr. Sidwell's foot. He didn't notice.

He stared at Gabe, a look of horror on his face. "Do you know who took it?"

"Not yet."

"Are the police investigating?"

"Scotland Yard hired me to investigate." Gabe indicated me. "Sylvia and I are working together."

"But shouldn't a proper detective be assigned to the case?"

Gabe took the insult in his stride. "I have experience."

"I assure you we're doing everything we can to find it," I said gently. "To that end, we have a question for you. Where were you the night before last?"

Mr. Sidwell barked a humorless laugh. "Here, of course. Miss Ashe, are you suggesting that I stole the book?"

"Very few people knew of its existence. You're one of them."

Mr. Sidwell blinked at me. "Well, it wasn't me." He picked up the teacup but, finding it empty, clicked his tongue and returned it to the saucer. "I never leave the house except in an emergency."

"Can anyone vouch for you?" Gabe asked.

Mr. Sidwell sniffed. "No. As you can see, there's no staff. The last maid left earlier this year."

"Do you mind if we look around the outbuildings?"

"Go ahead. You won't find a vehicle, if that's what you're looking for. Even the bicycle is broken. I don't know how to fix it."

Tension settled over us, and I wasn't inclined to linger. I'd liked Mr. Sidwell, but he took our questioning as an accusation. Rightly or wrongly, he was upset. It was best to get on with our investigation and leave.

Gabe and I headed outside and circled the large manor house to the stables and coach house. Beyond them was a potting shed that was bare except for some broken pots, and the ruins of a greenhouse. We carefully picked our way across the overgrown weeds and glass ceiling that had fallen onto the ground but found nothing of interest.

The stables and coach house were in equally poor condition with broken doors and rusted equipment piled up in the corners. Gabe shook his head sadly at the sight of a cracked leather saddle hanging on the wall, before inspecting the bicycle lying on the ground. The handlebars were loose and just needed some screws to be tightened.

He fetched the toolbox from the motorcar and fixed the bicycle. "For someone who delights in his family's possessions, he takes very poor care of them."

"I think the delight is purely in the possessing, not in the objects themselves. He admitted that he's never read the books in the library, yet he looks at them lovingly."

He gave the handlebars a good tug to test them. "Do you think he wants to possess his family's heirlooms badly enough that he stole the book to return it to where he believes it rightfully belongs?"

It was something I'd considered too, that ever since learning of the Medici Manuscript, he'd wanted it returned to Sidwell House. Knowing it was well cared for in the Glass Library wasn't enough for Mr. Sidwell. He wanted it in *his* library, alongside the other books Sir Andrew acquired from Dr. Adams.

Gabe sighed, as if he loathed to think Mr. Sidwell was the thief, but knew he had a sound motive and couldn't be dismissed. "He doesn't appear to have any means of transportation, so he would have needed to either catch the train to London or someone drove him. We'll ask at the station and check with the neighbors."

"Daisy's family seem to be his closest friends. I think it might be better if she telephones them and asks. They might not speak to us."

Gabe agreed.

We trudged back to the motorcar in silence. I waited for him in the passenger seat as he turned the crank handle then waited for him to join me. He didn't come straight away. He studied the manor house, a frown on his face.

"What's the matter?" I asked when he finally slipped into the driver's seat.

"I'm just thinking about these large houses and the trouble so many of them are now in. Sidwell isn't the only one with mounting debt, an enormous house to maintain and no means to maintain it. These homes used to be vibrant, filled with family and staff, and now they're little better than a noose around their owners' necks."

Not only was it a macabre opinion, but how much of it related to his own estate? As far as I was aware, his family's house now lay empty while his parents were overseas.

Gabe caught me staring at him as he put on his driving goggles and gave me a rueful smile. "My family are fine, don't worry. My father's business interests are vast enough to keep the old place in good shape. My mother loves it, although I don't think he cares where he lives as long as he's with her."

It was such a sweet sentiment that I couldn't help smiling. I'd only seen his parents in photographs, but it was easy to imagine the handsome couple strolling around a country garden. Not an overgrown, weed-infested garden like that outside Sidwell House, but something filled with flowers, broad lawns partitioned by hedges, and either a shaded pond or lake a short walk from the front door.

"And you?" I asked as we drove off. "What do you think of your family estate?"

"It was an excellent place to grow up. There was always an adventure to be had, whether in the garden, the house, or the village, especially when Alex visited." His smile suddenly vanished and his gaze hardened.

"And now?"

"And now I only visit when I have to. With my parents on an extended holiday, I won't go there unless the estate manager needs me. Ever since the war…" He shook his head and I thought he wouldn't go on, but he added, "It's a reminder of a time that's lost forever."

Gabe wasn't unusual in his avoidance of places he'd enjoyed as a youth. Many people our age refused to look back to those halcyon days. It was too painful.

"I don't blame you for wanting to stay in London." I had to raise my voice to be heard over the roar of the engine and the wind whipping past us. "There's an energy there, a sense of moving forward. I don't know if it was always so full of life or if it's something new since the war, but it's what I needed after James and my mother died."

He changed gear and glanced at me before concentrating on the road again. "You used to live in Birmingham, but don't really consider yourself a native."

"We only lived there a few years." I'd already told him that, so I wasn't sure why he was mentioning it.

"Is there anywhere that you do consider your ancestral home?"

"No. We never stayed anywhere long enough for me to think of a place as home, and I don't know where my mother's people are from. Or my father's."

I thought that was the end of the conversation, but he hadn't finished. "I hope we find out who made the silver clasps."

We turned a corner and I clutched at my hat, sitting on my lap. "What do you mean?"

"I hope it leads to finding out more about your family, about who you are." He glanced at me again, frowning. "Isn't that what you want?"

I shrugged. "It doesn't really matter if we don't find a connection to me. I've come to terms with not knowing my roots. I won't waste anyone's time by chasing down possibilities."

That was met with a charged silence.

"It won't change anything," I added. "I'll still be Sylvia Ashe, and my life will continue on as it is."

"But it could lead you to find family you never knew you had."

"And then what? I might write to these long lost cousins or aunts and uncles, and they might write back, but that's all. We're hardly going to become close after not knowing of the other's existence beforehand."

He shook his head. "You baffle me, Sylvia. If I were you, I'd be anxious to know more. I can't imagine not knowing my family. They're everything to me. Even the cousins I don't like are a part of me, part of my story." He glanced at me again. "I don't understand why you don't want to know them or find out more about yourself."

"I suppose it's a case of not missing what you've never had." While I could see his point, it seemed he couldn't see mine and nothing I could say would change his thoughts. I didn't want to argue with him, so I said nothing more.

He couldn't let it go, however. "Everyone needs to know their family, their past."

I bit back my retort, but when he looked at me again, with his brow furrowed, I couldn't help myself. "I don't need your pity, Gabe."

"It's not pity. I just want you to have what I do."

"I'll never have what you have." I turned to look at the meadows, but I saw nothing through the blur of tears.

The motorcar slowed until it came to a stop on the side of the road. Gabe kept the engine idling as he turned to me. I continued to stare at the meadow, not wanting to look at his face. Not wanting to see his pity.

"I'm sorry, Sylvia. That was thoughtless." His rich, warm voice enveloped me, soothing my tightly strung nerves. "Forgive me."

I shook my head and risked my voice. "There's nothing to forgive."

He touched my chin, gently coaxing me to look at him. I blinked damp lashes and dared to meet his gaze. What I saw in it shattered me even more. I saw a man who was used to always knowing the right thing to say, but was now lost for words. He knew he couldn't make me overcome my losses any more than he could magically overcome his.

The pad of his thumb wiped away the tear on my cheek.

His hand lingered. I thought he'd cup my cheek, lean in, kiss me...all the signs were there in his heated gaze, the parting of his lips.

But then, in a blink, the signs vanished. He withdrew his hand and faced forward. His profile hardened as he revved the engine and turned back onto the road. I stared ahead, too, and pretended nothing had passed between us in that charged moment.

But inside its cage, my heart thundered.

CHAPTER 13

*T*he stationmaster at Marlborough Station was quite the gossip. He knew Lazarus Sidwell and claimed he hadn't caught a train in years. He went so far as to say that he was sure Mr. Sidwell hadn't gone past the front gate of Sidwell House since war broke out. With the staff numbers declining over the years, his only contact with the outside world was with his neighbors, the Carmichaels, who visited once a week, and his nephew who continued to check up on his uncle every few months, even though he was treated appallingly and sometimes even chased off the property.

Gabe and I ate lunch at a teashop in Marlborough. Although we talked as if nothing were amiss between us, something had shifted since our conversation in the motorcar. I no longer felt at ease. An awkwardness had settled over us, and I wasn't sure how to throw it off. I wish I did. I wanted things to go back to the way they were.

Gabe returned me to the library and insisted on escorting me to the door. I wished he'd be more careful about his own safety and return home immediately where his friends could help protect him, but I didn't tell him that. He'd already snapped at me once today for voicing my concern, and after our conversation on the way home, I didn't want to test our friendship again.

He opened the door for me, but I stopped on the threshold and stared at the tall, elegant woman chatting to Professor Nash at the front desk.

"Ivy?" Gabe came up behind me. I stepped inside and let him past. "What are you doing here?"

She looked from Gabe to me and back again. Her throat moved with her swallow. "You weren't home. Willie said you might be here. I was just asking the librarian if he'd seen you and...well, here you are. You and Miss Ashe." She nodded a curt greeting. "How nice to see you again." Her voice trembled and her eyes watered. She was on the verge of tears.

"What's the matter?" Gabe asked. "What's happened?"

She showed him the newspaper she was clutching. "There's been another article. This time it's on the front page."

He breathed deeply and let it out slowly, as if relieved the problem wasn't something worse. But Ivy's face implied this was the most dreadful thing that had happened to her. For her to come looking for Gabe even after he'd ended their relationship must mean she had no one else to turn to.

I caught glimpses of the article as Gabe read. According to the reporter, the former soldiers who'd been protesting outside Hobson and Son's factory claimed their army issued boots were of inferior quality. The magic in them had been weak or non-existent. In some cases, they'd fallen apart. They'd developed trench foot, a condition where the soldier's feet stayed wet and cold over a long period, resulting in sores and fungus. In extreme cases, the foot had to be amputated after becoming gangrenous. The magical boots made by Hobson and Son had seen a dramatic decline in trench foot in this war compared to others, and the article pointed that out, but it did suggest that perhaps a batch of boots never received their spell. It speculated that some unfortunate soldiers had been issued the artless batch as part of their uniform.

Gabe handed the newspaper back to Ivy. "Has your father responded?"

"Yes."

"The article's not too bad. If a batch was missed—"

"Nothing was missed! My father is an excellent magician, not to mention our processes ensure that nothing could slip through."

"Mistakes happen, Ivy."

She stared at him, unblinking. Then she dipped into her bag and removed a handkerchief. She pressed it to her nose. "I expected support from you, Gabe."

"I do support you. You and your family."

She touched his arm. "I am so relieved to hear you say that. I need your strength now."

I wasn't sure Gabe had the sort of strength she required. When I first met him, I thought he had it in abundance, but it was his confidence that was so palpable. Now that I knew him better, I could see he struggled. Why couldn't she see it?

"Come to dinner tonight and you can write a statement with my father," she said.

"What statement?"

She glanced at me. I took the hint. The professor and I moved through to the library. He disappeared into the stacks, while I picked up some books that needed reshelving. I hovered near one of the marble columns where I could listen without being seen.

"A statement to the press, throwing your family's support behind Hobson and Son," I heard Ivy say. "Something to the effect that all our boots are superior in quality and any trench foot is a result of them not being worn correctly."

"They're boots, Ivy," Gabe said levelly. "There's only one way to wear them."

"I don't care what you say, but say *something*!"

The silence stretched so long that I risked a peek around the column. Gabe stood with his head bowed, and ran his hand through his hair. "Is this your price?"

"Price?" Ivy echoed.

"For ending our engagement. Is that what you want in return for releasing me?"

"Do you mean am I punishing you? Darling, no. Of course not." Her voice gentled as she closed the gap between them. "We've been through this; you know I'm on your side, that I understand you just need some time to yourself. It'll be all right. You'll see. You'll soon be yourself again. When you're ready, I'll be waiting."

"I haven't been myself in a long while. That's the problem."

She gave him a pitying look. "Darling, don't make rash decisions when you're not feeling yourself."

"I did make a rash decision, three years ago. That's the problem."

She gasped.

He winced. "Sorry. That was cruel." He dragged a hand over his face. When it came away, he seemed to have regained some composure. "When we met, I thought you were what I needed, that marriage was what I wanted. I acted hastily. But please understand, I wasn't myself then, and I'm still not."

"Gabe, there was nothing hasty about it. We were in love. We still are. As you say, you're not yourself now. It's all right. I can wait for you. You're worth it." She reached for him, but he caught her wrist.

"Our engagement has ended, Ivy. I'm not simply having some time off. I won't be back. The sooner you come to terms with it, the happier you'll be."

She jerked free. I couldn't see her face from where I stood, but from the rigidity of her shoulders, I suspected she was only just holding herself together. I felt sorry for her. She had been his fiancée for three years. She must have come to rely on him and lean on him, even though she struck me as a capable woman. To have that support removed from beneath her must be unsettling.

"We're good together, Gabe. Everyone says so. You'll be yourself again soon. Give it time. Then you'll see that I am your match in every way. There can be no one else as perfect for you as me." She strode to the door, but with the newspaper in one hand and her bag in the other, she had no free hands to open it.

Gabe opened it for her then closed it behind her. "Call me a coward, but I'll wait a few more minutes before I leave too." He didn't raise his voice. He knew I'd been listening the entire time.

I came out from my hiding spot. "You're not a coward. You're just…" I was about to say he was just tired, but instead said, "…keen to avoid unnecessary conflict."

He huffed a humorless laugh as he leaned a hip against the desk and crossed his arms.

I wanted to go to him, stroke his cheek to comfort him as he'd stroked mine in the motorcar. But he'd made it clear then that he didn't want anything to develop between us, and he'd made it clear to Ivy just now that he wasn't himself when he rashly asked her to marry him, and he still wasn't himself. I wasn't about to be another woman in his life who imposed herself on him.

I sat at the desk and reached for the telephone. "I'll ask Daisy to speak to her parents about Lazarus Sidwell's movements."

He blew out a breath. "Right. Good idea." He checked his

pocket watch. "And I'll go home and face Willie and Alex." He opened the door but didn't leave. "Sylvia."

"Yes?"

He hesitated then said, "I'll see you tomorrow."

Whatever he'd been about to say, I was quite sure it wasn't that.

* * *

GABE RETURNED THE NEXT DAY, as promised, along with his entourage of Willie and Alex. They ushered him into the library and quickly closed the door behind them. Alex blocked the door, arms crossed, feet apart. A formidable barrier to entry.

"Were you followed?" I asked.

"No," Gabe growled with a glare for Willie at his side.

"We don't want him running off again." She pointed at me. "Don't encourage him."

Gabe removed his hat and placed it on the coat stand. "Driving to Wiltshire was my decision and my decision alone. I would have gone with or without Sylvia."

She hooked her thumb into her waistband and grunted. "Is Daisy here?"

"No," I said. "Why?"

"I wanted to ask her how it went with the producer."

"She doesn't think he'll cast her, but he gave her some good advice about the business. She had Carl Trevelyan take some photographs of her to take to auditions."

Alex pushed off from the door. "Trevelyan? The suspect? Couldn't she find someone else?"

"He has a good reputation among actresses." I wasn't sure if I was defending him or her. Perhaps a little of both. "She chose him because he came highly recommended, and he's trustworthy. There are a lot of unscrupulous men out there who'll prey on vulnerable women."

Alex slumped against the door, causing it to rattle. "She's not vulnerable. She's smarter than she lets on."

I was pleased to know that he saw it, too.

"But she is naïve," Willie added. "Don't let her bravado fool you, Alex. She's as worldly as a kitten."

"Don't let Daisy hear you say that," I warned.

"That's why I like her. She might be a kitten, but she's got claws and teeth and she'll use them if she has to."

Alex crossed his arms again. "Heaven help us when she does become more worldly."

Willie poked a finger into his arm. "Heaven help *you*, my friend. The rest of us will do just fine. But she's gonna run rings around you."

Alex narrowed his eyes. "Stop poking me."

She poked him one last time then backed away, hands in the air.

Someone tried to open the door from the other side, only to be met with the brick wall that was Alex. He stepped aside, but not fast enough. The door flung open, smacking into his arm.

Daisy stood there with her bicycle, frowning. "Why were you blocking the entrance?"

"I'm keeping out undesirables."

"Do you mean me?"

He readjusted his crossed arms, doing his best to look formidable, but the flicker of his lashes meant she'd unsettled him. He wasn't sure how to respond.

"He means kidnappers," Gabe clarified. "He's trying to save me from another abduction attempt."

Daisy wheeled her bicycle inside and leaned it against the wall. "It's a library. You have to let some people in."

The professor came downstairs slowly, reading an open book. He reached the third lowest step before he realized we were all there. "Good morning, everyone. Who'd like some tea?"

I helped him make it in the kitchen of his flat then rejoined the others in the reading nook on the first floor. It was the larger of the two retreats, but even so, there weren't enough chairs for everyone. Alex remained by the staircase, keeping watch, and Gabe leaned against the desk.

I asked Daisy if she'd telephoned her parents as I handed out the teacups.

"I did. They doubt Lazarus left the estate at all. He's too frightened. If he did manage it, he wouldn't have gone all the way to London. They think it would be too overwhelming for him here. Too much noise and activity."

"He might have set aside his fears for something he really wanted," Alex said. "He wants that book back in his collection."

The professor wasn't so sure. "A recluse can't simply turn off their fears. If he has difficulty even leaving the house, London would be too great an effort."

It seemed reasonable to me, but he hadn't seen the way Mr. Sidwell talked about his ancestors and the library collection. He was proud, but also sad to have lost valuable assets that he believed belonged at Sidwell House.

"The professor has been reading up on famous medieval people," I said. "He hopes to match individuals to the symbols from the Medici Manuscript. The symbols we can remember, that is."

The professor withdrew a piece of paper from his inside jacket pocket and studied the list of symbols he'd drawn up. "So far we have the power-knot representing the pope."

"And the green onion representing the Medicis," Gabe added.

"Not necessarily. In the mid fourteenth century, when the

book was written, the Medicis weren't all that powerful. They gained more power in the fifteenth century, with Cosimo, the one who funded the library in Florence." The professor indicated the thick book he'd been reading. "I borrowed this from a friend at the university. It's a good overview of medieval and renaissance Europe. It mentions all sorts of influential people of the time, how they were connected, how they came to be influential, that sort of thing. Popes, of course, royalty, dukes and wealthy merchants, mostly. In the 1350s, aside from the pope, the various kings of Europe are the next most powerful people, but I would expect them to be represented in the book with crowns or their own heraldic symbols."

Gabe shook his head. "Too obvious. If the author is trying to keep it a secret, he wouldn't have used anything that could be easily attached to a particular person."

Willie threw her hand in the air while balancing her teacup and saucer in the other. "Then it'll be impossible to work out who is represented by the symbols."

"Perhaps." Professor Nash flipped through the book until he came to a bookmarked page. "Sylvia stayed back last night and told me all about your visit to Sidwell House, Gabriel. She said Dr. Adams acquired our manuscript from Niccolo di Mario, a doctor from Florence." He tapped his finger on the page and smiled. We all leaned forward. "I found him. There's a few lines here that mention him. He was purported to be an alchemist, and was a doctor to the Medici family. It doesn't say when he died, but he apparently saved the life of a Medici in 1558."

"A few years before he sold the book to Dr. Adams," I added. "And a hundred years after the Medici symbol was added at the front."

The professor pushed his glasses up his nose. "Which was probably added during Cosimo de' Medici's time. He funded the library so it makes sense the book belonged to him. But jumping forward to Dr. Niccolo di Mario, it's likely that as doctor to the Medici family, part of his payment was the book. They gifted it to him. Perhaps, as an alchemist, they thought he would appreciate it, perhaps even decipher it."

"Maybe he stole it," Willie said. When we all looked at her, she shrugged. "Why not steal it? It ain't like anyone would miss it. I reckon they had a billion books in their library by then."

"Not quite that many," the professor said wryly.

Gabe picked up the book and read the line about Dr. Niccolo di Mario. "However he acquired it, I think we can assume he never decoded it. He sold it to Dr. Adams without learning its contents, although he guessed—or was told—that the symbols were alchemical, hence Dr. Adams wrote the note in his catalog."

It seemed likely. Although it felt like we'd learned something today, the information about Dr. Niccolo di Mario only told us how the book had gone from the Medici's library to Dr. Adams' hands. We still knew nothing of the hundred years before Cosimo de' Medici obtained it.

Nor was I certain that filling in that gap was going to help us find out who made the silver clasps.

I picked up the book and began to read, not quite sure what I was looking for. The others finished their tea. I thought they were silent because they were considering the manuscript's origins, but Alex proved me wrong. He had something else on his mind.

He left his post by the staircase to stand beside Daisy. "Next time you want your photograph taken, ask someone to go with you."

She concentrated on the contents of her teacup, as if the tea was far more interesting than the man towering above her. "Sylvia was busy."

"You have other friends." He cleared his throat. "Or I can go with you."

"It wasn't necessary. Carl was the perfect gentleman."

"But you didn't know that when you went. In fact, he was a suspect in the theft. He still is."

Her nostrils flared. "Since I'm not a rare and valuable book, I decided I would be safe."

"You're naïve if you think you were perfectly safe from a man you hardly know."

She finally looked up at him. "Me? Naïve? Ha!"

"You—"

"Alex!" I picked up the tray and shoved it into his chest. "Would you be so good as to help me take the dishes back to the kitchen?"

He took the hint and obliged. My rescue attempt may have come a little late, however. Daisy shot him a withering glare as she dumped her cup and saucer on the tray when he lowered it to her level.

Willie watched on with a wicked smile.

The telephone downstairs rang and Gabe offered to answer it since I was on my way to the kitchen and the professor would never reach it on time. When Alex and I returned, Gabe had hung up and rejoined the others. They were all on their feet.

"That was Cyclops," Gabe told us. "His men have been questioning the staff at antique and rare bookshops. One claimed to have been visited by a man trying to sell a book that sounded very much like the Medici Manuscript. Grab your hat and coat, Sylvia. We're going to interview the shopkeeper."

I no longer bothered to question why he included me. I was simply pleased to be invited along.

Willie and Alex wouldn't let Gabe out of their sight, of course, but Daisy had things to do. Alex insisted on wheeling

Daisy's bicycle to the lane for her, but she refused. Willie watched them arguing, an amused gleam in her eye.

With a roll of his eyes, Gabe stepped outside and held the front door open for me. But before I could exit, he was grabbed from behind by a giant of a man. With his arms pinned behind him, Gabe couldn't defend himself.

Nor did he try. He glared directly ahead at another man, standing mere feet away, holding a gun. It wasn't aimed at Gabe, however.

It was aimed at me.

"Come quietly, Glass, and no one gets hurt," the gunman growled.

CHAPTER 14

What happened next was a blur. In the blink of an eye, the gunman inexplicably threw the gun away. It fell just out of everyone's reach on the cobblestones. He clutched his forearm, his face distorted with pain and confusion.

Willie barged past me, her own gun aimed at the man still holding Gabe. "Let him go! Let him go now, or I'll shoot you between the eyes!"

Alex also rushed through the door. He tackled the gunman to the ground.

Gabe wrestled free from the man holding him. There was no resistance.

"Hands in the air where I can see them!" Willie shouted.

The thug put up his hands, his eyes wide with shock. He didn't know how the tables had been turned either. Both kidnappers were stunned into silence.

As was I.

Gabe placed his hands on his hips and drew in several ragged breaths, as if he couldn't quite fill his lungs. Since no one moved, I picked up the discarded gun. I handed it to him.

"Gabe, are you all right?"

He nodded and took the gun. He removed the bullets and pocketed them before closing the barrel. "Are you?"

"Of course, but...what happened?"

"Daisy? Professor?"

They both stood in the doorway, watching in silence, mouths ajar. They nodded numbly.

One of the neighbors emerged, blinking in surprise at the sight of Willie pointing a gun at one man, and Alex hauling another to his feet. The professor went to speak to him.

Gabe drew in one more deep breath before ordering the kidnappers inside.

The professor returned and offered to telephone the police, while I stood with Daisy. She clutched my arm. I clutched hers. We stared as the thugs were marched into the library.

"What happened?" she murmured.

"Someone tried to kidnap Gabe again," I said.

"Yes, but...why didn't the man with the gun shoot?"

"You didn't see what happened?"

"No. I only heard him threaten Gabe. But when I looked through the door, he wasn't even holding a gun, just his arm. Then Alex and Willie rushed out. You must have seen what happened, Sylvia. You were right there. You must know why he didn't shoot."

Gabe wheeled Daisy's bicycle out.

I took the hint. "I'll speak to you soon." I hugged her and held the bicycle while she climbed on. "It's best not to mention this event to anyone. You know how persistent the newspapers have been when it comes to Gabe's life."

"I won't say a word." She made a locking motion at the corner of her mouth and pretended to throw away the key.

I watched her ride off then joined Gabe and the others in the library's ground floor reading nook. The two kidnappers sat side by side on the sofa like boulders. Willie made sure they didn't move. While she was half their size, she exuded a wild anger, leaving no one in any doubt that she'd shoot if necessary.

Gabe's first question wasn't the one I expected him to ask. "Did you both serve at the Front?"

The men nodded. It had been a guess on Gabe's part, but not a big leap. One man sported burn scars on his hands and face, while the other wore a patch over his eye. These were not the same men who'd tried to kidnap Gabe outside Burlington House on the first day I'd met him.

Willie adjusted her grip on the gun. "Why're you trying to kidnap him? What do you want?"

The men glanced at each other. "We're just following orders," the scarred man said.

"Whose orders?"

"We don't know. We never saw him."

"You must have. Answer me!"

Gabe put up his hand to silence her. "How did he communicate with you?"

"By telephone, and sometimes we met him in the park, but we couldn't see his face. He always wore a hooded cloak."

"It was definitely a man? Describe what he sounded like, how he seemed."

They both shrugged. "He had a quiet voice," Eye Patch said. "Maybe he spoke that way to disguise it. He wasn't tall or short, just average."

"Do you know why he wanted you to abduct me?"

They both shrugged.

Willie swore. "Is there a brain between you?"

Scarface narrowed his eyes. "He ain't about to tell us why he wants to kidnap you. Why would he? He hired us to do a job, no questions asked."

"Well, you failed to do your job and now you're going to prison."

Neither man looked concerned by the prospect of a conviction.

The professor entered and announced the police would arrive shortly before he retreated to the front desk again. He seemed unfazed by the presence of two criminals in his midst. Perhaps he'd been exposed to worse on his travels.

Gabe suggested we all sit while we waited. Alex remained standing, however, close enough to the men that he could tackle them if necessary, but out of Willie's firing line.

Eye Patch rubbed his wrist. "I know you did something to knock the gun out of my hand. But I don't know how."

No one answered.

The thug shook his head. "I don't understand. What happened?"

When we continued to remain silent, Scarface added, "He told us it would be easy. A quiet, dead-end lane outside a library that no one visits. He never warned us there'd be more of you. He never warned us..." He let the sentence dangle. He seemed unsure how to finish.

The police were mercifully quick. Cyclops accompanied the team and took statements from all of us, separately. When it came to explaining how the tables were turned and the firearm went from being in the gunman's hand one moment to discarded on the ground the next, I had no answer for him. To my surprise, he didn't press me to give one. He simply flipped his notebook closed and thanked me.

Before he left with his men and the two perpetrators, he gave Gabe and Alex a silent nod. Both nodded in return.

The four of us remained in the reading nook. Once we heard the front door shut, a thick silence descended over us. Willie glared at Gabe and Alex, but they pretended not to notice.

"Ready to question the bookshop owner?" Gabe asked me.

Willie moved to block our path, settling her feet apart and crossing her arms. "Sylvia, you can go." She jutted her chin at Gabe and Alex. "But you two ain't going nowhere until someone tells me what's going on. You're keeping secrets from me, and I hate secrets."

Alex went to pick her up by the elbows to move her, but she kicked him in the shin. He swore under his breath and hopped on one leg to the sofa. "Gabe. It's time."

"It sure is." Willie moved aside and pointed at me. "Go speak to the professor about books or something. We'll be there in a minute."

I copied her, crossing my arms and settling my feet apart. While I probably wouldn't kick anyone if they tried to move me, it was the symbolism that mattered.

It worked. Gabe asked me to sit down with Willie. "Sylvia saw more than anyone just now, so she deserves an explanation, too."

But that was the thing. I hadn't seen anything that could explain how the gun ended up on the cobblestones.

With Willie and I sitting side by side, looking up at him expectantly, Gabe released a long breath. He'd recovered from his earlier breathlessness, but he seemed even more out of sorts. He started to say something, paused, then said, "Essentially, I kicked the gun out of his hand."

I shook my head. "But you didn't move. Nor did he, except to rub his arm *after* the gun ended up on the ground."

Willie gave Gabe a challenging look. "She was right there. She saw it all. So don't try to fob us off."

"I'm not. I'm trying to explain, but…I don't really understand it myself."

"Maybe the prof can get us some more tea. It seems to help you English folk to think."

"I don't need tea."

Willie looked a little disappointed but focused again when Gabe sat opposite us.

He cleared his throat. "Let me begin with the war."

"The war! What's that got to do with it?"

"Shut up and you'll find out," Alex growled.

Willie pressed her lips together.

Gabe cleared his throat again. "The first time my battalion came under attack, I thought I was going to die. Men standing beside me one moment were dead the next. It was chaotic, noisy, bloody. Then it suddenly just...calmed. It didn't stop, but everything around me slowed. So much so that I could see bullets moving through the air. It was as if they were trying to push through a thick jelly that had somehow hindered their movement. It wasn't just the bullets. Everything slowed. Men and horses moved inch by inch, even the leaves in the wind, mud splatters, everything. Except me. I could move at regular pace."

As incredible as his story sounded, it made sense and explained a lot. Everything started to click into place like pieces in a puzzle.

"You were able to dodge the bullets," I murmured.

"And the gas and bombs. I could avoid them all before they hit. Sometimes, I pushed men out of the way, but I couldn't save everyone." He dragged a hand through his hair, and I wished we didn't have to dig up his painful memories.

"So that's how you got through the war," Willie said. "I thought you were just lucky. That someone up there was on your side." She looked to the ceiling.

"It wasn't something I could control. I couldn't turn it on or off at will. It only seemed to happen when my life was threatened."

"Which it was for four years," Alex added.

"Except it felt longer than four years," I said. "If time

slowed for you in every battle, it must have felt inter-minable." No wonder he was tired.

Gabe gave a small nod. "After the war, I thought every-thing would return to normal, that it wouldn't happen again. Then I witnessed the boat capsize off the coast of the Isle of Wight, and the boy and his father disappear under the water. I dove in and helped the boy out then I went for his father. It felt as though I found him quickly. He was tangled in the net. I was about to swim over to him, but I suddenly became short of breath. I had to resurface. I tried again to free the man, but realized he was already gone. The boy later told me that he thought I'd drowned too. I was down there far longer than I realized."

"Wait a moment," I said, thinking it through. "That's the opposite of what happened on the battlefield. There, you slowed down time. But for the underwater rescue, time—for you—sped up. Is that correct?"

"Yes. In the war, as bullets and bombs rained down on us, a second of real time felt like a minute to me. But that day off the Isle of Wight, several minutes underwater went by in mere seconds."

"A reporter wrote about you and the miraculous rescue of the boy. It was the article that made me go in search of you at the exhibition. He also speculated that there was something... curious about the rescue and your extraordinary good fortune in the war. That reporter knew something wasn't right."

Gabe nodded. "A few other reporters picked up the story, but none more than Scarrow, particularly after the first kidnapping attempt."

"Which you escaped by slowing down time."

"And the second attempt," Willie added. "And the third, just now."

"The second time, Alex witnessed it," Gabe said. "I slowed down time and managed to take the gun off the kidnapper and turn it on him. When time restarted, Alex helped me capture them and frighten them off. I thought that would be the end of it."

"I pressed him on how he got free," Alex said. "He told me everything."

Willie grunted. "You could have told me, too."

"And this third time?" I asked. "The gunman was close enough for you to kick the gun out of his hand during that... window of opportunity?"

Gabe nodded. "I couldn't get out of the other kidnapper's grip, however. I was...finding it difficult to breathe."

"That's when I came to the rescue." Willie patted the hilt of her weapon, protruding from her waist band.

"I would have freed him," Alex said defensively.

I thought it through, trying to grasp the facts. But when it came to magic, did facts even apply? Because this *had* to be magic, of some sort. "So while time slows or speeds up for you, it operates at normal pace for everyone else. But if you do something during the slowed window, it looks as though things have happened in the blink of an eye for the rest of us. That's why it seemed to us that the thug threw the gun away even though he didn't move. But you'd kicked his hand and the weapon flew through the air."

He parted his hands. "That's it in a nutshell."

I remembered the time he'd saved me from an attacker by running up the stairs incredibly quickly. One moment I'd heard his voice downstairs and the next he'd been tackling the fellow to the ground. Gabe must have used his magic then too.

"It doesn't just save you, this...skill. You used it to save me, too."

He must recall the incident I was referring to. His hands parted again. "It seems to occur instinctively. I can't control it. I heard you were in trouble and I just ran. I thought I'd be too late, but when I arrived at the scene, you'd all slowed down. It allowed me to capture him."

"You had trouble catching your breath that time, too."

Gabe's nod was barely perceptible.

Willie sat forward. "It makes you tired?"

He nodded.

"What about your chest? Does it hurt?"

"No."

She sat back again. "Well that's something, I suppose, but you got to be careful. Don't go slowing down time again unless it's to save your life."

"I told you, I can't control it. It just happens."

"You've got to try! You understand me? There will be a way. All magic can be controlled. Some magicians don't always know how, especially when they're new to a spell. India could control them. What did she say when you told her?"

"I haven't told her or my father, and nor will you. I don't want to worry them. Let them enjoy their holiday. I'll tell them when they get home."

"What can she do anyway?" Alex asked. "If this is magic, it's completely different to hers. She won't understand it any more than Gabe does."

"It is magic, and it ain't that different. Not really. Sure, Gabe ain't using a spell and he doesn't have a craft, but India didn't always use a spell to make her magic work. And she's got that watch of hers."

"What watch?" I asked.

Willie seemed reluctant to explain, so Gabe told me. "Her watch knows when she's in trouble and can save her. It chimes a warning, amongst other things."

I stared at him. Magic was more complicated and interesting than I realized.

"India's extraordinary," Willie said with a hint of fondness in her voice. "She ain't like other magicians. She's got real talent." She pointed at Gabe. "So do you, it seems."

Gabe shook his head. "If this is magic, then it's strange magic."

"It *is* magic and it ain't all that strange. Not when you know what happened to you when India was carrying you." She wagged a finger at him, thoughtful. "That must be how you got your magic. I reckon you'd have been born completely artless like Matt if it weren't for what happened when India was pregnant."

Gabe and Alex turned sharply to her. This must be a story neither was familiar with. "What happened?" Alex asked.

Willie chewed her lower lip. "Um… Maybe I should check with Cyclops before I say anything. I don't want to get the details wrong. It was a long time ago."

"My father knows?" Alex asked. "Why didn't he say so?"

"Because we all thought it meant nothing at the time. All right, I'll tell you what I remember. When Gabe was born, he was healthy and normal. We didn't know if he was going to be a magician or not, but as he grew up, it became clear he had no natural affinity for timepieces. He wasn't drawn to them like India. There's a bunch of magics on your mother's side, Gabe, not just watches, but you didn't seem to have inherited any of them. We all thought you were artless and that what happened to India when she was pregnant meant nothing."

"What happened?" we all prompted in unison.

"She had a lot of magic blasted into her. If you want the full story, you got to ask her. I don't remember it too well. But I do remember we were all worried until the day you were born. But you came out fine. A little wrinkly and small but apparently all babies look like that." She smiled and I thought I saw her eyes become misty, but she quickly hid her face by looking down at her lap. "Looks like all that magic did affect you. But no one could have guessed how it would manifest. It ain't never happened before."

We fell into silence. Willie's story proved we knew so little about magic. Within Gabe, an entirely new magic had been born, one without precedent. We didn't know its rules. What were its possibilities? And what were its limits? Why was Gabe breathless afterwards? Did that pose a danger to his health? What would happen to him if he used it again? And how could he stop himself using it?

Alex clapped Gabe on the shoulder. "So...are you a magician or not?"

Gabe shrugged. "I don't think so. I don't use spells. I can't create a watch or anything else and make it exceptional. I can't feel magic in objects that contain it. I'm just ordinary."

Willie got up and did the most curious thing. She took Gabe's face between her hands and kissed his forehead. I'd never witnessed her be so maternal. "You ain't ordinary, Gabe. You weren't ordinary before the war when we didn't know you could affect time, and you ain't ordinary now. Not to us."

Clearly Gabe wasn't used to seeing this softer side of her because he hugged her somewhat awkwardly.

She withdrew and looked away again, but this time I definitely saw tears in her eyes.

"You say your mother's watch saves her," I said. "And it seems time saves you, Gabe. Those two things are not all that different from one another."

Willie liked the connection. "Nicely put, Sylvia. Now let's go get drunk to celebrate."

"It's the middle of the day!" Alex cried. "Even I have limits, Willie."

"A cigarette?"

"You've given up with Gabe." He reached inside his jacket

and pulled out a cigarette case. "I, on the other hand, have not. I'll wait outside."

Willie gazed longingly at his back as he left.

Gabe watched me through his long black lashes. "I know it's a lot to take in, especially when magic hasn't been a part of your life. I've always been around it, and around people who talk about it. While this is new and different for you, bear in mind it's strange for me too."

I nodded, but the strangeness of it all wasn't utmost on my mind. "The four of us are the only ones who know about it?"

He nodded. "Not even Cyclops knows. Although I think he suspects something. I'll probably have some explaining to do later. Scarrow and the other journalists also suspect something, but they don't know what. They probably don't even have an inkling. None have witnessed me affecting time."

He seemed unconcerned. The journalists didn't worry me either. They were merely seeing an oddity they could exploit to sell more newspapers.

But the kidnapper was different.

"Someone has an inkling," I said. "Someone suspects magic is involved and will go to extraordinary lengths to question you to find out more."

"I don't think they merely want to question me. They could try to do that anywhere. I don't have to be taken away for that."

Willie swore loudly as she realized what Gabe was implying.

I realized too, and it sickened me to the core. "Someone wants to take you away to study you."

CHAPTER 15

*B*arstow's Rare and Antique Books was a booklover's feast. The tightly packed shelves housed gems dating back four hundred years according to the sign painted on the front window. Most were bound in leather, but some were missing covers altogether. I inspected an illustrated bible, sitting open on the round central table as a display. The ink colors were bright and the lettering bold, but it was in Latin. I bent to take a closer look.

"That's near enough." The shop owner, Mr. Barstow himself, had been speaking to Gabe at the desk, but he broke off to snap at me.

"I can't turn the page?" I asked.

"No. It's for looking at only."

I bit back a retort that books should be read and enjoyed, not simply be decorative objects. It wouldn't be wise to antagonize him. We needed him.

I smiled as I joined Gabe, prepared to strike up a friendly chat with another booklover. But he scowled down his sharp nose at me, his even sharper chin thrust haughtily forward. I'd let Gabe do all the talking. Mr. Barstow had already made up his mind to discount me, and I doubted a rapport could develop between us, despite our mutual interest.

"Can you describe the man who tried to sell the book to you?" Gabe asked.

"Oh, he didn't come in." Mr. Barstow reached into the top drawer and removed a piece of paper. "He sent this letter."

I read the typed letter over Gabe's shoulder. It was signed by Mr. John Smith who claimed to have inherited an old book that was once owned by the Medici family. Mr. Smith went on to describe it and asked if Mr. Barstow would be interested in purchasing it. The description matched the Medici Manuscript.

"Did you reply?" Gabe asked.

"I did."

"You wanted to buy it?"

"I wanted to see it before I made a decision. If it was genuine, then yes, I would put in an offer. A book with a connection to the Medicis is valuable."

The return address on the letter was in St Giles. My hopes soared. It was now simply a matter of seeing who lived there.

"Did you suggest meeting him so you could see the book?" Gabe asked.

"I sent a response yesterday asking him to bring it here. I haven't yet received a reply."

"Please notify us when you do." Gabe held up the letter. "May we keep this?"

"Of course."

Gabe turned to me. "Do you have any questions, Sylvia?"

"Just one. Mr. Barstow, you must know the other antique bookshop owner." I pointed to the window, although the other shop was several doors down on the same side. "Do you know if Mr. John Smith offered to sell the book there as well?"

"We're competitors. It would be foolish of me to discuss it with Mr. Chiffley."

Gabe and I made to leave, but Mr. Barstow quickly skirted the desk to join us.

"Can I assume that the engagement of the police in this matter means the book *is* genuine?" he asked. "It was once housed in the Medici library?"

Gabe placed his hat on his head and opened the door. "We can't be entirely sure if it was owned by the Medicis, but we do think it's old."

"Oh? Has an expert verified its age?"

"An ink magician."

Mr. Barstow's eyes lit up. "Does it contain magic?"

Gabe doffed his hat. "Good day, Mr. Barstow. Thank you for your time."

Mr. Barstow followed us outside. "Mr. Glass, please tell the owner that I'll put in an offer, sight unseen."

"I will."

"In exchange for my assistance today, I'd like the opportunity to be the first to make an offer. If he gets the book back, of course. If he doesn't..."

"He will. I gave him my word."

Mr. Barstow smiled. "Of course. I look forward to speaking to him."

I waited for Gabe to say something, but he merely indicated that I should walk ahead of him. I did not. "Mr. Barstow, the book won't be for sale," I said. "The owner plans to keep it."

"He can be persuaded to sell," Gabe said with a charming smile which I wasn't sure was for my sake or Mr. Barstow's.

Mr. Barstow returned to his shop and closed the door. Gabe suggested we call at the other antique bookshop. Alex and Willie shadowed us, although I doubted there would be another kidnapping attempt. With his two thugs arrested, the leader needed to find replacements. He'd also be foolish to try again while Gabe was on high alert.

"Why did you let Mr. Barstow think the book was for sale?" I asked.

"Because he wants it. If he thinks it's not for sale, he might warn the thief and suggest they do business discreetly."

I gasped. "You think he'd deal in stolen goods?"

"Anything's possible. At least Barstow admitted to the police that someone tried to sell him a book that matched the description of the Medici Manuscript. The other dealer did not." He nodded at the second antique bookshop.

"You think he received a letter from the thief too?"

"The thief wants to sell it. What better way to drive up the price than have two dealers vie for it? He may have even approached others."

It made a lot of sense. While we were here, we ought to question the second shopkeeper.

Cecil Court was known for housing literary and artistic businesses. There were publishers, a private library, art galleries, and a number of bookshops specializing in different subjects. There were only two antique bookshops, however. Mr. Barstow's establishment and the one owned by Mr. Chiffley, a pale and somewhat cadaverous fellow who looked as though he never set foot in the sunshine.

Gabe introduced us and explained the reason for our visit. Unlike Mr. Barstow, Mr. Chiffley claimed he had not received any correspondence from a John Smith about a book that was supposedly once owned by the Medicis. He looked annoyed at being questioned and returned to reading the book open on the desk in front of him while we still stood before him.

"He may have used another name," Gabe persisted.

"The police have already asked me and I gave them my answer," Mr. Chiffley said without looking up from the book.

"No, I have not been approached about a book belonging to the Medicis. Now, if you don't mind, I have work to do."

It didn't look like it to me. The shop was empty, and he was reading a book about archaeology.

On the way back to the motorcar, Gabe asked if I believed Mr. Chiffley.

"No. Do you?"

"No. I'll ask Murray to watch both shops. I want to know if anyone goes in carrying something the size of the Medici Manuscript." He paused and nodded at a lamppost on the other side of the street. "If he stands there, he can see both shops."

"You don't trust Mr. Barstow either? But he alerted the police."

"He didn't come to the police of his own accord. They went to him as part of their investigation. If they hadn't, would he have reported the letter?"

"Not if he assumed it was genuine. Which he didn't," I added. "I see your point. Just because he's a little more honest than Mr. Chiffley doesn't make him one hundred percent trustworthy."

He smiled as he opened the motorcar's door for me. "Now you're thinking like a detective."

I slid across the back seat and watched as Gabe climbed in beside me. "The thief doesn't know the book contains magic," I said. "If he did, he would have added that detail in his letter."

Gabe removed the letter from his pocket to re-read it. "Not only that, but the thief also has no knowledge of the black market for rare books. If he did, he wouldn't have approached Chiffley and Barstow in that manner. It was a risk writing to dealers directly, not knowing if they were honest or not."

"But it was a risk he had to take since he knew of no alternative," I finished.

We used the public telephone at the nearest post office to call their footman, Murray, and give him instructions to watch the Cecil Court bookshops. Then Alex drove us to the return address on the letter Mr. Barstow had given Gabe. My heart sank as Alex pulled the motorcar to the curb. The address was a vacant shop. The window was boarded up and the recessed doorway reeked of urine. It had been empty for some time.

Willie checked around the back and returned to report that the door was easy to unlock for someone with a little skill in lockpicking. Apparently she had this skill and neither Alex nor Gabe were surprised that she suggested they look around inside.

We entered the shop via the small courtyard at the back of the premises. The smell inside was worse than outside and I pressed a gloved hand to my nose as we picked our way through discarded newspapers, broken crates, and stained rags. Except for the small creature that dashed out from beneath a threadbare blanket, the shop was otherwise devoid of life.

"Someone's sleeping rough here at night," Gabe said.

Alex indicated the three distinct piles of rags. "Probably more than one person."

Gabe picked up an envelope propped on the window sill. "It's Barstow's response to John Smith. It's still sealed."

"And placed there, out of the way, as if waiting for someone to collect it," I added.

Gabe agreed. "Our thief doesn't live here. John Smith merely has his mail sent here."

"Probably just his mail for the negotiation of the manuscript's sale," Alex said. "It was the only way to ensure anonymity. We could wait for the vagrants to return and ask them to describe the man who comes to collect his mail."

Willie disagreed. "He's obviously paying them something for the mail service. They might not betray him. Besides, we better go before Sylvia faints from the smell."

I lowered my hand from my nose to my side. "I'm fine."

She brushed past me, heading for the back door. "You look green."

"That's a result of the poor lighting."

I followed her outside where I drew in a lungful of air. It wasn't fresh—this was London, after all—but it was far better than the smell inside.

"I'll stay here," Alex said. "We have no other choice but to wait for John Smith to collect his mail."

"Not necessarily." Gabe gazed at the corner where the small street on which we stood intersected with a larger one. "We're not far from Trevelyan's studio. It's just around that corner."

I followed his gaze and realized what he was implying. "He probably often walks by here. He would know that shop is vacant. He might even know the vagrants who call it home." A sense of disappointment washed over me. I'd liked the photographer, in a way. I didn't want him to be the thief.

Willie, Gabe and I walked to Trevelyan's studio while Alex drove the car. Gabe and I entered the studio alone and found Mr. Trevelyan about to leave. He was inspecting his camera at the desk, the satchel opened in front of him.

He looked up upon our entry and sighed. "What are you accusing me of this time?"

"We've come to search your studio," Gabe said.

"Again?"

"Do you have a problem with that?"

"If I do, you'll think I'm guilty." Mr. Trevelyan indicated the door to the dark room. "Be my guest. But I have to go.

Close the door when you leave." He hoisted the satchel onto his shoulder and headed for the door.

Gabe moved to block his exit. "May I look through that bag?"

"It just contains my camera and extra film."

"Then you won't mind showing it to me."

Mr. Trevelyan's fingers tightened around the strap. "This is a violation of my privacy."

Gabe held out his hand. "The bag, please."

The muscles in Mr. Trevelyan's jaw bunched. "I'll ask you one last time to step aside, Glass. I'm running late."

"Then you should want to get this over with quickly. Show me what's in the bag so I can—"

Mr. Trevelyan swung the satchel, but Gabe blocked the blow with his forearm. Before I'd registered what was happening, Mr. Trevelyan punched Gabe in the stomach.

Gabe grunted but recovered quickly. He landed a punch on his opponent's jaw, but must have pulled back. It didn't seem to hurt his hand or affect Mr. Trevelyan overmuch. It turned out that the punch was a decoy. The blow Gabe landed with his left was much harder.

Mr. Trevelyan doubled over, backing away at the same time. He coughed and gasped for air.

Gabe held out his hand. "The bag."

Mr. Trevelyan dumped the satchel near his feet to free himself up, and ran at Gabe with a snarl. The two men collided with a sickening thud against the wall. I ought to scream to alert Alex and Willie, but a glance at Gabe showed that he had the situation under control. He wrestled Mr. Trevelyan and grabbed his wrist. Mr. Trevelyan swung his other fist, but Gabe dodged it. The punch hit the wall. Mr. Trevelyan sucked in air between his teeth then grunted as Gabe twisted his arm behind his back.

I went in low on hands and knees and snatched the

satchel off the floor. By the time I'd wrapped my fingers around the strap, Gabe had Mr. Trevelyan in a firm grip, his arms immobilized behind him. Gabe breathed normally. He'd hardly exerted himself.

"Are you all right?" he asked, glancing over his shoulder at me.

I stood and dusted off my skirt, feeling a little foolish for my dramatic maneuver to retrieve the satchel when it turned out to be unnecessary. I cleared my throat and stroked an errant strand of hair out of my eyes. "Perfectly well, thank you."

Mr. Trevelyan struggled but Gabe's grip was too firm. "Don't open the bag, Miss Ashe. I beg you. Let Glass do it. I promise not to try to stop him when he lets me go."

Gabe frowned, considering the suggestion. He was clearly as intrigued as me about the reason for Mr. Trevelyan's request. But his hesitation acted to my advantage. Now that I'd been warned not to look, I very much wanted to.

I opened the satchel before Gabe decided to oblige and release Mr. Trevelyan. Aside from the camera and rolls of film, there was an envelope. I pulled it out and removed the photographs inside.

I gasped and almost dropped them in my shock.

Mr. Trevelyan groaned. "It's not what you think."

"So I'm not looking at a naked woman?"

I flipped through the four photographs and tried to keep my features schooled, although a little heat flushed my cheeks. The model was naked from the waist up only, but I'd still never seen anything so explicit in a photograph before.

Gabe released Mr. Trevelyan. The photographer didn't try to escape. He pressed his forehead to the wall and sighed. He looked utterly defeated. Or, rather, disappointed.

"Were they taken here?" I asked. If he placed a cloth backdrop over the cupboard to block it out, they could very well have been done here. The lighting was good.

"Does it matter?"

I supposed it didn't. I handed the photographs to Gabe, but he placed them on the desk without looking. He peered into the satchel, but there was nothing in there except the camera and film. Certainly no Medici Manuscript.

I suspected we wouldn't find it anywhere else in the studio either, but we searched high and low to make sure. Mr. Trevelyan remained in the front office, seated behind the desk. He buried his head in his hands, only looking up once I emerged from the dark room.

"Your book isn't here," he said. "I'm not a thief."

"Just a purveyor of pornographic material?" I asked.

He lowered his hands. "I'm just a photographer, and these were done at the behest of the model, not a publisher."

"You expect us to believe that?" Gabe growled. "You took advantage of the girls who came to you."

"No! They *asked* me to photograph them naked! I swear to you."

"Why would they do that?" I asked.

"Because it increases their chances with some producers. Some girls, like this one, know it. They might not like it, but they're prepared to do anything to become famous. I was about to take these to her. I don't like having them here any longer than necessary."

"Because you know how it will look if anyone sees them," Gabe said.

"It's not illegal. I'd argue it's not even immoral. The girls *ask* me to photograph them like that. That's all I do, I assure you. I don't take advantage of them."

Daisy had come here to have her photograph taken. Had she taken her clothes off in front of this man? Was she prepared to go to such lengths for a role in a movie?

I dismissed the idea. Daisy might be adventurous, but Willie was right. Daisy was naïve. She acted worldly, but she wasn't. She would have been shocked if a producer asked her for nude photographs. Shocked enough to confide in me, at least.

Gabe and I made to leave.

"Miss Ashe, wait." Mr. Trevelyan shot to his feet and rounded the desk. "You believe me when I say the girls wanted their photograph taken like this, don't you? I don't sell their photographs to anyone else. I don't take advantage."

Beside me, Gabe stiffened, but he didn't interrupt or tell Mr. Trevelyan to leave me alone. I appreciated it. I didn't require protection at that moment, and I was perfectly capable of answering for myself.

The problem was, I wasn't sure how to answer. If Mr. Trevelyan was speaking the truth, was there anything wrong with what he was doing? "Does it matter what I think?"

"Yes. Very much." This man, who had seemed confident to the point of arrogant, now held his breath in the hope my opinion of him hadn't been tarnished.

It was an odd sensation to be afforded such high regard, but not an unwelcome one. "I haven't yet formed an opinion. Goodbye, Mr. Trevelyan. Thank you for your time."

I walked out of the studio, my own words ringing in my ears. I'd sounded so formal and stiff, but I couldn't help it. I found it difficult to face him now, let alone speak normally with him. Before we entered his studio, I didn't want him to be the thief because I liked him. Did I still like him? I supposed that depended on whether I believed if he was telling the truth.

Gabe pushed the door at the base of the staircase open and light poured into the stairwell. "Are you sure you're all right, Sylvia?" His voice was warm and reassuring. There was no judgement in it. Whatever he thought of Trevelyan's activities, he gave no hint.

"I'm just rattled. Those photographs were unexpected." I moved past him to join the others by the motorcar. "If he does have the book, he's not keeping it in the studio. Perhaps it's at his house." I clicked my tongue in frustration. "We should have found out where he lives."

Gabe's smile was smug. "I saw it on a label printed inside his satchel." He uncurled his fist. "I also found this set of keys."

"Gabe! We can't just break into his home!"

He held up the keys. "We won't be breaking in."

Alex and Willie grinned. They clearly had no qualms about searching a man's flat without his knowledge.

"He lives a few streets away," Gabe said.

"In the direction of the vacant shop?" Alex asked.

Gabe nodded to our left. "The other way."

"Are you all right?" I asked as we climbed into the backseat. "Did he hurt you?"

He seemed a little amused that I was concerned about him. "I'm fine."

"Time didn't change for you. I mean, it didn't slow down and allow you to get the upper hand, unlike with the kidnappings."

He shrugged. "I suppose I never felt truly threatened. I instinctively knew there was nothing to worry about."

Instinct. His was very finely honed.

We drove to the address Gabe had seen inside the satchel, even though it wasn't far. I didn't know the area, but I recognized the name of the basement nightclub we passed: the Buttonhole. I hadn't been there before. Daisy must have mentioned it.

Mr. Trevelyan lived in a garret at the top of a run-down lodging house. Gabe charmed his way into the landlady's good graces by telling her that Mr. Trevelyan had given us his keys and asked us to fetch a camera he'd left there. He was too busy to come himself.

Gabe and I searched the flat under her watchful eye, claiming to be looking for the camera. We never found it. Nor did we find any nude photographs or the book, despite a thorough search. Gabe handed her the keys and asked her to return them to Mr. Trevelyan with our apologies.

"He'll know it was us who took them and why," I said as we headed back to the motorcar.

"Yes, but he won't make a formal complaint."

"Because he is doing something illegal with those photographs?"

"I think it's more likely because he's embarrassed."

"Trevelyan doesn't strike me as someone who embarrasses easily." Although the look on his face had certainly been filled with a kind of horror at being caught. "You believe he told the truth, don't you? That he's not exploiting anyone?"

"I do, although I can't explain why. Instinct, perhaps."

There was that word again. "You have good instincts, Gabe. If you trust Mr. Trevelyan, then so do I."

"Ah." He sounded like he regretted admitting his thoughts about Trevelyan to me.

He opened the motorcar door and held out his hand to assist me inside. I placed my hand in his and watched as his fingers closed around mine. I rubbed my thumb across his knuckles.

As I slid onto the seat, I overheard Willie and Alex talking about the Buttonhole, the club we'd just passed. "I heard it was good," he said. "Have you been?"

"No. Who said it was good?"

"That ink magician, Huon Barratt."

That's where I'd heard the name. It wasn't Daisy who'd been there, it was Huon. And he was one of our suspects.

I turned to Gabe. "Trevelyan isn't the only one who regularly passes the vacant shop. Huon Barratt does too. And he knew about the Medici Manuscript. He even commented on how valuable it must be, *and* he hinted that his Uncle Oscar was the one to find it and therefore it ought to belong to his heirs now."

"I remember the conversation. He backed down from the argument very quickly and easily. He's also desperate for money after his father tightened the purse strings. Alex, drive to Barratt's house. We need to have another chat."

CHAPTER 16

*H*uon Barratt was not at home and his butler claimed not to know when his master would return or where he'd gone.

With no more leads to follow and the day growing late, we returned to the library. Something was amiss. Professor Nash tried to warn us when we entered. He pointed through the passageway to the reading nook then pointed at the door. I couldn't decipher what he was mouthing at us.

There was no opportunity to ask. Lady Stanhope suddenly appeared between the two black marble columns marking the entryway, a full-stop between two exclamation points.

"There you are. I've been waiting." She slapped the pair of black gloves she held against the palm of her other hand. "The librarian said he didn't know when you'd return but suggested I wait. I was about to give up."

The professor gave us an apologetic shrug. Lady Stanhope didn't seem to notice. She was too intent on Gabe to see anyone else.

"Come in, dear boy. Miss Ashe, we'll have tea in that little sitting area."

"I don't want tea," Gabe said without moving. "Madam, I can't stay long. If this is about a timepiece for your collection, then I'm afraid I have to remind you that they're not for sale."

"It isn't about that." Her gaze shifted to me. "We will speak privately. What I have to say is personal and shouldn't be overheard by staff."

"Sylvia and the professor are friends, not staff."

"Friends already?" She bestowed a condescending smile on me. "How remarkable. You must be special indeed, Miss Ashe."

"The reason for your visit, madam?" Gabe bit off.

"I spoke to Ivy just now and came directly to see you. Your butler said you weren't at home and suggested I try here."

Gabe sighed. "So this is about Ivy and me."

"She told me she ended the engagement, but I know she was lying. The poor girl looked distraught." Her tone was chastising although it was edged with a hint of smugness. It was an odd combination. "Your timing is dreadful, considering the difficulty the family business is facing."

"If you're here to plead her case, I'm afraid there's no point."

Her chuckle was low, ominous. "If you insist with the charade that she ended it then I will play along, in public but not privately." She rested a hand on his arm. "I don't blame you. She wasn't right for you."

I raised my brows at that. Last time we spoke to her, she claimed Ivy was perfect for Gabe. Something about them both being tall, beautiful and from magician families. I could have added wealth to that mix, and probably a dozen other virtues they both possessed. If people were keeping score then yes, on paper, they were perfect for one another.

"Her family's predicament proves it," Lady Stanhope went on to say.

Gabe had seemed disinterested in her reasoning up until then. "What has the protest got to do with my suitability for Ivy, or lack thereof?"

"You have it around the wrong way. It's she who isn't suitable for you. Her family may never detach themselves from this scandal. If they can't, then it's best for the Rycroft heir to distance himself from the Hobsons. I can see it bothers you, but it's just the way of things. You know I speak the truth. She's beneath you now."

"I think you should leave," Gabe said tightly. "And stay out of my business, as well as Ivy's."

She tilted her head to the side and regarded him with sympathy. "You're such a proud, honorable gentleman. I commend you for it. But don't look a gift horse in the mouth, dear boy. I came here to warn you." She stepped closer and peered up at him through her lashes. "Be careful you haven't made an enemy there."

Gabe blinked at her, taken aback. Then he strode to the door and opened it.

Willie stood on the threshold, her hand extended to reach for the knob. "You said you weren't staying long, Gabe." Her gaze fell on Lady Stanhope behind him. "You."

Lady Stanhope swanned across the floor to stand before her. "Lady Farnsworth. A pleasure."

"Bullsh—"

"Willie!" Gabe glared at his cousin until she moved aside to let Lady Stanhope past.

She obliged, albeit grudgingly.

Lady Stanhope smiled her superior smile at Willie then drew on her gloves. She walked off along the lane, her black silk skirts swaying with the seductive motion of her hips.

Willie swore under her breath as she watched. "That

woman thinks she's so much better than me, but *I* outrank *her*. My late husband was an earl, and hers is a viscount. That means I can order her about."

The professor cleared his throat. "It really only means you get to walk into a room ahead of her at official functions."

"Well, then I'm going to attend the same function as her and rub her nose in it as I march right on past. That'll show her. So what'd she want?"

Gabe shrugged. "I don't know. She doesn't seem to want anything. I thought she was going to try to convince me to resume my engagement to Ivy, but she said the opposite. She says I'm better off."

She'd warned him about making an enemy of the Hobson family, but he seemed unconcerned. I wasn't so sure that he should dismiss the warning. The Hobsons were wealthy, and wealth gave them power.

"I think she was here to offer her support to you," I said. "To show she's on your side."

"I don't know why."

"Because she wants something she thinks you have —magic."

Magic that I now knew he possessed. Did Lady Stanhope know, too? Had she guessed?

* * *

GABE DECIDED the best way to corner a man like Huon Barratt was to hunt him down in his natural habitat. He sent me a message to meet him at the Buttonhole, one of Huon's favorite clubs, just around the corner from the abandoned shop where the thief's mail was sent.

Instead of sneaking out, I told my landlady where I was going. She insisted I take Daisy.

Daisy was only too happy to accompany me. She wore a

black dress I'd seen her wear before, but it was much shorter, reaching only to her mid-calf.

"I cut it off. It's easier for dancing." She kicked up her heel and strolled into the club with a confidence I could never possess. She might be unworldly now, but I suspected that wouldn't last. Dance halls and clubs were the perfect venue for a girl with a pretty face, open character and a desirable figure.

Alex certainly couldn't keep his eyes off her. He and Willie accompanied Gabe as his ever-present guards, flanking him to the edge of the dance floor. All three watched Daisy and me dance the foxtrot with our partners until the music finished. While I excused myself, Daisy continued when the band struck up Tiger Rag.

I joined Gabe and Alex, but Willie disappeared into the crowd. "He isn't here," I told Gabe. "Daisy and I arrived thirty minutes ago, and we had a good look around before we danced."

"We'll give it more time." He held out his hand. "Shall we?"

Gabe was a good dancer. He moved seamlessly between the more traditional styles and the jauntier modern ones without breaking into a sweat. After almost two hours, I needed a rest. We joined Alex and ordered drinks from a waitress dressed like a hotel porter in a red double-breasted jacket with rimless hat.

Alex blew out cigarette smoke without taking his gaze off Daisy.

"Why don't you ask her to dance?" I shouted over the music.

"Who?"

"You know who."

He drew on the cigarette and tilted his head back to blow out the smoke above our heads. "She's not short of dance partners."

"That doesn't mean they're the ones she wants to dance with. They're just the ones who asked."

He lifted a shoulder in a nonchalant shrug but continued to glance her way until the music ended and she parted from her partner. The gentleman grabbed her hand, begging her to dance one more time, or to have a drink with him, or simply keep him company. She laughed and tugged her hand away, only for him to catch it again. She tried to leave, but he wouldn't let go.

Alex stubbed out his cigarette butt in the ashtray and stood. He strode up to Daisy and said something to her. The gentleman gawped up at the towering man above him. Alex didn't move or speak, but the gentleman backed away, hands in the air. He stumbled into another man who took offence. Daisy's partner shoved him. The other man shoved back. The crowd around them dispersed, creating space for the two men circling one another, hands closed into fists.

Alex stepped between them and ordered them both to go home or be thrown out. The men made a show of lingering, squaring their shoulders and scowling at one another until Alex grabbed them both and marched them off.

Daisy joined Gabe and me, but her gaze tracked Alex until he was out of sight altogether. Then she sat back with a huff. "Why did he have to go and ruin things?"

"Alex?" I asked.

"The man I was dancing with. He was nice, friendly, and I enjoyed his company. Then he ruined it by not letting me go. Honestly, are there no decent men left in the world? Just tonight, I've learned that Mr. Trevelyan takes nude photographs of women and now this fellow."

"Not all men are like that." I indicated Gabe, beside me. "And there's Alex, too."

Her gaze wandered in the direction Alex had gone.

Willie arrived followed by a waitress carrying a tray of drinks. "You look like you need one of these," she said, handing Daisy one of the two cocktail glasses. I took the other as I assumed the whiskeys were for the men and Willie.

"Lord, yes." Daisy gulped it down as if it were water.

Alex returned, but before he could resume his seat, Daisy leapt up, wrapped her arms around his neck and kissed his cheek.

"My hero."

He blinked back, bemused. He scratched his chin. "I don't like men who bother women."

Willie raised her glass in salute. "It's true. Alex can't sit by and watch a man treat a woman like his possession. Any woman, not just you. Ow!" Willie winced and reached down to rub her shin. She shot a glare at Gabe then turned a sweet smile onto Daisy. "But I reckon he took partic'lar delight in ejecting that pigswill on account he was bothering *you*." She looked pleased with her efforts until she received another kick under the table, this time from Alex, if I wasn't mistaken. She rubbed her other shin and swore under her breath.

Daisy didn't seem to notice the exchange. She was too busy batting her eyelashes at Alex. "You really are my hero."

He picked up his glass. "You're drunk."

She plucked the glass out of his hand, drank it all down, then got to her feet. "Dance with me."

He looked like he was going to protest, but Willie spoke before he had a chance. "He'd love to." Daisy sashayed onto the dance floor, but when Alex didn't move, Willie glared at him. "Don't make me kick you under the table because you know it won't be soft."

He got to his feet. "She's drunk."

"It's just dancing. Now go, before someone else takes advantage of her drunkenness and gets there before you."

That got Alex moving. He finally joined Daisy and they were soon swallowed up by the other dancers.

Willie picked up her glass, smirking. "Now maybe we'll get some peace at home."

"Oh?" I asked. "Has Alex been unbearable?"

"He's moping. I reckon it's on account of him liking her but won't admit it because he reckons she doesn't like him back." She jerked her thumb at the dance floor. "This proves she does."

I wasn't so sure Alex would agree. But I did like that they were finally being nice to one another.

I looked to Gabe to get his opinion, but his mind seemed elsewhere. He was watching the crowd, his thumb tapping on the edge of his glass. When Willie asked a passing man if she could have one of his cigarettes, Gabe eyed it as if he'd fight her for it. The thumb tapping grew more rapid.

Now that we'd stopped dancing, he was growing edgy. I wasn't sure if it was the crowd or the noise, or perhaps both, but he looked like he wished he could be anywhere but in the club.

Willie noticed too. "You need a distraction."

His thumb stilled. He released the glass and closed his hand into a fist. He shot me a self-conscious glance before resuming his observation of the crowd. "I'm looking for Barratt."

"Perhaps we should go," I said. "If he hasn't shown up by now, he probably won't."

"It's still early."

He rubbed his knuckles, grinding his palm as if he had an itch he couldn't scratch. Every time someone passed holding a cigarette, he looked desperate enough to snatch it off them. I'd never seen him so agitated.

I placed a hand on his arm to get his attention. "You should dance some more."

He raised his brows, inviting me to partner him.

I was about to complain that my feet hurt, but instead, I smiled and stood. Sore feet was nothing compared to whatever was going through Gabe's mind.

We never made it onto the dance floor, however. The crowd parted and spat out Alex, followed closely by Daisy.

"He's here." Alex nodded in the direction of the door. With his superior height, he could see over all the other heads.

Gabe charged off, a look of determination on his face. Alex followed.

Beside me, Daisy sighed. "Will you dance with me, Sylvia?"

"We're here to speak to Huon Barratt."

"I know, but I was enjoying myself."

I grabbed Willie's arm and hauled her off the chair. "Dance with Willie instead."

Willie pulled a face. "I don't dance."

I didn't wait to see how the exchange turned out. I pushed through the crowd until I found Gabe and Alex with Huon. By the way Huon missed his mouth as he attempted to put the cigarette to his lips, he must be drunk.

He saw me and threw his arm around me, sloshing some of his drink down my dress. "It's my favorite librarian!" He frowned, pouted, and frowned harder. "No, that's not right."

"You have another favorite librarian?" I teased. "Is it Professor Nash?"

He tapped my nose. "I meant, it's not much of a compliment saying you're my favorite librarian since I only know you and Nash. I should have said, you're my favorite girl."

"Now I believe you even less."

"You *are* my favorite girl. At this moment." He managed to slot the cigarette between his lips where he left it dangling.

"But I guarantee you will *always* be my favorite librarian. Now, I need a drink. Who'll buy me one?"

Gabe stepped forward. "We will."

Alex headed for the bar.

I carefully removed Huon's arm from around my shoulder and lifted his hand to show him he still held a glass. "You already have a drink."

"Good lord! Did you just make that appear out of thin air? Sylvia, you're a magician." He downed the remainder of the contents, almost losing his balance as he tipped his head back.

Gabe steadied him and removed the empty glass before he dropped it. "May we have a word?"

"We already are."

"In private."

"This is private. No one can overhear us. Music's too loud. Also, everyone's drunk. Some folks can't hold their liquor." He poked Gabe in the chest, sending a shower of ash onto Gabe's shoes. "I'd wager you can, Glass. You've got every-thing else going for you, so why not that too?"

"That's enough, Barratt."

Gabe's irritation only spurred Huon on. He nudged me with his elbow. "Have you seen all the girls staring at him?" I had, but I wasn't going to acknowledge it to him, drunk or sober. "Shame he's already taken, eh?"

Gabe's jaw firmed. "There's a vacant shop not far from here. Do you know it?"

Huon squinted at Gabe. "What are you talking about?"

"Have you seen the empty shop down the street? There are vagrants camping in it."

"Christ, Glass. I don't know. Is this about the stolen book?" He tapped his chest. "*My* stolen book, I might add. It belonged to my uncle."

"He purchased it on behalf of the Glass Library. Legally, it belongs to the library."

"Ah. But *morally*?" He was distracted from the argument by the return of Alex with a glass of whiskey. "Good man! You're a champion." He leaned in as Alex handed him the drink. "I bet you do well with the ladies, too."

Alex gave him a benign smile and looked to Gabe. "Are you done?"

Gabe nodded. "Enjoy the rest of your night, Barratt."

"I will if you leave Sylvia here."

A muscle in Gabe's jaw twitched in time to the passing seconds before he answered. "Sylvia may do as she pleases."

Huon reached for my hand, but I withdrew it before he managed to trap it. "I'm going home. I have an early start tomorrow. Goodnight, Huon."

He pouted but was soon distracted by a pretty girl he knew.

Gabe, Alex and I returned to where Willie was sitting, flirting with a young woman dressed in a gentleman's evening suit. There were several empty cocktail glasses on the table. Daisy was dancing, but abandoned her partner upon seeing us and approached.

Willie sent her friend away with a wink and a promise to telephone her. "So?" she asked when we were alone. "What did you discover? Does Barratt know the place?"

"He revealed nothing," I said. "That doesn't mean he's innocent. He can lie just as well when he's drunk as when he's sober."

Willie didn't seem to want to hear my version of events. She turned to Gabe and Alex. "Well?"

Alex pulled out a brown leather bi-fold wallet from beneath his jacket sleeve and passed it to Gabe. Neither Gabe nor Willie showed surprise.

I gasped. "You stole that from Huon?"

Alex merely shrugged. "How else can we find out more about him?"

With his back to the room, Gabe rifled through the contents of the wallet. I wasn't sure what he was looking for. Perhaps a key to the vacant shop, or a scrap of paper with the address, or the number of a bank deposit box where the book might be stored. But he closed the wallet with a shake of his head.

"Nothing."

Alex stealthily returned the wallet to its owner and met us in the club's entrance foyer, collecting our coats. "He was too drunk to notice a thing." He eyed Daisy as she struggled to put her arm into her sleeve. "Speaking of which…"

She had no idea he was referring to her, and allowed him to assist her. "We don't have to leave now. Why don't we stay?"

"I think you should go home," Alex said.

She grasped his jacket lapels. "Dance with me."

"Another time."

She pouted. "But I want to dance all night. I want to have fun. Don't you?"

He removed her hands from his jacket only to release them again. "I have to make sure Gabe gets home safely."

She sighed.

"I can make it home on my own," Gabe growled.

"Or Willie can escort him," I suggested.

Willie shook her head. "I'm going back inside. I got unfinished business to attend to in the shape of a pretty woman." She clapped Alex on the shoulder. "He's all yours."

"I'm fine," Gabe ground out.

Alex ignored him and waited for Daisy to give in and say she was ready to go home too. But she did not. I was torn between staying with her to make sure she was all right and wanting to leave. I was tired and there was nothing for me at the Buttonhole.

It was Alex's imploring look over the top of Daisy's head that convinced me of the best thing to do. I hooked my arm through hers. "You need to sleep it off. Let's go home."

To my surprise, Daisy didn't protest. She fell asleep on the way home. Alex carried her up the stairs to her flat and I put her to bed while they waited. Other than an unintelligible murmur, she didn't stir.

"Sorry about that," Gabe said as we returned to the waiting cab.

"You don't have to apologize," I said. "It's not your fault."

"It's Willie's, but I often find I need to apologize for her."

"Why is it Willie's fault that Daisy is drunk?"

"Because she kept buying Daisy cocktails and Daisy drank them like they were cordial."

Alex settled into the front passenger seat and glanced over his shoulder at us. "She's dangerous when she's drunk."

"Daisy?" I asked. "She's only a danger to herself. Unless you count the men she flirts with then abandons when they become too insistent."

He merely grunted as he turned back to face the front. I got the feeling that was exactly what he meant. Perhaps he even included himself in the abandoned category. But Alex was the perfect gentleman and had treated Daisy gently all night. He'd never insist she be with him.

Gabe was another matter. While he'd enjoyed the dancing, after we finished, he was keen to locate Huon Barratt and leave as soon as possible. He was listless while we sat and waited. It seemed he didn't like being still. He wanted to keep moving, whether that be dancing or getting on with the investigation. Indeed, that could be said about him all of the time, not just tonight. He needed to be active.

Perhaps that was his way of putting the war behind him,

of forgetting. Activity of the body and mind left no time or energy for dwelling on the past.

* * *

I FOUND it difficult to concentrate the following morning. I was tired, and none of the books I was cataloguing intrigued me. At any other time, I would have settled on the sofa and read a few pages at the very least, but I was unable to focus. It wasn't simply the late night. It was the frustration at not getting anywhere in the recovery of the Medici Manuscript. We were relying on the thief showing up at the shop to collect his mail, and until he did, we must wait.

A telephone call changed the trajectory of my day. It was from Gabe's footman, Murray. Apparently Gabe had instructed him to watch the vacant shop overnight. "I telephoned the Park Street house, but Bristow said Mr. Glass was coming to the library after he called on Miss Hobson."

Gabe's business with Ivy was none of my business, but I nevertheless found myself wondering why he'd gone to see her.

"Miss Ashe? Are you there?"

"Sorry, Murray. Mr. Glass isn't here. Can I pass on a message when he arrives?"

"Tell him someone came to the shop a short time ago. He spoke to one of the occupants then left. I followed him to a house in Spitalfields. I'll return there after I hang up, but I reckoned Mr. Glass would want to come and question him."

I reached for a pencil and notepad. "Give me the address and I'll pass it on when he gets here."

It was another thirty minutes before Gabe and Alex arrived. I watched for them through the window and wrenched the door open before they reached it.

I waved the piece of paper in Gabe's face. "Murray is

watching our suspect's house in Spitalfields. Come on. There's not a moment to waste." I called out to the professor that I was leaving then grabbed my bag and raced out of the library.

Gabe waited for me, but Alex was several steps ahead and reached the motorcar first. I showed Gabe the address and he nodded. He knew how to get there.

Gabe drove as fast as he could through streets clogged with the usual weekday traffic and parked a few doors down from the address Murray had given me. We spotted the footman leaning against a lamp post, pretending to read the newspaper. He folded the newspaper up and strolled toward us.

"He's still in there," he said. "Medium sized fellow. I didn't get a look at his face. He wears a homburg."

Many men wore homburgs. The style of hat wasn't uncommon, particularly when worn with less formal daywear. Yet I didn't associate it with any of our suspects. I did associate it with someone, however. I just couldn't quite remember who.

"Want me to knock?" Alex asked.

Gabe shook his head. "I'll do it. You go around the back in case he tries to leave that way."

"And me?" I asked.

"Wait in the motor."

"I'm not coming all this way merely to watch from afar."

"'All this way?' It only took us ten minutes to get here."

I arched my brows at him.

He sighed. "I'm not going to win that argument, am I? Very well. Stand a few feet back. If the suspect sees that he's caught, he may try to flee. I don't want you getting hurt."

An elderly woman answered Gabe's knock. She must be the landlady, Mrs. Wright. According the sign in the window, she managed the boarding house for "Respectable

Gentlemen." Those with genuine references could apply within. She smiled at Gabe, no doubt assuming he was a potential boarder. She didn't see me, standing beyond.

He asked after the homburg-wearing boarder who'd recently arrived home.

"I'll fetch him for you." She smiled. "Who may I say is asking?"

Gabe hesitated. He would hate to lie, but if he told her his name or that he worked for the police, the suspect might flee out the back. Although Alex was watching the rear door, Gabe wouldn't want to put his friend in danger if he could help it.

If he stayed silent, he wouldn't have to lie to her. And I knew a way he could stay silent. I'd finally grasped the image that had been teasing me ever since learning about the homburg.

I knew the identity of the thief.

I stepped forward. "Tell him Miss Sylvia Ashe would like to see him. Tell him I have some information that he will want to hear."

She asked me to wait inside the entrance hall while she headed up the stairs. Once she was out of earshot, I turned to Gabe.

"Stay out of sight until he's standing before me. We don't want him running off the moment he sees you."

He glanced up the staircase. "Very well. But first, tell me who we're up against."

CHAPTER 17

*G*abe stood on the front porch beside the open door, out of sight from anyone coming down the stairs. I clutched my bag tightly and waited for Mr. Scarrow.

Now that I knew the journalist was the thief, it all began to make sense. He'd not been seen at work for a few days, nor had he come looking for Gabe again. We'd also seen him leaving Mr. Trevelyan's studio on the day we called there to inspect the photographs of the book's signature page. Mr. Scarrow must have seen the Medici Manuscript on the desk and realized how valuable it was. He didn't know its clasps contained magic, only that it was connected to the powerful Florentine family. He merely wanted to make some money, and fast. He'd stolen it at the first opportunity.

Hopefully he wouldn't know I was here about the book and assumed I wanted to talk to him about Gabe. Hopefully he hadn't given up journalism altogether and still wanted an exclusive.

But the longer time dragged on, the more doubtful I became. Surely he'd connected me to his crime. Surely he was wary of any visitor to his home, particularly one he'd never given his address to.

I adjusted my grip on my bag's shoulder strap. My fingers ached from clutching it too tightly.

"Miss Ashe? How did you find me?" Mr. Scarrow asked as he came down the stairs. He didn't hurry. His step was slow, cautious, and his gaze darted back and forth. He was suspicious. He wouldn't let down his guard unless he thought I was alone.

I needed to get him standing as close to the front door as possible. If he suspected I was lying, he might dash back up the stairs where he may have a weapon hidden in his room. I couldn't risk him retrieving it.

This required all the courage I could muster as well as any acting skills I might possess. "Good morning, Mr. Scarrow. I apologize for the intrusion. I hoped to see you at the library, but I've watched for you for two days now, and you haven't returned."

He took another step down, but he was only halfway. "I've been busy."

"Are you still interested in Mr. Glass's story?"

Going by the way his gaze sharpened, he certainly was. "You know something about his secret, the reason he survived the war for so long? Something that would interest my readers?"

"I overheard him talking to his friend, Mr. Bailey."

He took two more steps down. "Tell me."

"I'm not a fool, Mr. Scarrow. I won't give it to you for nothing. I expect some compensation for my efforts."

His smile was slippery. "Very wise. I suspect a librarian's wages aren't very much."

"Assistant librarian. And every wage can do with a little bolstering from time to time."

"You're not as naïve as you look." He was a mere four

steps away from the bottom of the staircase when he stopped. "Would you mind closing the front door? It's chilly out there." He wasn't going to trust me. Not yet.

He gave me no choice. I closed the door, blocking out Gabe. I was alone with Mr. Scarrow with no way of capturing him. I wasn't strong enough and I had no weapons.

So I had to be smart.

His confidence grew once the door was closed. He trotted down the last few steps and joined me in the foyer. "Tell me the information and I'll decide how much it's worth."

I shook my head. "We negotiate first."

"Miss Ashe, come now. I can't agree to terms without knowing if it's worth my while."

I thrust my chin out, doing my best to look offended. "It is. You'll simply have to take my word."

He rubbed a hand over his jaw as he thought about it. "I'm afraid I can't. Not without a hint. I've had too many jilted women make up lies to get revenge on former lovers."

I stiffened. "I didn't come here to be insulted." I turned and strode toward the door, flinging it open.

Gabe charged inside and ran at Mr. Scarrow.

Mr. Scarrow was far enough away that he had a moment in which to shout, "Bitch!" He also had time to reach out and grab the umbrella from the stand.

I'd not been smart enough. I hadn't ensured he was far enough from any potential weapons before I let Gabe in.

He thrust the umbrella at Gabe's chest. Gabe dodged to the side. He thrust again, and this time Gabe caught it. Gabe pulled on the umbrella, jerking Mr. Scarrow closer.

He landed a punch on the journalist's jaw. Mr. Scarrow would have reeled backward, but Gabe grabbed his arm and twisted it behind Mr. Scarrow's back.

It was over in seconds. Gabe hadn't even broken a sweat.

My heart was thumping, however. There'd been a part of

me that worried Gabe's powers would activate if he felt threatened. Using his magic would sap his strength, and I didn't like seeing him weakened.

I accompanied the wide-eyed landlady to the kitchen. I settled her on a chair and placed the kettle on the stove before letting Alex in through the back door. "It's Scarrow," I told him as we returned upstairs.

We found Mr. Scarrow still struggling to free himself from Gabe's grip. It was hopeless, however, and he gave up upon seeing Alex. He tried denial instead.

"I didn't steal it! I don't know anything about your book. Where would I have learned of it?"

"At Carl Trevelyan's studio." I pointed up the stairs. "If you didn't steal it, then I won't find it in your rooms, will I?"

"You can't search my flat! That's a violation of my rights!"

Gabe passed Mr. Scarrow over to Alex. "Mind if I join you, Sylvia?"

Mr. Scarrow lowered his head and his shoulders slumped forward. He didn't try to fight or escape when Gabe released him. It was a sure sign of guilt.

It wasn't difficult to find the manuscript. It had been carefully wrapped inside a blanket and stored on top of a wardrobe where I began my search. I passed it to Gabe then accepted his assistance down from the chair.

He studied me with a small crease between his brows before letting me go.

I nodded at the Medici Manuscript. "We should check the book hasn't been damaged."

"Yes," he muttered. "We should." He unwrapped it completely from the blanket and handed it to me. "How did you know it was up there?"

The cover looked fine. The boards might be old but they were sturdy and protected the pages within. "It seemed like a good place to start." I sat on the chair and opened the book. I passed my hand over the Medici family symbol then turned the page.

"But why not leave the higher places for me to search?"

I shrugged as I turned more pages. "I don't know. I didn't put much thought into where to begin." The book was undamaged, thank goodness. The pages and silver clasps were in perfect condition. I expected nothing less from magician craftsmanship.

"That's what I thought."

I looked up. "Gabe? Is something the matter?"

He glanced at the top of the wardrobe. He could have reached up there himself, although he couldn't have seen the book, stored in the blanket toward the back. "It seems like a strange place for the shorter of the two of us to start searching, that's all."

"Is that a comment on my height, or lack thereof?"

He smiled. "Not at all. Come on. Let's take Scarrow to Scotland Yard then return that book to where it belongs."

* * *

To say the professor was pleased to see the book again was an understatement. He was like a lover who'd not seen his love for a long time. His first act was to sit with it and check there was no damage, as I had done. I didn't tell him I'd already checked. I doubted it would have made a difference.

When he finished, he clutched the book to his chest. "I'm so glad it's safe. I've been dreadfully worried."

Willie snorted. "It ain't a child, Prof." She was already at the library when we arrived. Her annoyance at being left out of the arrest was written all over her scowling face. She'd complained vehemently, until Alex reminded her she'd slept in after a very late night out.

"What will you do with it?" Gabe asked the professor.

Alex gave him an odd look. "He'll shelve it. The cabinet has been fixed and new magician-made glass is in place. It won't break again for some time."

Gabe looked to Professor Nash. The professor merely sighed.

I sat beside him and asked to see the book. "It's not going anywhere until we decipher it."

"And if we can't?" the professor asked.

"I have a feeling we can. We know some of the symbols. Gabe, could you ask your friends to come here tomorrow and we'll all put our heads together. Mr. Stray, the mathematician, of course, but also Stanley Greville and Juan Martinez. They've already helped us, so perhaps they can offer more insights."

Gabe telephoned his friends then returned with Daisy in tow. She'd just arrived on her bicycle, and her face was flushed and her hair windswept. She touched it self-consciously while studiously avoiding Alex's gaze. Her attempts at fixing herself up were pointless as he was avoiding looking at her, too.

She gave me a fierce hug. "I'm so glad you have the book back, Sylvia. I know how much the theft was troubling you."

"How much?" Gabe asked.

She waved her hand. "Enormously. It's all she could talk about."

"That's not true," I said. I'd been holding the book tightly, but released it and placed it on the desk beside me.

"It is true. From the moment you found it, you've been obsessed with either learning its secrets or trying to find it after it was stolen. Now two mysteries are back down to one, and hopefully that won't be a mystery for long."

"Why? What do you know?"

"Only that with three clever people poring over it, you can't fail to discover what it's about."

Alex and Willie looked at one another, then both turned to Daisy. "What about us?"

"Dear Willie." Daisy clasped one of Willie's hands between both of hers and gave her a sympathetic look. "You are special in so many ways."

Willie looked pleased with that. "It's true."

"And you, Alex." Daisy patted his cheek. "You're tall, athletic and handsome. You don't need to have brains too. That's just being selfish."

Unlike Willie, he didn't take it as a compliment. He crossed his arms and narrowed his gaze at her.

She smiled sweetly and perched on the edge of the desk. "Now tell me how you rescued the book from that villain."

I repeated the story for her, all the while growing more self-conscious with every passing moment. Gabe was watching me intently. It was unnerving.

It wasn't until just before he left, when we were alone, that he drew me aside and told me what was on his mind. "You found the book very quickly."

"So you've already said. Is that important?" For one horrible moment, I thought he was going to accuse me of colluding with Albert Scarrow to steal it.

He must have seen the horror written all over my face, because he quickly put my mind at rest. "The only thing I'm accusing you of is being a magician."

My mouth fell open. I stared at him.

"Think about it," he went on. "You went directly to it when it would have been easier to leave the top of the wardrobe to me. Something made you search there. Perhaps the magic in the silver clasps called to you, and you responded on a sub-conscious level. You've also been obsessed with it, as Daisy put it."

I began to protest but closed my mouth. It was possible, I supposed. The top of the wardrobe was an odd place for me to begin the search. And I did want to find out more about it, very much. But that was the thing. I was obsessed with the book itself, not the clasps.

"I want to learn more about it, it's true," I told him. "But all of it, what's between the pages, what the symbols mean, what knowledge it contains. The clasps are beautiful but I don't find them as interesting as the rest of it. Does that make sense?"

He nodded slowly. "It does. And while it means you're probably not a silver magician, perhaps you are another sort. Perhaps the magic in the silver was strong enough that yours responded to it."

"Is that possible?"

"There's one way to find out. I have to make another telephone call."

* * *

GABE'S FRIENDS arrived at the library the following morning, but we didn't get started until Huon Barratt turned up. He entered the library with a flourish of his cape and a deep bow.

Willie rolled her eyes. "You're a proper magician, not a sideshow trickster. Have some class."

Alex snorted. "The day someone takes lectures about class from you is the day I'll start calling you Lady Farnsworth."

Willie gave him a rude hand gesture.

As much as I wanted to ask her about her marriage to a lord, I had a more pressing matter to address. Now that Huon had arrived, we could begin. I took his cape and hat and hung them up before inviting him into the reading nook on the first floor where Gabe's friends waited to see the book.

But the book was hidden and only the professor knew where.

"We're running a little experiment," Professor Nash told Huon. "Yesterday, Sylvia found the book very quickly in Mr. Scarrow's flat. Was it luck or was she drawn to it, as a magician? She claims she isn't particularly drawn to the silver clasps, so Mr. Glass suggests she might not be a silver magician but some other sort, and the silver magic is calling to her nevertheless. Does that theory seem plausible to you?"

Huon stood with hands on hips and nodded. "As a magician of a discipline other than silver, you want to test whether I can find it just as easily?"

"Precisely."

Huon spread out his arms. "Everyone stand back. Allow me to work unencumbered." He closed his eyes and pressed his fingers to his temples.

We all followed him as he wandered down one aisle, then the next and the next. "There is a lot of interference," he mused.

"Interference?" I asked.

"There are so many magical disciplines in here." He pointed to a vase, the glass-fronted cabinets, some of the shelves. "It's everywhere, both up here and downstairs. I find it difficult to separate one magic from another. I can identify ink magic quickly, but other magic takes me longer. Do you want me to point out which books are written with magician-made ink, Professor?"

"No need," Professor Nash said. "Your uncle identified them years ago. So you can't locate the magical silver clasps?"

"I can, I just need time."

It took a few more minutes but he eventually removed the Medici Manuscript from the shelves. He brandished it above his head in triumph.

I suddenly needed to sit. I reached behind me and lowered myself onto the chair by the desk.

Gabe crouched in front of me. "Sylvia? Are you all right?"

I nodded. But I wasn't all right. The blood thrummed through my veins. I felt light-headed, yet also very aware of Gabe, crouching close, and of the book now in the professor's hands. I'd guessed precisely which aisle it had been hidden in.

Perhaps it hadn't been a guess.

"You knew, didn't you?" Gabe asked. "The silver magic called to you, called to your magic."

"I don't know. It's not as though I *felt* anything. It was simply a...fact." That didn't quite explain it, however. The fact hadn't been stored in my head, available to draw on when required or push aside when not. "It's more of a deep understanding, a consciousness. Just as I am conscious that you are here, that I am seated, that I breathe air...I was aware of the book's location in here." I tapped my chest.

One corner of his mouth lifted with his half-smile. "Then you must be a magician. The question is, what sort?"

It was the most logical explanation. And yet, how could I have gone my entire life without knowing I was a magician? I'd never even had an inkling. My brother had. James's diary suggested as much, and his simple jottings had set me on this path. Had his own magic been more developed than mine? Had he been more aware of his capabilities?

Gabe grasped my hand, jolting my mind back to the present. "We'll work it out, Sylvia. I'll help you."

Whether it was the warmth of his hand, the touch of skin against skin, or the tenderness in his voice and eyes, but I had complete confidence in him. He would help me learn more about myself. I was sure of it. And I would enjoy every moment we spent together in our search.

I didn't have the opportunity to consider my magic further. Gabe's friends got to work on the symbols in the book. Professor Nash, Gabe and I joined them at the desk, but

I soon left them to it. There were too many of us to pore over a single book.

I found Alex, Willie and Daisy at the front desk as they saw Huon Barratt out. He threw his cape around his shoulders, knocking over the desk lamp. Alex caught it and righted it.

Huon gave a shallow bow. "My apologies. Not all of my faculties are working yet. It's still early in the day."

"Are you still drunk?" Willie asked.

"My dear, strange little...person, I haven't been sober since I demobbed in January '19. Now if you'll excuse me, I have a luncheon to attend."

He walked out of the library with another flourish of his cape.

I was about to follow Willie and Alex back into the library when Daisy grasped my hand. She waited until the others were out of earshot before speaking.

"How did I get home last night?"

"We took you in a cab." At her blank look, I added, "Alex, Gabe and me."

She blew out a breath. "So it was you who put me to bed?"

"Yes."

She clutched my hand harder. "Did Alex say anything?"

"About what?"

"About me. Did he comment on my drunkenness?"

"No. He's a gentleman, and Willie is partly to blame for that. Anyway, why do you care? Everyone drinks to excess these days." I indicated the door through which Huon had just left.

She eyed Alex's broad back until he was gone from sight. "Not everyone."

"You like him, don't you?"

She let go of my hand. "Who?"

"You know who."

"I suppose I do. But he thinks of me as a feather-brained, spoiled girl. And until his opinion of me changes, nothing will happen." She marched off, but not in the direction of the library. She grabbed her bicycle and wheeled it toward the door.

I opened it for her and watched her ride off along Crooked Lane. Perhaps she was right. Perhaps Alex did think she was a little silly and somewhat spoiled. Whether it was true or not, the fact was, she *thought* it was true and she wouldn't feel like his equal until her own opinion of herself changed.

* * *

PROGRESS WAS SLOW. Copies of some pages were made so we could split into teams. Juan recognized one more Catalonian symbol, and the professor thought two of them could be ancient Greek and went looking for a source to verify them. But it wasn't until Stanley Greville came across a sequence of four letters beside the knot symbol that we were quite sure represented the pope. After the four letters was another symbol that Stanley suggested represented the female genitalia.

Once he pointed it out, I could see it, too. We all could.

"A female pope," I said. "Surely not."

Willie had been resting on the sofa with her eyes closed, but now sat up. "Why not? It'd be easy to hide a woman's curves under a pope's cassock."

The professor pushed his glasses up his nose. "There's a story about a female pope: Pope Joan, from the early middle ages. Apparently her name was struck off the list of popes once her gender was discovered."

"But the story has been discredited," Gabe said. "Most

scholars think it was just a fiction made up at the time. There's no evidence she was real."

We all looked at the four letters squeezed between the symbols for pope and woman. They had to represent the letters J O A N. There was no doubt in anyone's mind. It was the key to cracking the code.

With those four letters of the code now deciphered, we wrote the actual letters they represented on the copies every time they appeared. It should have helped us decode more words, but no one could make sense of them.

I returned to the book, wanting to see the original source. The first page of text was laid out like the first page of most books with three lines in large print. Could they be the title, subtitle and author name? Below that was smaller writing, perhaps the publisher or scribe's name, and a location.

Where the author name should be was three creatures with a large body and skinny legs. Tiny hairs sprouted from the legs and vertical lines were drawn on the body. The head was small. "This is an insect," I said. "Three of them, all the same."

Gabe leaned closer to get a better look. "They're very well drawn. Alex, pass me the magnifying glass." He peered through it. "There are even tiny hairs on the insects' backs. I think they're fleas."

"Are you certain?"

"Don't ask how we know about fleas," Alex muttered.

"So why are there three fleas to represent the author's name?" I asked. "Why would the author call himself fleas?"

"Perhaps that's his name," Gabe said.

"Flea?" Juan wrinkled his nose. "You English have very strange names."

The professor suddenly gasped. "It's not English. In fact, none of it is."

"What language is it written in?" I asked.

"My guess is, the most common language in Florence at the time this book was written."

"Latin?"

"Latin was the most common *written* language, it's true. But few people could write and most spoke a version of Vulgar Latin or Italian." He pushed his glasses up his nose and regarded me through them. "What we now think of as the Italian language developed in Tuscany, of which Florence is the capital."

I stared at the diagram of insects. "So what's the Italian for fleas?"

"Pulci. And I happen to know there was a well-known man living at the time this was written named Pulci." At our surprised looks, he admitted that he'd been reading up on the Medici family over the last few days. It was in one of those that he'd read about Luigi Pulci. "He was from an aristocratic family, and was something of a wit, famous for his insults. He had a biting sense of humor, and regularly skewered his contemporaries in taverns, which sources say he frequented often."

"Sounds like my kind of fellow," Willie chimed in from the sofa.

Gabe tapped his finger on the flea symbol. "I think we can assume we've found our author."

"And the language the book is written in," I added.

I did not know Italian, but Juan, Gabe, Stanley, and the professor did, to varying degrees. They settled in and got to work, stopping only to eat dinner which Mrs. Ling sent to the library with the chauffeur and footman. Between them, and with Francis Stray the mathematician's assistance, they decoded the entire manuscript with only some of the symbols left.

One symbol in particular had them both excited and confused in equal measure. The pentagram, the traditional symbol for the occult and witchcraft, appeared more than any of the others.

"This must be a book about magic," the professor declared, only to shake his head. "But very little of these passages seem to refer to magic. Indeed, most of it is just gossip."

Willie peered over his shoulder at the deciphered and translated text. "Gossip about what?"

"People. For example, the reference to Pope Joan being female implies that the author, Pulci, has seen evidence to prove it. He claims to have seen a letter in a monastery that was kept locked away in a vault with heretical books. The letter was from a doctor who'd given the pope a medical examination, and she was indeed a woman."

"And pregnant," Gabe added, pointing to the relevant line.

"Pulci wrote about other scandals, some from well before his time like Pope Joan, and others about his contemporaries. He claimed to have seen proof of every scandal he wrote about. He calls one distinguished scholar a cheat for copying another's work. He accuses the member of one particularly well-known family of theft. He says the queen of France had a sexual relationship with one of her maids, and a certain cardinal frequented brothels."

"No wonder he needed to write it in code," I said. "The consequences of this information being discovered would have been dire indeed for Pulci."

"There is only one reference to magic and that is associated with the devil symbol. Pulci states that the devil, whoever that may be, smuggled a silver magician out of the Ottoman Empire, and forced him to use his spell. So if Pulci uses the word 'magic' in his own code, the pentagram must mean something else. But what?"

I flipped through the pages of the book I'd been reading

while they worked until I found the pentagram symbol. "It represents truth in Hebrew, according to this. Pulci is reminding us that he speaks the truth in this book." I was more interested in the Ottoman silver magician, however.

As was Gabe. "Pulci states that the silver magician was able to improve the quality of a silver object. Imagine buying low quality silver cheaply then improving it with a spell. You could sell it at a higher price. Profits would soar. Who do we know who became wealthy very quickly and is considered the devil? Or his profession is, at least."

"Money lenders," Francis said.

"Bankers," Alex added.

"The Medicis," more than one voice chimed in.

The professor wagged his finger. "Of course! Not Cosimo. He inherited his wealth. His ancestor, Giovanni, is considered the forefather of the Medici empire. Although he didn't start the bank, he took it from a small enterprise and turned it into a powerful center of finance, and he did it quickly. Not only that, he was alive during the time of Ottoman expansion. It's not clear how he came to steal the silver magician, but Pulci believes he did. Indeed, he states it's the truth. The Medici bank was founded on the hard work of an illegally obtained silver magician. Ha! What a story."

It certainly would have been an explosive accusation at the time, considering Europe was purging magicians, accusing them of heresy and driving them underground.

Gabe turned the pages back until he reached the first one showing the balls and *fleur de lis* of the Medici family. "How ironic that the book ended up in Cosimo de Medici's library, the descendent of the man Pulci accuses of using magic to obtain wealth."

"Pulci sounds like someone who would have been secretly pleased," the professor said, sounding quite satisfied with the circular nature of it himself.

While it was all very interesting to finally know what the book was about, it shed very little light on who made the silver clasps.

"The silver magician stolen from the Ottomans had children," I pointed out. "The magic was passed down through the lineage until one of the descendants made those clasps."

I wondered if they knew their ancestor had been mentioned in the book. It was most likely a coincidence brought about by the fact that the wealthiest family in all of Europe was able to buy this very beautiful, mysterious, and expensive manuscript for their library. They may not have known anything more than we did when we first saw it.

Juan leaned back in the chair, his hands clasped behind his head. He'd removed his tie some time ago and rolled up his shirt sleeves, as had Gabe and Alex, but the other men kept themselves buttoned up. "I wonder what happened to the silver magician family. Where are they now?"

"Silver magic is extinct," Stanley said.

We did not correct him. Indeed, he might be right, if Marianne Folgate died without children.

Gabe got up to serve drinks from the decanter that Bristow had packed with the food. He handed out glasses of sherry, but Francis Stray didn't accept his. He was too distracted to notice Gabe standing before him until Gabe cleared his throat.

Francis accepted the glass. "It would be beneficial to keep track of all the magician families, past and present, particularly when it comes to rare magic like silver. Perhaps the silver magician mentioned in the book has descendants who are unaware of their talent. You could find them and tell them, Gabe."

"I'd have to know the name of the original magician," Gabe pointed out.

Francis dismissed the roadblock with a flick of his wrist. "I could create the records for you, if you like. They will act a little like a library's card catalogue, with cross references, et cetera. The project would also require family trees, which could get quite cumbersome to store. Does anyone know a historian?"

Nobody did, and Francis lost interest as he realized how little of the concept involved mathematics. He didn't want to execute the idea himself.

We remained quiet because we knew such a catalogue already existed, although I was yet to see it.

"What will you do with the book now?" Juan asked.

"Shelve it," Willie said. "Behind magician-made glass in a cabinet locked with magician-made locks."

Gabe leveled his gaze with the professor. "I'm not sure it belongs here."

Professor Nash pressed his lips together. After a moment, he nodded. "You're right. It has another home."

"Sidwell House?" Willie blurted out. "But Lazarus Sidwell's got a few screws loose. Can he be trusted with it?"

"He's eccentric and a recluse, not mad," Gabe said. "And we'll provide him with a specially made cabinet to keep it safe. But I feel like the book belongs with the rest of the collection Sir Andrew purchased from Dr. Adams. What do you think, Sylvia?"

"I agree. It had a home long before the Glass Library and should be returned there. Mr. Sidwell will be very pleased."

Despite the late hour, no one wanted to leave. We felt triumphant. Solving the mystery of the Medici Manuscript was like winning a battle, one fought in the library with books as our weapons. I was very aware that we'd not won the war, however. We still didn't know if Marianne Folgate was connected to the magician who made the silver clasps, and we didn't know if I was related to her.

Although it was looking likely that I might very well be a magician, I was quite sure I wasn't a silver one.

So why had my brother thought he was?

A clock on the mantel chimed three AM.

"That can't possibly be the time," Stanley said, tapping the face of his wrist watch.

"Of course it is," Professor Nash said, somewhat defensively. "Lady Rycroft's magic is in that clock."

Willie pushed to her feet. "And her magic ain't never wrong. All her clocks run on time."

Juan stood to inspect the clock. "But the magic must fade. All magic does. And then the clock will lose time."

"India's not like other magicians. Time marches to *her* beat. *She* don't march to it."

Stanley went to pass his empty glass to Gabe but dropped it on the carpet before Gabe could properly grasp it. He tucked his hand inside his jacket, but not before I saw it shaking.

Gabe picked up the glass and set it on the tray. He clasped Stanley's shoulder. "It's all right," he said quietly. "How is the treatment going?"

"Fine. I'm just tired."

"It's been a long day. Thank you for your assistance. Our thanks to all of you."

Francis shook Gabe's hand. "No need to thank me. I haven't had so much fun since my university days."

Willie laughed. "What were your university days like? Because when Gabe went, he wasn't decoding mysterious books. He was getting drunk, swimming naked in the river, and stealing the coat of arms."

"You stole the university's coat of arms?" I asked him.

"Only the one, from above the grand hall's door. And I returned it the next day."

Willie opened her mouth to say something further, but

Gabe flung his arm around her shoulders and gave her a friendly but vigorous shake. "That was a long time ago. I'm a changed man now."

She sighed, looking somewhat disappointed by the fact.

The evening edition of one of the newspapers the professor subscribed to had been delivered while we were upstairs. I picked it up to hand to him, but a small article on the front page caught my eye.

"Famous magician family defends Hobson and Son", the headline read. According to the article, "Mr. Gabriel Glass, son of watch magician Lady Rycroft, gave his assurance that the quality of the boots worn by the British Army was outstanding, and that any trench foot cases were not the result of poor craftsmanship."

Gabe frowned. "Sylvia? What is it?"

I showed him the newspaper. Willie and Alex moved closer to read it too.

Willie swore. "That ain't right, is it, Gabe? That don't sound like something you'd say."

"I didn't," he growled. "I never said any of this."

"So..." Alex indicated the article. "Who did?"

"That's what I'm going to find out first thing in the morning."

CHAPTER 18

*T*he following day was Sunday so I was able to sleep in. I awoke to see a message written in Mrs. Parry's hand slipped under my door saying that Gabe telephoned and asked me to join him for lunch at his house if I was available.

I caught the omnibus part of the way and walked the rest. It was a beautiful day with enough of a breeze to freshen the air but not so much that I had to worry about my hat blowing off. I tried not to think about why I was invited to Gabe's house. He'd left the library in a troubled mood after reading the newspaper article claiming he supported Hobson and Son. I doubted he wanted to see me about that.

Bristow showed me through to the drawing room where Gabe was seated, reading the newspaper. He folded it up and stood to shake my hand. It was oddly, awkwardly formal, considering the friendly terms we'd been on recently. He must have thought so too, because he dipped his head and gave a self-conscious laugh. At least he seemed less troubled this morning. He must have resolved his issue with Ivy's family.

"Willie and Alex will be down in a few minutes," he said. "And Cyclops, Catherine and their daughters will arrive soon, too. But I wanted to have a word with you before lunch." He invited me to sit. "I wanted to talk to you about Marianne Folgate."

"Have you learned something more about her?"

"No, but that's the thing. I wanted to suggest we investigate her in more depth. We've only done a cursory search for information about her. We should try harder. Even though we don't think you're a silver magician, your brother seemed to think there was a family connection. Marianne is the only known silver magician of recent history and it might be worth pursuing that line of inquiry."

It was something we could have discussed over the telephone or waited until I was in the library. He didn't need to invite me to luncheon to tell me he wanted to help me. But I was glad he had.

"Someone must know her," he went on. "We'll start with her last known address, as noted by my parents on her file."

"You don't have to do this, Gabe. You must be very busy."

"I want to do it. Besides, my father's business affairs largely run themselves, so I'm at a loose end until Scotland Yard assigns another magical investigation to me."

It was tempting for more reasons than I cared to admit, even to myself. "I'll have to fit it around my work at the library."

"Of course." He glanced up as Alex and Willie entered the drawing room. "We make a good team, Sylvia."

Willie glared at him, hands on her hips. "*We* make a good team. We don't need a fourth wheel."

Alex rolled his eyes at her. "Vehicles work better with four wheels instead of three, and Sylvia is good company." He held out his hand to me and smiled. "She'll be an excellent addition to our team."

I shook his hand. "Thank you, but I don't want to step on any toes."

"You're not," Gabe assured me.

Willie grunted.

"It'll just be until we find out what we can about Marianne Folgate," I told her. "It's not permanent."

The arrival of Bristow was a welcome interruption. He wasn't there to announce the Baileys, however. Someone else had come to visit. Mr. Hobson pushed past the butler before Bristow had even finished speaking.

Ivy's father rushed through the pleasantries, clearly disinterested in them. He looked as though he might burst if he couldn't say his piece soon. He asked to see Gabe alone.

Bristow departed, closing the door, but Gabe didn't ask the rest of us to leave. He gestured to a chair. "Thank you for calling on me, although a telephone call would have sufficed. I know you're busy at the moment."

"Some things can't be discussed over the telephone." Mr. Hobson perched himself on the edge of the armchair, ready to spring up at any moment. "I came as soon as I received your message. Glass, I implore you not to go to the press. Please tell me you haven't already done so."

"I have not. I told you that I would wait until I'd spoken to you and I'm a man of my word."

"Precisely!" Mr. Hobson thumped his fist on his knee. "You are known as an honest man, your reputation and that of your family is beyond reproach. That's why I beg you not to go to the press. Do not retract your statement now. It will damage your reputation."

Willie scoffed. "*His* reputation?"

Gabe put up a hand to stop her. She wasn't the only one disgusted with Mr. Hobson, however. Alex's nostrils flared and his jaw firmed. He looked as though he was barely containing himself.

Gabe was calm by comparison. If it weren't for the slight tapping of his thumb on the chair arm, I'd have thought him completely unconcerned. "First of all, I never made any statement in support of Hobson and Son's army boots. Not to you and certainly not to the press. You went to the newspapers. Not me. Secondly, by speaking to them, *you* have damaged my reputation. Reputable journalists know I'm not a magician." He picked up the newspaper he'd been reading. "They're already pointing out that I'm unable to give my word that your boots were well made. My reputation and, by extension, that of my family, is being questioned." He slapped the newspaper down on the table. "Why did you say it?"

I'd never seen Gabe so angry. He was always so amiable, even under pressure. But he sat there, as rigid as a pole, his stare unwavering. His reputation meant everything to him.

Mr. Hobson fidgeted with his tie and swallowed heavily. "When you came to see me to support us after that disturbance outside the factory, you said yourself you knew our boots were well made, that the magic made them strong. It was on your own mother's recommendation that we won the contract with the army, for God's sake!"

"She didn't test every batch. No one did. When I spoke to you, all I said was that there must have been a genuine mistake. Perhaps a batch got through without having a spell put on them, and some unfortunate soldiers received that batch instead of the magician-made ones." He stabbed his finger on the newspaper. "But that's not what the article stated. There is not a single word in the so-called quotes from me that I actually said to you."

"You expected me to tell the journalist that?" Mr. Hobson snorted. "Are you mad? It could destroy us!"

"Over a genuine mistake?"

Mr. Hobson drew in a deep breath and let it out slowly. Those few moments allowed him to gather himself. "I merely told the journalist what I believed you would have said anyway, had you had the opportunity."

"You had no right."

"I had *every* right. You jilted my daughter!"

Gabe flinched. Even though he must have expected the accusation, it still rocked him.

"You ruined her," Mr. Hobson went on.

Gabe said nothing. His thumb tapping grew more insistent.

Willie took it upon herself to defend him. "He's letting her say *she* called it off. Her reputation is intact. She'll be fine."

"Will she? The thing is, she loved you, Glass. She still does. You've upset her."

"And this is your revenge," Alex sneered.

Mr. Hobson shot him a flinty glare but otherwise ignored him. He focused on Gabe. "Don't hurt Ivy further by going to the press. If you damage our reputation, it will destroy her chances of finding a good husband. Her friends will abandon her. She'll be devastated. I beg you, Glass. Leave the statement as it has been reported. It's the least you can do."

Gabe's chest rose and fell with his even, deep breathing. But he remained silent, unblinking, as he regarded Mr. Hobson.

Mr. Hobson swallowed heavily. "Good man."

"He's given no promises," Willie snapped. But from the way she glanced at Gabe, she wasn't sure what he would do, let alone what he was thinking.

"Glass?"

Alex stepped closer to Mr. Hobson and indicated the door. "It's time you left."

Mr. Hobson jutted out his chin as he peered up at the man towering over him. "I don't take orders from the likes of you."

"You will unless you want to be physically bundled out by the likes of me."

Mr. Hobson stood and buttoned up his jacket. "Think of Ivy," he said to Gabe. "Think how much you've hurt her already."

Willie grabbed his arm and marched him out of the drawing room.

Alex shook his head as he watched him leave. "Normally I'd call him a few colorful names right now, but he's not worth the effort." He clasped Gabe's shoulder. "I know it's early, but do you need a drink?"

"I'm fine," Gabe muttered. He turned to me. "Sorry, Sylvia. I didn't think it would be that way. I thought he'd come to tell me he'd spoken to the journalist and retracted his statement. I didn't think he'd be so defensive and angry for a batch that accidentally missed the spell casting process."

Willie returned with the Bailey family in tow. The mood lifted. No one mentioned Mr. Hobson's visit or what Gabe claimed to have said in the newspapers. The Baileys seemed unaware of the saga, and no one was keen to enlighten them. We wanted to put it behind us and enjoy our lunch.

Conversation grew louder as the meal wore on, mostly thanks to Willie, Alex and his three sisters disagreeing on almost everything, from their favorite moving picture to whether the eldest sister, Ella, should be allowed to learn to drive.

"There's no point," Alex said. "You can't afford a motorcar."

"Gabe will let me borrow his." Ella was the boldest of the three girls. Indeed, she wasn't a girl. She was twenty-two and fiercely independent, according to her mother. She was something of a tomboy, enjoying sports and outdoor pursuits, even beating men at tennis. Her competitive nature probably had something to do with that, too.

"He will not," Cyclops boomed with a glare for Gabe.

Gabe gave him an innocent look. "I haven't said a word."

"My girls aren't going to drive."

"Why not?" more than one female voice asked.

Cyclops took a sip from his wine glass, wisely taking time to consider his answer. "It's dangerous."

"We ride in vehicles all the time," Ella pointed out. "Wouldn't you prefer me to know how to drive myself safely around the city instead of relying on a cab driver who could be drunk or easily distracted, or simply careless?"

Cyclops appealed to his wife but received no help from that quarter.

"She has a point," Catherine said.

"If Ella learns to drive then so do I," Mae, the middle sister said.

"And me," added Lulu, the youngest.

Mae clicked her tongue at Lulu. "You always copy me."

"I do not!"

Cyclops spotted Willie and Ella whispering at the end of the table. "Don't you dare promise to teach her to drive, Willie."

"I wasn't," Willie said with a sly smile.

Cyclops narrowed his one good eye. "Then what were you two whispering about?"

Willie simply continued to smile, leaving it to Ella to respond. "She said she'll teach me how to fly a plane."

"Willie," Cyclops growled. He poked the dessert around his bowl a few times before lowering his spoon. "Fine. If it's all right with Gabe, you can ask Dodson the chauffeur to teach you to drive, but only in the old Hudson Super Six. The Vauxhall's too flashy."

Gabe, seated beside me, muttered, "Well played."

"Willie can fly?" I asked.

"She's a good pilot. She wanted to fly in the war, but women weren't allowed."

"If only the prime minister had met her, perhaps he would have changed his mind."

"He has met her."

"Really?"

He nodded. "My parents advise Cabinet from time to time on magical matters. When he learned that my father's cousin was Lady Farnsworth, he invited all three to dine at his house along with some important people. Let's just say he got more than he bargained for when she arrived dressed in a tuxedo and insisted on smoking cigars with the men after dinner."

"At least she wore formal attire."

"She insisted on keeping her gun holster on."

"Oh dear."

He smiled. "It was wartime, after all."

I laughed.

Cyclops, seated on my other side, had been listening in. "She withdrew the gun at one point when someone asked her how her husband died. She threatened to shoot him if he asked again."

I was considering whether it was appropriate to ask how he had died, and whether the rumor was true and she had a hand in the deaths of both her husbands, but Willie got in first.

"I can hear you, Cyclops. You think you're whispering, but you ain't. Your voice is like thunder."

"And yours has all the sweet melody of fireworks," he shot back.

Catherine rolled her eyes. "My apologies for those two, Sylvia. They seem even less mature these days. If India were here, she'd put them in their place. She and Matt know how to handle them."

"You're wrong anyway," Willie said to Cyclops. "They

didn't want to know how my husbands died. They wanted to know why Davide married me in the first place."

"We all want to know that," Cyclops muttered.

Gabe leaned down to me. "Davide is Lord Farnsworth."

"He was drunk," Willie went on. "We both were. Getting married seemed like a good idea at the time. Maybe it was. Being married to him was fun. Let that be a lesson to you, girls." She pointed her spoon at each of them. "If you're not sure if you should marry someone, just drink to excess and you'll naturally do what you want. Just make sure you ain't too drunk to stand up at the altar."

Catherine sighed. "Do you have to, Willie?" She indicated the three girls, listening intently to Willie's story.

"They've got to learn about the world some time. Ain't that right, Ella?"

"Absolutely," Ella declared.

Mae and Lulu giggled.

We managed to get through lunch without anyone being insulted or another argument breaking out. I suspected a lot of that was because Gabe steered the conversation to the Medici Manuscript and how we'd solved its mysteries. The three Bailey girls hung on his every word.

Cyclops reported that Albert Scarrow admitted to stealing the book after seeing it in Mr. Trevelyan's photography studio. He'd recognized the Medici family symbol and suspected it would be worth a great deal of money. With no understanding of the black market or having any contacts, he'd taken a risk and approached the antique book dealers in Cecil Court. It had been his downfall.

I hated to think what would have happened if someone with better connections had stolen it. It may have been lost to us forever.

We retreated to the drawing room for tea after the meal was over. No one was inclined to leave. Catherine, Cyclops and their girls seemed at home, even speaking to the servants as if they were their own. They must have spent a great deal of time here over the years.

As dusk settled outside, and Murray turned on some of the lights, the Baileys left. I decided to head home, too. I had one last question to ask Gabe, however. A question I wasn't sure I should ask. It might dampen his mood and he'd seemed so content these last few hours. Despite his earlier encounter with Mr. Hobson, Gabe had been relaxed all afternoon. There hadn't been a thumb-tap in sight. It was a testament to how much he enjoyed the company of Alex's family.

I waited until he'd said goodbye to them before I stepped aside to have a quiet word with him. "Are you all right, Gabe? Mr. Hobson was very cruel."

He clasped his hands behind his back, pressed his lips together, then said, "I am. Thank you."

"You hesitated."

"Ah. Yes. I assure you I am all right. Hobson was only lashing out because he hates what I did to Ivy. He wanted to punish me. I can't blame him for that."

I gave him a flat smile, nodded and turned away. It was his affair and none of my business.

But I suddenly turned to face him again. I couldn't let him excuse Mr. Hobson's actions because he felt guilty about Ivy. It wasn't fair. "He acted appallingly. It's one thing to be upset about your engagement ending; it's quite another for him to ask you to stake your reputation, and that of your mother, on the quality of his boots. And to do it so publicly, too!" I could have gone on. I could have told him he was better off not tying himself to such a man, that he deserved a better father-in-law. But I'd already overstepped.

I could see his surprise from the way he stared at me, his lips slightly parted. Like most people, he probably thought me mild-mannered and quiet, the clichéd librarian. But I did have a temper. It generally lurked well below the surface and was slow to flare, but when it did, I found it almost impossible to contain. Much to my own horror.

I grasped my bag in both hands and lowered my head. "Good day, Gabe. Thank you for lunch."

He caught my elbow as I turned to go. "Wait. I…"

"Yes?" *Ugh*. I sounded breathy, girly. "I'm sorry," I quickly added. "It's none of my business."

"It's nice to have someone leap to my defense." He gave me one of his crooked smiles, the sort that made my insides do a little flip. I hoped my reaction didn't show on my face. The breathy girlishness had been bad enough.

"You have a lot of people to do that for you." I indicated the drawing room where Willie and Alex were waiting for him. "You don't need me."

"Don't I?" It may have been said quietly, but those two words ricocheted through me, leaving shattered nerves in their wake.

Gabe's fingers caressed the bare skin at my wrist before letting me go. He stepped back, suddenly rigid, his gaze hard. Whatever warmth he'd felt toward me, he'd shut it out.

Mr. Hobson's visit had left a deep, jagged scar on Gabe, one that had nothing to do with the damage to his reputation. Mr. Hobson had brought Gabe's guilt over ending his engagement to Ivy to the fore once again. It stopped Gabe from completely letting her go and moving on.

As much as I wanted to help him, there was nothing I could do. Just as those of us who'd remained behind in the war could do little to help the men in our lives after they demobilized, I couldn't actively help Gabe overcome his guilt. Some battles had to be fought alone. All the rest of us could do was stand by their side and be a sturdy crutch to lean on when necessary.

Despite the coolness of the evening, I felt cozy as Dodson

the chauffeur drove me home. The echo of Gabe's words and touch kept me warm, lingering well into the night.

Available from 5th September 2023:
THE UNTITLED BOOKS
The 3rd Glass Library novel

DID you know the Glass Library series is a spin-off of the Glass and Steele series? Go back to where it all began with book 1, The Watchmaker's Daughter by C.J. Archer.

A MESSAGE FROM THE AUTHOR

I hope you enjoyed reading THE MEDICI MANUSCRIPT as much as I enjoyed writing it. As an independent author, getting the word out about my book is vital to its success, so if you liked this book please consider telling your friends and writing a review at the store where you purchased it. If you would like to be contacted when I release a new book, subscribe to my newsletter at http://cjarcher.com/contact-cj/newsletter/.

ALSO BY C.J. ARCHER

SERIES WITH 2 OR MORE BOOKS

The Glass Library

Cleopatra Fox Mysteries

After The Rift

Glass and Steele

The Ministry of Curiosities Series

The Emily Chambers Spirit Medium Trilogy

The 1st Freak House Trilogy

The 2nd Freak House Trilogy

The 3rd Freak House Trilogy

The Assassins Guild Series

Lord Hawkesbury's Players Series

Witch Born

SINGLE TITLES NOT IN A SERIES

Courting His Countess

Surrender

Redemption

The Mercenary's Price

ABOUT THE AUTHOR

C.J. Archer has loved history and books for as long as she can remember and feels fortunate that she found a way to combine the two. She spent her early childhood in the dramatic beauty of outback Queensland, Australia, but now lives in suburban Melbourne with her husband, two children and a mischievous black & white cat named Coco.

Subscribe to C.J.'s newsletter through her website to be notified when she releases a new book, as well as get access to exclusive content and subscriber-only giveaways. Her website also contains up to date details on all her books: http://cjarcher.com

Follow her on social media to get the latest updates on her books:

facebook.com/CJArcherAuthorPage
x.com/cj_archer
instagram.com/authorcjarcher

Made in the USA
Coppell, TX
07 March 2024

29852711R20164